# EXECUTE THE OFFICE

DANIEL BAILEY

An Imprint of The Overmountain Press
JOHNSON CITY, TENNESSEE

This book is a work of fiction. All names, characters, places, and events are either the product of the author's imagination or are used fictitiously. Any resemblance to actual events or persons, living or dead, is entirely coincidental and beyond the intent of either the author or the publisher.

Book design by Cherisse McGinty

Hardcover ISBN 1-57072-282-X
Trade Paper ISBN 1-57072-283-8
Copyright © 2004 by Daniel Bailey
Printed in the United States of America
All Rights Reserved

1 2 3 4 5 6 7 8 9 0

*To Mom and Dad
for letting me explore and grow
and for encouraging all of us to chase our dreams.*

*As with all my writing,
I dedicate this work to my public-safety family,
and especially to those members
who have been called to serve their country on foreign soil.
May their sacrifice never be forgotten or taken for granted.*

# ACKNOWLEDGMENTS

Special thanks go to FBI Special Agent-Retired Larry Bonney, who taught a session during an FBI training seminar I attended in Charleston, South Carolina. He likely doesn't remember me, but I know he planted the seed that matured and grew into this book. While captivating the entire class with his in-depth knowledge of the inner workings of extremist groups, he mesmerized us with his firsthand investigative accounts of some of the most notorious cases. Without question, the creation of the fictional Free Confederacy grew from our discussions, but any glaring errors that may appear are mine alone.

Thanks also go to The Tarheel Gumshoes, Charlotte's Sisters in Crime chapter. This brother truly appreciates the support and encouragement he receives from each of you.

I would be remiss if I didn't acknowledge the support my family gives to my craft by understanding my grumpiness when the urge takes hold and by allowing me the solitude to flesh out the bones of my next idea with minimal interruption. Writing can be a lonely exercise—and should be at times—but it is nice to know that sanity lurks on the other side of the closed door.

Finally, as always, I want to thank my publisher, Silver Dagger Mysteries, for giving me a chance to tell my stories in my own way. To Sherry, whose relentless scrutiny during the editing process makes me look far more learned than I am; and to Beth, who keeps all of us on course. To Karin, who suggested a title change, a great inspiration for which I am indebted; and to all of my authorial siblings, who e-mail encouragement and respond to requests for help. Thank you!

# Chapter · 1

CHARLESTON, SOUTH CAROLINA

For three days the category five hurricane had churned the seas off the coast of Charleston, South Carolina, like a playground bully hurling threats at timid playmates. As gale winds mounted, tourists and vacationers jammed the roadways leading west, away from the angry squall. Business owners and residents boarded up windows and tied down outdoor furniture. Some prepared to leave with what belongings they could cram into their cars and trucks. Others, old salts who had grown up weathering the periodic turbulences, planned to stay. Fear ruled the emotions of some, opportunity drove others.

During the predawn hours of the fourth day, a warm October morning, the nautical terror attacked with a vengeance. Tidal swells hurtled the rock walls of the Battery. The wind wailed, and palmetto trees bowed as if in prayer to the sea god, Neptune. Savage winds sucked stately antebellum homes off their foundations, spitting them out in pieces all across the Lowcountry. Two-hundred-year-old buildings along Meeting Street, all having weathered lesser assaults, rocked and began to crumble. The sides of a popular seafood eatery split open like a flounder gutted with a fillet knife.

When the winds subsided some four hours later, the sun peeked from behind darkened clouds, revealing the extent of the disaster. The once vibrant port city, a historical pearl of the South, revealed devastation unparalleled since William Tecumseh Sherman's fiery march through the Carolinas near the end of the Civil War. Shards of glass poked from the sandy soil like porcupine quills. Splintered lumber floated in brackish pools. Broken brick and severed roofing littered courtyards and streets. Out in the harbor, swamped pleasure boats sank slowly out of sight, leaving a greasy rainbow of oil and gas glistening on the now calm waterway's surface.

Jefferson Lee walked slowly through the melee of storm victims and their rescue personnel, toting his bulky television camera on his shoulder, shaking his head in disbelief. Steam rose all around him as the sun turned Church Street into one long asphalt griddle. He wore a blue bandanna tied around his shaven brown head to stop the sweat from leaking into his eyes. A black mesh T-shirt stretched tightly over his muscular chest, and cutoff denim shorts bulged across the rock-hard thighs of the former NFL wide receiver. Thick-soled brogan boots protected his feet from nails protruding from broken boards hidden under carpets of windblown sand. Born 31 years before, just south of Charleston, he had experienced his share of storms and their destructive aftermath, but none the likes of what he witnessed now.

"Over there!" Cassie O'Connor's voice pealed, ripe with urgency. "That old church steeple's about to fall. Get a shot."

Jefferson jerked his camera around and peered through the viewfinder. He focused in on the cross at the top of the steeple listing hard to one side of the church's precipitous roof. Just as he did, a sharp crack flushed a flock of white birds from a nearby tree. The resultant loud fluttering noise drowned the commotion caused by nearby rescue personnel.

The steeple wobbled, thrust forward, then slammed down onto the roof and slid like a sled on an icy hill. It fell over the roof's edge, landing with a board-ripping crash on a row of centuries-old tombstones in the graveyard below.

"You get that? Tell me you got that!" Cassie shot around Jefferson for a closer look.

"I got it." The words slid out of his mouth like molasses pouring from a Mason jar. Jefferson glanced away from the eyepiece as the diminutive, New Jersey-born, auburn-haired woman dressed in khaki culottes and a navy silk blouse ran by. "You shoulda worn somethin' a mite more rugged," he said.

The five-foot-two-inch reporter from CNN in Atlanta didn't bother so much as a nod back at her six-foot-eight-inch cameraman. "I'm fine. Just keep shooting." She jumped over a fallen streetlamp and ran through ankle-deep water toward the wrought-iron gate of the stone wall surrounding the church graveyard.

"You'd better slow down, or you'll break your fool neck." Jefferson grimaced, shaking his head as he watched the woman he used to work with in Columbia, South Carolina. She was impetuous, with a volatile Irish temper. She was impatient, sometimes arrogant, and often irritating. But he respected her journalistic instincts, the determination and fearlessness required to break a controversial hard-hitting story. He had witnessed her daring firsthand, when she took on powerful people to uncover a conspiracy involving a drug cartel, local and federal politicians, and a police officer's killer who had escaped from a neighboring county jail. She revealed the entire plot on her station's national affiliate and earned an invitation to move to Atlanta to report for one of the most-watched television news networks in the world. Once she got her big break, she never looked back.

Now everyone who watched CNN knew Cassie O'Connor, and Jefferson felt flattered that she had requested to be partnered with him again, to cover the aftermath of the state's worst hurricane disaster. He chuckled to himself. *Flattered, but wary.* If he could only keep her from getting them both killed. That always seemed to be the challenge with her.

Jefferson wiped sweat from his brow as he watched Cassie high-stepping, wearing only leather tennis shoes to protect her feet as she splashed through the dingy water covering Church Street. "If a nail rams through those soft rubber soles into your dainty foot, I want to be the one to jam that tetanus needle in your ass."

As usual, she paid no attention to his warning. "Get some footage of the wreckage." She looked back with a glare of impatience, then turned and craned her neck to peer into the graveyard.

Before Jefferson could lumber up behind her, Cassie leaned across the wall and pointed. "What's that?"

He lowered the camera, holding it by the handle the same way he would a suitcase, and stepped up behind the reporter. "What's what?"

"Over there, near that section of roof, next to the pile of palmetto branches. Is that a chest or something?" Cassie pulled on the old gate, but debris had collected at its base, preventing her from pulling it open.

Jefferson surveyed the area where the eager reporter pointed. He saw the fallen tree and the piece of collapsed roof. He also saw what looked like an ornamental box sitting amid the rubble. "Pirate's booty! Vast, me hardy, ye landlubber may have discovered Blackbeard's treasure." He let loose with a thunderous, deep laugh as he eased his camera on top of the wall.

"Smart ass! It might be important."

He propped his left hand on the wall and vaulted over the top. "Yes'm," he said in a tone of subservience, "I'll check it out." A low grunt escaped his mouth as he landed. He held his hand high in the air and waved. "Hang tight, Miz Patience. I be right back."

Cassie rolled her eyes, planted her fists against her hips. "I've told you before, don't use that movie-slave bullshit on me."

Jefferson laughed harder but stopped abruptly as he got closer to the box.

His eyes narrowed, but he wasn't looking at the treasure chest Cassie had spotted. Something under the roof caught his attention. *That's peculiar*, he thought.

He kicked away a palmetto frond with his size-fifteen brogan and knelt down by the piece of roof. He pushed away loose shingles. His features expressed surprise. "Get a cop over here." He popped back to his feet and spun around to look at Cassie. Before the words were out of his mouth, he saw her scrambling over the wall.

"What is it?" she said, breathless, as she jumped down and ran toward him.

"You might want to stop right there," Jefferson said, holding up his large hand. "There's a foot under here, and there's a very dead body connected to it."

# Chapter · 2

HISTORIC DISTRICT, CHARLESTON, SOUTH CAROLINA

Jefferson leaned against a brick column marking the entrance to a tiny courtyard across Church Street from the cemetery where he had first discovered the body. For the past ninety minutes, he had watched an assortment of police officers measuring and photographing everything around the corpse he had found. Over the same time period, he had watched Cassie pacing in front of him like an expectant father.

"Why don't you sit a spell?" he said. "You're gonna wear a hole in the sidewalk. You know they're not gonna tell us anything until they're good and ready."

"What I know," she muttered as she passed by Jefferson's resting spot, her eyes locked on the officers' every move, "is that *we* found the body. *We* showed them where it was, and all *we* got for our trouble was junior, over there, directing us to stand over here. The nerve." She pointed and glared at the pencil-thin, uniformed officer positioned at the entrance to the church cemetery.

"'This is a crime scene.'" Her voice mocked the high-pitched tone of the young officer, likely the newest recruit and the one delegated to remove unnecessary people from the area where evidence was being sought and retrieved. He now stood vigil in front of the wrought-iron gate, letting only authorized police and medical personnel past. Inside the stone wall, yellow tape stretched around the area where the body had been found. "I know what a damn crime scene looks like," Cassie said.

"You expected them to let us stand there and film while they worked? You've been away too long from the way local police do things."

"They could have let us stay until they uncovered the body. At least we would have found out who it is." She glanced at her watch. "We've been over here almost two hours now. You'd think they'd tell us something."

"Yeah, right." Jefferson pushed away from the column and picked up his camera. "Come on, there's plenty more for us to cover. Besides, it'll likely turn out to be the preacher, and you couldn't air his name until notification of next of kin, anyway."

"Why are cops so arrogant? That pimply-faced kid out front wouldn't even let us do a stand-up with them working in the background."

Jefferson chuckled. "Do your stand-up here. I can zoom in and capture them working in the background."

Cassie frowned. "You know it isn't the same." Her tongue extended her cheek as it traced circles inside her mouth. She glared toward the activity inside the yellow tape. "Zoom in where they're working. Can you see the body—the head and face?"

He pulled the viewfinder to his right eye and shook his head. "Nope. I can only see the lower part of his leg and foot. Nice slacks and shoes, though. You want to take a look?" He held out his camera and grinned.

"Very funny. Come on, we'll go down and check out the City Market over on Meeting Street. Maybe the Neanderthal heading up the investigation will give us something from here later on." Cassie whirled around to leave, then stopped. "What's all that about?"

Jefferson looked back across the street. The young police officer guarding the gate was arguing with a short, blonde-haired woman wearing cutoff jeans and a grimy tank top. Holding a stern expression, the officer pointed away from the crime scene. The woman appeared to ignore his demands, pushing around him as if it was important for her to get inside the cemetery.

"Get that." Cassie's eyebrow lifted. "He wants her to leave, but she insists on going inside. Wonder if she knows the victim?"

Jefferson looked askance at Cassie, then he looked back toward the argument. "Whatever." He pulled the camera to his shoulder.

"Her father, maybe, or her husband, something like that?" Cassie asked, verbalizing every thought rushing through her brain.

Jefferson angled the camera toward the encounter. "Can't say, but if she don't back off, she's getting ready to get locked up."

Just as he spoke, the woman threw her arms in the air and stormed down the street. She stopped, yelled back at the young officer, then continued away from the church.

"Come on." Cassie swung her arm in a sweeping arc. She started across the street toward the irate woman.

Releasing a long sigh, Jefferson fell in behind his energized reporter. Life before and after Cassie had been pretty laid-back. A weary grin spread across his face. *Wonder if Charleston will be able to survive both the hurricane and Cassie O'Connor?*

"Ma'am! Ma'am, may I talk to you?" Cassie jogged toward the woman.

The woman stopped, stared, and wiped a dirty strand of hair from her face. She looked behind her with an expression that begged to know if Cassie was referring to her.

"Do you know the victim over there?" Cassie fired the question just as she stepped up on the sidewalk. She motioned for Jefferson to hurry up.

The surprised woman shook her head. She studied Jefferson suspiciously, then looked back at Cassie. "Who're you?"

"Cassie O'Connor, CNN." She waited for the expression of recognition that usually appeared on the faces of people when she told them who she was and where she worked.

The woman shrugged her bare shoulders. An unimpressed expression disguised her face as she touched a bandage taped to her forehead. Distrust flickered in her pale brown eyes.

"You were arguing with that officer. Weren't you trying to get inside to see the victim?"

"No."

"Well, why—"

"You a reporter?" The woman's words flowed slow. Her gaze locked on Jefferson's camera.

"That's right. I'm covering the hurricane for CNN. You do know CNN?"

The woman frowned. "Course. I'm not ignert."

"If you didn't want to get inside, why were you and that cop arguing?"

"I seen something, wanted to tell him, but he was too dumb to care." She glanced back over her shoulder. The young cop's eyes narrowed as he glared back. "Look, I gotta go."

"What did you see? When?"

The short, pudgy woman began to walk away. "Uh-uh. I know a detective. He pay good for what I know."

Cassie glanced back at Jefferson.

His eyebrow raised. With a reluctant expression, he shoved his hand into his pocket. "I'll pay. How much?"

The woman stopped, turned, and tilted her head. She studied Cassie from top to bottom. "I tells you, I gets in all kinds o' trouble. Trouble I might get into is worth as much as what I seen."

"How much?" Cassie's voice rose an octave. She felt her blood pressure inch even higher.

Propping her hands on her hips, the woman appeared to be in thought.

Cassie thrust her hand in the pocket of her culottes, pulled out a small purse. "How about twenty dollars?"

"Ha! Crazy woman tink what I know no good." She whirled around, mumbling just loud enough to be heard. She started down the street.

Jefferson stepped around Cassie. "What about a C-note?"

The woman stopped. She slowly turned around. "You be gettin' closer."

Cassie's face flushed. "What do you mean—"

Jefferson pulled a hundred-dollar bill from an old worn wallet and waved it in the air. "That's the only offer. If you saw something, somebody else probably did too. Maybe they'll be more interested in doing business than you."

The woman's eyes closed to tiny slits. She eased toward Jefferson, reached her grimy hand out, and snatched the bill. She held it up to let the sun filter through the paper. With a nod of satisfaction she said, "I seen a big black somethin' drivin' fast away from here, right as the storm hit."

Cassie stepped toward the woman. "What kind of black something?"

"Can't say. Don't know for sure. Ain't ever seen nothin' like it afore. It were squatty like—and wide. Some kind o' cross twixt a car and truck."

"That sure as hell ain't worth a hundred dollars." Cassie rolled her eyes and stared up at Jefferson as if he had just been had.

He set his camera down on the sidewalk and stepped beside the woman, who was a good inch or two shorter than Cassie. Glaring down, his muscular arms folded across his broad chest, he spoke in a low voice that reminded Cassie of a bear's growl. "Where were you when you saw this black thingamajig?"

"Over there, under that there loading dock."

Cassie thought she detected a slight trembling in the woman's voice as she spoke. She followed Jefferson's gaze as he cast a long look at the back of a nearby store and the concrete loading dock that looked like a war bunker.

He looked back at the woman. "That where you live?"

"Sometimes. When big storms come, it's the safest."

"Did you see this black vehicle stop in front of the church?"

"Huh-uh."

Jefferson rubbed his hand across the unshaven stubble of his jaw. "What else you see?"

"Folks scurrying around in the dark. That's all. They weren't there more'n a couple of minutes."

"How many folks?" Cassie wiped her face with a handkerchief from her pocket.

"Two, I tink. No more than three. It was dark. The wind whipped at the shadows, makin' it hard for a body to tell how many really be out there."

Jefferson nodded, as if he understood. "Then what?"

"Then they left. Fast, like they seen an old hant rising out of one of them graves."

Jefferson looked over at Cassie. He shrugged, then looked back down at the woman. "Thanks. By the way, the least you can do is tell me who copped my C-note."

"Folks round here call me Rowdy . . . Rowdy Dubois—SSB!" Her tone mocked Cassie's earlier introduction.

Cassie glowered; Jefferson smirked, as if he knew what was coming next.

"Street Smart Bitch," Rowdy cackled. She wadded the hundred-dollar bill in her fist and hurried away.

Cassie watched as the woman splashed through puddles in bare feet. "Humph! 'Bitch' fits," she said. "What kind of accent was that?"

Jefferson smiled. "Sea island. I grew up hearing relatives of mine speak that way. Folks raised in the Lowcountry call 'em Gullahs, descendants of slaves brought over from Angola. Their ancestors settled along the barrier islands just off the coast. Some whites who grew up with the Gullahs picked up the dialect."

"You believe her?"

"I believe she saw something peculiar, some kind of strange vehicle—maybe military."

"Military? Why military?"

"Just a hunch. A squatty, wide cross between a car and a truck sounds like something the military would be driving—a Humvee, maybe. She probably saw National Guardsmen trying to find folks like her to get them out of harm's way before the storm hit. What she saw likely doesn't have a damn thing to do with the body we found."

"What if it does? What if she saw the killers?"

Jefferson grinned and rolled his eyes. "Can't rightly know, but for now we better be getting some footage for you to feed back to Atlanta, or I *do know* what'll happen there."

# CHAPTER · 3

WASHINGTON, D.C.

In his District of Columbia office, Finley Sawyer, Director of the United States Secret Service, studied the communiqué he had just been handed by Bryson James, his deputy director. Sawyer's forehead furrowed. "When did we get this?"

James settled into one of two leather wing chairs positioned in front of the director's desk. "Just now. I brought it in as soon as it arrived."

Sawyer stroked his tanned chin with his thumb and index finger. "Who found him?"

"CNN news crew. We're checking out the reporter now. I understand her name is Cassie O'Connor. Her cameraman actually found the body in a churchyard, buried under hurricane debris."

Sawyer, an athletic 55-year-old South Carolina native and graduate of Princeton University, where he was an All-American baseball player, shook his head. "I hear the city's destroyed."

"Yes, sir," James answered quietly. "Do you have relatives there?"

"No. We're from upstate, along the North Carolina state line. Hurricanes rarely make it that far inland, but it's happened. What about our Charleston office?"

"Everyone got out like you directed, but the building is gone. Probably out in the Atlantic somewhere by now. We evacuated, once the storm turned and landfall was imminent."

Sawyer glanced back at the report. "CNN? Does she have any idea how big a story she stumbled into?"

A wry smile slid across the deputy director's face. He chuckled. "No, sir. As far as I know, she and her cameraman don't even know who they've found."

"Talk about an exclusive." The director rocked back in his chair and massaged his graying temples, the only sign he might be over fifty. With charcoal black hair, except for his temples, a perpetual tan, and a body maintained by six-mile-a-day runs, he could pass for someone in his late thirties. "If this reporter's worth her salt, she'll know soon enough who she found. What about the Bureau, are they involved?"

"They dispatched agents as soon as word got out. I'm sure by now they've offered to assist, but you know how that goes. They can't come across too pushy, so until something turns up in the investigation that looks like a federal violation, they're pretty much just observing."

Sawyer slid the report back across his desk. "What about the election? Intelligence picking up anything?"

"The usual number of crank threats. We're checking them all out." James formed a steeple with his index fingers. "I've never seen an election where both candidates had so many detractors. How'd either one get so far along with so much animosity out there?"

"Well, the President can thank his resident pit viper, Randall, for a large dose of the ill will directed toward the Oval Office. Him, and all the rumors swirling around the former VP's alleged suicide."

The deputy director's right eyebrow lifted. "Alleged is right. Now Clark Randall's slithered his way from chief of staff into the vice presidency. Kind of coincidental, don't you think?"

Sawyer's voice lowered and his eyes narrowed. "More than coincidental. Damned suspicious. And on top of everything else, the VP's death made us look bad." He leaned forward, glared at his deputy director. "If Samuel Griffith committed suicide, then Ulysses S. Grant is gonna be named the next patron saint of the South. The whole incident smells, and I have a hunch Clark Randall would like to make it all go away."

James nodded his agreement.

"But that isn't going to happen," Sawyer said. "The FBI director and I are in agreement. We both want that investigation to continue. Mark my words, we'll have our day—just you wait and see."

"No doubt in my mind, sir."

"What about that rumor coming out of South Carolina? The one concerning that right-wing group and possible threats to the candidates."

James frowned, pursed his lips tight, and nodded. "They're a credible threat."

Sawyer pinched the bridge of his nose. He recalled the antiwar demonstrations he had witnessed as a Princeton student. "Some things never change. There's always going to be some fringe group out there with a bent toward anarchy—one that doesn't give a rat's ass about the sanctity of human life. When you think about it, these right-wingers aren't all that different from those radical groups of the '60s. They blew up government buildings and shot at cops then, just like they do today."

"They're all cut from the same cloth," James said. "If they don't like the way it's done, they use bombs and bullets as an exclamation point for their messages. Sad."

"The big difference between the groups then and now," Sawyer said, "is that today's knuckleheads hide in the pages of the Bible. That's what really galls me. They kill a cop or one of our people, then claim their action as God-inspired."

"At least the '60s radicals owned up to their Communist teachings. They preached Marxism on the street corners of Haight Ashbury. The only Marx today's militants know about is Groucho."

Sawyer shook his head. "Why didn't we get out of this business while we were young?" He flashed a sly smile at his deputy director.

James shrugged his shoulders. "Gluttons for punishment, I guess."

Sawyer thought about the environmental and religious issues that produced the occasional zealot, the heightened awareness international terrorism had brought to America. But, in his mind, the single greatest threat to the country was an old nemesis of the Secret Service—the homegrown, domestic terrorist, who blew up abortion clinics and thumbed his nose at the stabilizing laws of the land.

Since the end of the cold war, when Americans no longer held a common bond to ferret out Communists and foreigners dedicated to overthrowing the American way of life, this anarchist ideology had flourished. Born in the nation's heartland, where banks had foreclosed on family-owned land handed down through generations, the growth of armed citizens as militias had spread across the country, sewing seeds of discontent.

Sawyer leaned forward in his chair. "Our man in place?"

James nodded. "Code name is Johnny Reb. He hasn't been able to make contact with the UNSUB yet, but he thinks it'll happen soon."

"He damn well better. The election's a month away."

"His controlling agent seems optimistic. Says he's developed a friendship with some men, a couple of whom who have openly embraced anarchist ideals. It's not clear if they belong to the group making the threats, though."

"What does this group call itself?"

"The Free Confederacy. They're headquartered in a fortified church, supposedly located somewhere in the middle of the Congaree Swamp. Leader's name is Eustace Hanley—a real psycho, by some accounts."

"We have anything on Hanley?"

A sarcastic grin slid across James's face. "U.S. Army-trained. A Ranger. Served in Laos. There's some unconfirmed intelligence indicating members of his unit participated in some recon missions in and out of Iraq after Desert Storm, but the Army won't verify any official involvement by any Ranger units after hostilities supposedly ceased."

"Company operation?"

"CIA is suspected, yes, sir. Information is, he soured on the—and I quote—'spineless bureaucrats in the Pentagon' soon after he returned. He's supposed to still have military connections. Probably more of the mercenary variety."

"Sounds like a real hardcase. Anybody else noteworthy linked to those unconfirmed operations?"

"We're checking, but we keep running into the usual interference at Central Intelligence. They deny knowing anything. Still, we have a source. We hope to have something in a few days."

"So when is the next scheduled communication with our Johnny Reb?" Sawyer asked.

"Sunday. Maybe he'll have made contact by then."

"He'd better. We're running out of time."

President Wagner Flint stared out the window of his Camp David office. "What else can go wrong?"

With his hands clasped behind his back and the skin around his dark eyes pinched inward, causing the deep furrows across his forehead to narrow, Clark Randall, newly appointed vice president of the United States, turned and glared at the solemn expression on the President's face. "Plenty, if we don't keep attacking."

Minutes before, he had glared out the same window, watching a lean gray squirrel jump from limb to limb, an acorn wedged in its mouth. He imagined catching the agile creature in the crosshairs of a rifle, imagined squeezing the trigger, and felt an unexplainable feeling of euphoria, knowing if the rifle were real, he alone would hold the tiny animal's continued existence in his hands.

Until a month before, Randall had been Flint's chief of staff, and most observers on Capitol Hill considered the surly malcontent little more than the White House hatchet man. But after Vice President Griffith was found in a Washington, D.C., park with a bullet in his temple, Randall moved with unexpected swiftness to have Flint push through his appointment as the new vice president.

On Capitol Hill, eyebrows raised at such a notion; opinions of Randall crept even more toward the dark side. However, with the election so near and the race so close, Flint's party muscled the nomination through Congress, despite misgivings by more than just a few, on both sides of the aisle, who despised Randall and his strong-arm tactics.

From the time the former vice president's body had been found, many on the Hill openly questioned the curious coincidences that had seemingly led to his suicide in the midst of a campaign-contribution scandal. Persistent murmurs inside the halls of Congress hinted that the investigation had been tampered with and suicide ruled without sufficient evidence to substantiate it as a viable cause of death. Doubters in both the House and the Senate suspected Randall had been pulling the strings for his own ascension to the vice presidency all along, and some wondered quietly what role he might have had in the surprising allegations about illegal campaign contributions being solicited by the former VP, a man believed to be of unimpeachable character.

"Attacking!" Flint leaned forward in his chair. "Jeff Hart has me on the defensive at every turn. He's like a rabid dog with teeth bared."

*Rabid dog indeed*, Randall thought with just the slightest of smiles creasing his thin lips. He admired Flint's opponent as much as he despised his own president. To the new vice president, Jeff Hart was everything Wagner Flint could never hope to be. Hart displayed the ruthless, take-no-prisoners attitude that Randall revered. He didn't mind taking chances and, Randall suspected, didn't mind playing dirty when needed. Hart's intelligence dwarfed Flint's, and his popularity seemed to be growing with every campaign stop.

Randall grimaced as he spoke. "You've got to go for the jugular. Attack his antibusiness stands. Paint him as a liberal . . . anti-NRA, proabortion. A man who wants the Government to strip industry of its power. A traitor who favors subsidizing those interlopers from foreign countries who come here and steal our way of life."

Flint slammed the palms of his hands on the top of his desk and shot out of his chair. Not particularly athletic, but an avid golfer, he was decidedly thinner and six years younger than Randall. His graying hair, along with the wrinkles he blamed on the stress from the past six months, made him look older. He even attributed some recent stomach problems to the former vice president.

"Griffith killed me." Flint inhaled and exhaled as if he were about to hyperventilate. "The son of a bitch solicits illegal contributions—from the Arabs, no less—then tries to claim he was being made a scapegoat. Made it sound like I was the one receiving the damn illegal contributions. If that's not enough, the chicken-shit bastard goes and kills himself, leaving me looking like some sinister SOB."

A furtive smirk crept across Randall's face. Through Flint, Randall had attained power, a need for him as real as the need to breathe. He had recognized the potential years before, when he first decided to carve out and then finely sculpture a plan that allowed Flint to ascend to the White House. And like an artist who gave birth to his creation, he wasn't about to see it end after four years. In fact, if plans went accordingly, Randall fancied himself as the man to move into the Oval Office soon after the beginning of Flint's second term.

"What hurt you were the lies spread by that bastard Laney. He convinced Griffith that he could shift the blame to you. Laney had his own ambitions, and he planned on using Griffith to achieve them."

"If that's so, why did Griffith commit suicide?"

"Laney was only using Griffith. Griffith must have found out. By the time he realized it, Laney had boxed him in. Griffith had no other choice but to take his own life."

"And make my life miserable," Flint muttered as he shuffled to the window, where his gaze wandered deep into the surrounding forest. "At every campaign stop, the only thing the reporters want to know about is Griffith—his death, the illegal contributions, how come I didn't know. I've rarely had a chance to mention Hart, much less attack him." He turned and faced Randall. "So, what do we do about Laney?"

"We don't have to do a thing. Good ole Mother Nature took care of the problem for us."

"What do you mean?"

Randall pulled a piece of paper out of his coat pocket. "Word came in this afternoon. The hurricane that hit the South Carolina coast this morning claimed several lives—including one U.S. senator." He handed the e-mail printout to Flint.

The President took the paper, scanned it. "Laney?"

Randall's momentary smile faded into a more serious expression. "You need to fly down today. Show your concern for the city and the people who died. You don't have to land, just fly over in a military chopper, be seen."

"Laney didn't live in Charleston, and that storm had been forecast to hit near there for several days. What the hell was he doing there?" Flint trudged back to his desk and dropped into the soft leather chair. With fallen features, he stared at Randall. "Besides, my day will be slammed when I get back to the Oval Office."

"Campaigning for Hart or vacationing—who the hell cares what the old bastard was doing? He's one less distraction we have to deal with between now and the election."

Flint glowered. "The man's dead, killed in a damn horrific storm. He was a United States senator, a man with a family. Doesn't that chunk of ice you call your heart ever thaw?"

Randall, who had headed toward the door, whirled around. His face flushed the color of a beet. "Don't toss that bullshit compassion at me. Save it for the press. Laney hated your guts. He would have done anything—*anything*—to see you defeated in November. Mother Nature did us a favor. It was his time, so good riddance." He jerked the door open and glared at the President. "Air Force One is ready, and the chopper's waiting to take you there."

# Chapter · 4

HISTORIC DISTRICT, CHARLESTON, SOUTH CAROLINA

Jefferson bent over to avoid raking his head against the doorframe of the Red Cross tent that had been erected near what was left of the old City Market on Meeting Street. The multitude of emergency lighting set up around the devastated city cast harsh, eerie shadows against the crumbled buildings. He cradled a Styrofoam cup full of black coffee in one huge hand and steadied the balanced television camera on his shoulder with the other.

Watching the flickering silhouettes of hurried rescue workers bounce and dance around the broken buildings reminded him of apparitions from the past, flushed from their haunts by the storm to roam the streets. Tales his grandmother told him in her lilting Gullah dialect seemed to come alive as he watched the larger-than-life images skitter from broken wall to graveyard tombstone, then disappear altogether in the darkness shrouding the city. He imagined the hags and hants and plat-eyes—all restless spirits painted so vividly on his mind's wall by the master storyteller and self-proclaimed conjurer—dancing to celebrate the disaster they had wrought on the city.

He also remembered how indestructible some of the surrounding buildings had looked to him as a child. Back then, all stood so tall and sturdy. He could have never imagined their destruction by a mere gale wind, or even one measured in excess of 155 miles per hour. He recalled how he used to come with his dad and cousin, Tree, to sell oysters and shrimp they had caught in nearby Lowcountry canals and creeks.

Jefferson had always looked forward to coming to the city, but as he looked toward the ruins of the old buildings, the place where Gullah women sold their wares and weavings, he remembered how he had felt a bit intimidated too. This also had been the place where families were bought and sold, separated forever from one another, a historical fact he had never quite comprehended. Now he just felt sad that a part of his heritage had been destroyed.

As he looked to the far end of Meeting Street, he knew that out in the harbor, the veil of darkness hid Fort Sumter, the location of the first battle of the Civil War, when Confederates took the fort from the Yankees. He wondered how much of that Southern treasure remained. So much history gone. Blown away, as if the Big Bad Wolf had stopped by for a visit.

What a day. First the discovery of the body in the graveyard, then the President flies over in a helicopter without even bothering to get out and walk around to see what had happened. Jefferson recalled how Cassie had glared up at the chopper, cursed about not being able to get a sound bite from the President, and then flipped her middle finger at the helicopter. The moment had been hilarious, if not irreverent, in Jefferson's mind, and he wondered how many Charleston citizens felt like flashing the same greeting to their country's leader.

As he looked around the busy streets, he searched for Cassie, who had grown restless after interviewing only a few of the volunteers and victims inside the crowded Red Cross tent. She had approached Jefferson, with flushed cheeks and a sickly expression. She spoke as if she was out of breath, telling him to stay and shoot some footage for later use. Then she rushed out the door before he could ask if something was wrong. That had been almost thirty minutes earlier, and now he didn't see her anywhere around.

A block away, Jefferson did spot a familiar face, one he hadn't seen in over a year. In a floodlight beam shining down from what was left of a nearby popular seafood restaurant, he also spotted Rowdy Dubois, the homeless woman he and Cassie had encountered earlier in the day. She stood in the middle of Meeting Street in ankle-deep water, gesturing wildly to Brock Elliot, a lieutenant with SLED, as the South Carolina Law Enforcement Division was locally known. Jefferson knew Brock because the lieutenant, then a sergeant, had been Cassie's boyfriend, the man the ambitious reporter had left behind when she left the Lowcountry to pursue fame and fortune with CNN.

"Well, well, looky who we have here," Jefferson said as he walked up and peered down at Rowdy through squinted eyes. "This here wouldn't happen to be the detective who pays better than me, would it?"

Brock glanced around, surprised. "Jefferson. I guess you're here covering the disaster."

"Yep. Personal invite from CNN." He flashed a sly grin.

"C... NN." The last two letters crawled out as if they had been momentarily stuck in Brock's throat. "Anybody I know?"

Jefferson pursed his lips and nodded.

Brock looked past Jefferson. "Where is she?" he asked, his voice filled with anticipation.

"That's a damn good question. She interviewed a few rescue workers in the tent over there, and then she skedaddled, a panicked expression on her face. She told me to shoot some file footage, which I did. I'm a bit concerned about her, 'cause I ain't seen her since."

"Was the tent crowded?"

"Very. Why?"

"Claustrophobia."

"Yeah, now that you mention it, that's how she acted. Just like someone with claustrophobia."

Brock finished rolling one sleeve of his blue dress shirt up to the elbow. He started on the other. "Not an act. She *is* claustrophobic. When she was a kid, she got lost in some caverns on a trip with her parents. Ever since, she can't stand closed-in places."

"Didn't know that, but it explains a lot." Jefferson looked back at the wide tent. "Can't say that place is exactly close quarters, though."

"Doesn't matter. If there were a lot of people inside, it would have boogered her. Sometimes it just happens—comes out of nowhere."

"Interesting."

"How's she look? She said anything about me since she's been back?"

Jefferson flashed a bemused look. "She looks good." He placed a finger to one side of his mouth, rubbed the crease of his lips. "Let's see, what else did you ask?"

"Very funny. I was just curious."

"Oh, yeah. You wanted to know if she's mentioned you since she's been here." Jefferson winked. "If I told you, I'd have to kill you."

Brock sneered. "Thanks, old buddy—for nothing."

Jefferson cackled. "Well, when we first arrived, she may have asked whether or not I thought you'd be sent here."

"Yeah?"

Jefferson thought he spotted a twinkle in the lieutenant's eye. "That's about all, though."

Brock shrugged. His expression of indifference didn't hide the interest in his eyes. "That's good. Since I hadn't heard from her lately, I figured she'd hooked up with one of those news-anchor prima donnas down in Atlanta." He looked over at Rowdy, whose dirty-blonde hair looked like it had been chopped off with an ax. "What's this about me paying more than him?" he asked her, motioning his thumb back at Jefferson.

"He and that pushy reporter lady asked about the body over by the church."

The color washed out of Brock's face, Jefferson noticed.

"What'd you tell 'em?" Brock asked, looking at Jefferson, then back at the woman.

"Just that—"

"Hello, Brock. What's SLED's premiere detective up to tonight?"

Jefferson wheeled around to see Cassie walk up behind him. "Well, well," he said. "Thought maybe things around here had gotten too humdrum for you. Figured you'd decided to pack it in and head back to Atlanta."

"Actually," she said, her gaze fixed on the long-unseen features of her former boyfriend, "things are just starting to get real damn interesting. Isn't that right, Brock?"

Jefferson looked back and forth between the two, a quizzical expression on his face.

Brock cast an empty stare. "I'm pretty sure I don't know what you're talkin' about, beautiful. How've you been?"

"Cute." She glanced up at Jefferson, then over at Rowdy. "He does that. He'll flatter me and ignore the point of the conversation. Then he'll ask something—anything—unrelated to what you want to know." Cassie folded her arms across her chest. "All right, we'll do it your way. The body Jefferson and I found today happened to be a prominent person, if my source is right. Am I warm?"

Brock maintained his deadpan expression. "Yes, I'd say so."

Rowdy's gaze widened. "The body I seen dumped last night was somebody important? Who?"

"You saw a body dumped?" Cassie stood with her arms akimbo, her expression incredulous. "You told us you only saw the vehicle."

"I gave you a hunnert dollars' worth o' information," Rowdy said in response to Cassie's stern look. "No more."

Jefferson cleared his throat, making sure he did it loud enough to be heard by all parties. "That happened to be *my* C-note, and you didn't give me my money's worth—not by a long shot."

Cassie pointed up the street in the direction she had come from. "A little while ago," she said, "I wandered by a couple of cops taking a smoke break and overheard one say the body belonged to Rembert Wade Laney. The only Rembert Wade Laney I know of is South Carolina's United States senator—

at least, he was. Surely, no other poor child fifty years ago got saddled with a name like that." Cassie grinned like the proverbial cat who ate the canary. "Bet I'm hot, huh?"

Brock leered. "Darlin', if I had known that was all it took to get you hot, I'd have told you myself."

Cassie hit him with a disapproving glare. "Chauvinism doesn't become you. So, how'd he come to be in the cemetery, and how'd he die?"

"Maybe," Jefferson said, "our little friend who took my hundred dollars could shed more light on the situation than she already has."

Brock shook his head. "Not so fast, folks. I'll be doin' the questioning of Miss Dubois from now on. She's a material witness and off limits to the press."

"Brock!" Cassie's face flushed. "A U.S. senator is dead, and the people of this state and nation have a right to know how he died."

He laughed. "Says who? What the good citizens have a right to is a thorough investigation into what just might be a natural death."

"So what you're sayin' is, whoever this woman saw dump off the body last night, in the middle of the biggest hurricane in the history of the state, was probably only the mortician, preparing to bury him in the church cemetery." Cassie released an exasperated sigh. "What is it you used to say? 'I was born at night, but not last night.'"

"I can't comment on the investigation, and you know it. There'll be a press conference—"

"Come on, hon, help me a little here. I—" Cassie glanced at Jefferson. "We found the body. Don't we have the right to break the story?"

Jefferson couldn't help the grin that spread across his face. *The girl is good,* he thought. He had watched Cassie's performance change, as if someone had flipped a switch inside her, from railing with anger to blinking her eyelashes like Scarlett O'Hara pleading for understanding from Rhett Butler.

Brock smiled too. "I always did love that little sparkle in your eyes when you got riled. Fair enough. You found him, so you'll be first on any releases that don't hamper the investigation."

She sighed and fixed her fists back on her hips. "But—"

"That's the best I can do, okay. I'll have to clear it with Charleston PD—it's their case. But I think they'll go along."

Cassie looked up at Jefferson, who nodded. She raked her fingers through her auburn hair. "Okay, but we get at least a six-hour advance notice ahead of any others."

Brock shook his head. "One hour . . . *if* the PD will go along."

Cassie jerked a thumb at Rowdy. "When can I talk to her?"

"Not tonight. Maybe tomorrow, depending on what she knows and how sensitive it is to the case."

Rowdy protested. "Wait a damn minute. Ain't nobody gonna ask me if I'm willing?"

Jefferson hit Rowdy with the same glare he'd used to intimidate opposing corners when he played wide receiver for the Saints. "We'll make it worth your while—after I get what I paid for today."

"Humph." The woman turned to leave.

"Not so fast, Miss Dubois." Brock grabbed her flabby upper arm. "You're in my protective custody as of right now." He escorted her toward the police command post two blocks away.

Jefferson glanced at his watch and then looked at Cassie. "Why don't we crash for tonight and start again tomorrow?"

"What? And miss something? We're gonna conduct our own investigation into the senator's death, and I know just where to start."

He moaned as Cassie walked away. He shook his head. *Way, way too much energy for one girl to possess.*

Ambrose Wade Thornton—Thorn to a select few, Lieutenant Colonel Thornton to the former members of his Army Ranger unit—stood at the window on the twentieth-floor of a black and shiny building in downtown Atlanta. His eyes, as dark as the windows of the building he stood inside, narrowed, pulling the lines across his forehead taut, as he watched the lighted outline of the outside elevator glide up and down the cylindrical Weston Hotel Tower on nearby Peachtree Street. "Any word yet?"

A voice came from the darkness behind him. "No, sir. But the storm has moved out of the area. Forecasters project it will continue up the east coast and finally track out to sea."

"Washington?"

"Heavy rains are expected for the next twelve hours, then clearing. There aren't any expectations that travel will be disrupted."

"Are both parties still expected?"

"Yes, sir. No changes. Secret Service agents have already begun their sweeps."

Thornton squeezed the back of his neck with his thick fingers. "What about the polls?"

"Too close to call, sir."

He shook his head. "Damn! The last thing this country needs is a treasonous coward as president. We have to make sure that never happens. There's too much at stake."

"It's very close, sir; could go either way. Ever since the convention, he's been rising in the polls."

Light from the hallway flooded the room as a door opened. "Sir, call on line three. Said it's urgent."

Thornton glanced at his aide, motioned for him to leave. As the door closed and the room grew dark again, he picked up the phone and pushed the blinking button. "Go ahead."

"The Board will meet tomorrow afternoon," the caller said. "We had to wait on the storm. Two members will be delayed because of it."

"Will he be there?"

"Yes. He's coming in early, before the others. We'll hammer out an agreement that will benefit us all."

Thornton looked out at the flashing light of a distant aircraft. "Let me know how the meeting goes. And don't take no for an answer. We need their capital and their support to succeed."

He hung up the phone and stared back outside at the city lights. *If everything goes as planned,* he thought, *Washington's lights soon will be just outside my window.*

# Chapter · 5

SAND HILLS STATE FOREST, UPSTATE SOUTH CAROLINA

Barry Lynch dropped to one knee on the forest floor of damp humus, concealing himself in a thicket of honeysuckle vines. He sucked the sweet-scented air into his aching lungs like a man afraid of drowning, while his vision picked at objects concealed in the shadows. All around him, tall hardwoods—oak, hickory, ash—rose like skyscrapers alongside towering pines, their limbs blotting out the sun, turning midafternoon into dusky twilight.

Inside his chest, his heart pounded against his diaphragm with the fury of a captive desperate to escape. Sweat poured from the sides of his face, soaking the collar of his olive-drab crew-neck shirt, dripping down onto his camouflage fatigue pants. With his attention trained on the still woodland and his ears perked for the slightest hint of someone approaching, he reached up, removed the green sweatband encircling his head, and wrung it tight. Careful not to jostle the limbs and vines of his protective cocoon, he slipped the band back over his head, positioning it just above his thick eyebrows. A cool breeze rustled overhead leaves and filled his nostrils with more of the fragrant honeysuckle blossoms surrounding him. His gaze continued to prowl the landscape.

After several minutes of allowing his body to recover from the onslaught of overexertion, Barry drew a deep breath and listened to the woodland sounds. He released the air trapped inside his lungs, then listened again. An eerie quiet suffocated him. None of the birds chirped. Even the blue jay, Mother Nature's intruder alarm, had grown mute. He glanced from tree to tree. Not one squirrel.

*Someone's close by.*

Fifty yards behind him, a ravine ran to the north side of the forest and to the highway where he had parked his pickup truck. If he could make it there, he could escape the men stalking him. Easing up out of his crouch to look across the forest floor, he squeezed the grip of his pistol so hard, his knuckles turned white. Halfway up, he paused and listened. Nothing moved, absolutely nothing. *They're out there.* He could feel them, just like the animals could.

Drawing another deep breath, he shifted, careful not to shake the foliage around him. He peered through a small opening in the thicket. No one in sight. *Damn, not a hint of sound or movement.*

Earlier, he thought he had seen one of the men after him, near the old logging road. He had concealed himself behind some boulders to wait in ambush, figuring he was better off taking the offensive when he had the opportunity, but no one ever came near. He wondered at the time if the shadows in the forest had been playing tricks on him, causing him to see things that weren't really there, but he had quickly dismissed the thought, sure he had seen somebody, not just a figment of his imagination.

He glanced through the branches of his hiding place and saw where the ground sloped toward the ravine. He had to risk getting there. If he did, he was sure he could work his way to safety.

Only two were left, so if either or both followed him, he could lure them as far as the beaver dam. The thick foliage would give him the advantage, and he'd be able to take both out. He glanced at the Swiss Army watch on his left arm; he had about another forty-five minutes before the sun began dropping below the tree line. Then the forest would grow darker, and he would find himself consumed in an inky pitch. He needed to make his move before then. He couldn't risk using his flashlight, but moving through the darkness without one would be plain insanity.

He feared the one called Dane the most. Barry didn't know him very well, but he knew he was a crack shot, an Army marksman. He had arrived just a few weeks before from somewhere in Georgia.

Barry had witnessed Dane's marksmanship firsthand when he saw him shoot Yates Arden. The image of the attack was still vivid in his mind. It had occurred hours earlier, when Barry, hiding in a hollowed-out tree, spotted Dane—all six-foot-three-inches of the lean, muscled man—sneaking across the forest carpet of pine needles, brittle leaves, and dry twigs without making a sound. Yates never heard or saw his assailant. Just like a cunning assassin in one of those secret-agent movies, Dane walked right up to him, shot him dead in the chest, and then disappeared, before Barry could position himself for a shot. The agile assailant vanished into thin air, like one of the ghosts rumored to roam this state forestland outside Chesterfield, South Carolina.

Now, instead of being the hunter, Barry was the hunted. Sweat rolled off his forehead, filtering through his eyebrows, before dripping like liquid fire into his eyes. He blinked, wiped his sleeve across his face, and then squinted to clear his vision. A chuckle rose in his throat as he recalled the look on another pursuer's face earlier in the day.

Barry had positioned himself in a deer stand and sat quietly for over an hour, watching the forest floor beneath him. About the time his legs were beginning to cramp and he had decided to abandon his lookout point in favor of stretching his calf and thigh muscles, he heard Lance Mackenzie. Like a dysfunctional Indian trying to track his quarry, Lance moved slowly and deliberately, while clumsily stepping on dried leaves and dead branches. He wouldn't have been successful if he had tried to sneak up on a group of deaf campers.

Every step or so, Lance would pause and study the ground in front of him to make sure he didn't step on any telltale foliage. Even so, his big feet would find the most brittle around, and a loud crack would resound through the quiet forest. Each time, he would freeze momentarily, scan his surroundings, then begin the ritual all over again.

With his long blond hair peeking from under his green John Deere hat, and his focus on the ground in front of him, Lance had stepped right under Barry's deer stand.

Barry recalled how he couldn't believe his good fortune. With one thrust, he leaped from the stand and dropped down right in front of Lance. The surprised man's eyes bulged. A low-pitched, startled-sounding grunt escaped his mouth, and his gun dropped on the forest floor just as Barry squeezed the trigger of his own weapon, hitting Lance flush in the chest.

Barry grinned at the recollection. *James Bond couldn't have done better.*

He peeped out through the thicket of vines, mouth still curled with amusement. He glanced back at his watch. Time to move. He'd already been in this place too long.

Adjusting his headband to catch the moisture leaking from his brown crew cut, he popped his head up out of his cover. *No one in sight.* As he wriggled through the twisted vines, they wrapped around his legs as if they were tiny hands trying to pull him back to safety.

He broke free, started for the ravine.

A twig snapped behind him. He spun around, gun raised. He never saw the shot, but he felt the impact against his chest. He thought he had been punched at first, but when his head dropped and he looked down on the middle of his jacket, he spotted the red ooze.

He raked his fingers through the thick goo, glared at his hand, then stared in disbelief at Dane Everett. "Shit! Where the hell did you come from?"

Dane's blue eyes twinkled. "Been watching you ever since you slid in there." His deep voice chortled with amusement. "Thought you'd never come out."

Laughter broke out to Barry's right. Like ghosts risen from the dead, Yates Arden and Lance Mackenzie stepped from behind a moss-covered boulder.

"Hellfire," Lance said. "All three of us have been sittin', just waitin' for you to make a move." He spit a stream of brown tobacco juice between Barry's feet. Goggles splattered with blue paint hung from an elastic strap just under his chin. A bright blue splotch decorated the front of his green fatigues. "After what you done to me, I had to watch your skinny ass go down."

Yates didn't laugh. His face produced a pronounced scowl. "I f-for one, am t-tired of these d-damn games." His stutter, an affliction that had made him the butt of many childhood pranks, always got worse when he grew excited or angry. "I w-wish we had a real b-b-battle to fight."

Barry grinned. "If we did, you'd be dead." He looked around. "Where's Jimmy Joe?"

Dane pointed toward a patch of thick undergrowth. "Nature called."

Lance hollered through the forest. "The BODAB's probably wipin' his ass with poison sumac again." He turned to Yates. "Iffen you're serious about some action, I know some folks who'll fix you up."

"Hell, yes, I'm s-serious."

A loud rustle of leaves seized everyone's attention. "Who you calling a BODAB?" The scratchy, high-pitched voice came from a clump of bushes. Jimmy Joe stumbled into the clearing, buckling his belt above a wet spot on his jeans.

Yates shook his head. "Lance is right. You *are* a Big Ole Dumb Ass Boy."

The group laughed, all except Jimmy Joe, who grimaced and motioned to Dane before walking away. "Gonna miss vittles. If we ain't home when Mamma puts supper on the table, we don't eat." His words came slow, like his lumbering, stoop-shouldered strides.

"All you ever think about is s-stuffing your face." Yates returned his attention to Lance's offer. "When can you fix me up?"

"Soon. Anyone else interested in freedom?"

The skin between Barry's eyes pinched together. "What kind of freedom are you talking about?"

"Freedom from oppression." Lance pulled his driver's license from his wallet. "Freedom to not have to carry one of these."

Barry looked at Dane, smiled, and shrugged his shoulders.

Lance's face turned red. "There's a war comin'. If them traitors in Washington keep screwin' everybody over, there's gonna be one big ass-whoopin' war—count on it!"

Dane slid his paint gun into the holster he was wearing. "So, who are these folks—your freedom fighters?"

"Leader's name is Eustace Hanley."

Barry shook his head. "Never heard of him. Where's he from?"

"Not sure." Lance looked around at the group. "Some say from around Columbia, others say Sumter. Folks call him a modern-day Swamp Fox. I've heard that when the law gets after him, he disappears into the Congaree and won't be seen for days or weeks. He drives this black Humvee with no tag, and he ain't had no driver's license in more than two years."

"How's he get away with it?" Yates asked.

"Just does." Lance bent down and picked up a piece of broken limb. "Way he figures, no state or federal laws apply to him or his kin. He has two sons, Ira and Dewey. Dewey moved away a couple of years ago. Ira served in the Army with me—"

"Federal laws don't apply to him," Barry interrupted, "but his son served in the U.S. Army. That don't make sense."

"M-maybe he wanted to learn fightin' ways." Yates spoke up like someone listening to a story that he didn't want interrupted.

Lance nodded. "Maybe. All I know is I ran into Ira a few weeks back, down at Waldrop's. Over the course of a few beers, he told me he and his daddy done joined a bunch of other folks to form their own government— with their own laws."

Barry's expression revealed his suspicion. "How they gonna do that?"

Yates glared at Barry. "Let him finish. I think they're onto something great."

"You sound like you're ready to sign up," Dane said as he slapped Yates on the back, nearly knocking him off his feet.

Yates balled his fingers into a fist and shook it. "Hell, yeah! I'm r-ready. Let's all join. We'll go k-k-kick some ass."

The other men all looked at the willow-thin man, whose tan camouflage ball cap covered most of his short, bright orange hair, causing his oversized ears to fold down. All began laughing except Yates, who just stared, his hazel eyes wide and eager.

As the group of men emerged from the woods, Jimmy Joe leaned against Dane's red Dodge Ram truck, a look of exasperation painted on his face. He pointed to the dim last glimmer of the sun's rays painting soft hues across the graying sky. "Mamma's gonna be mad."

Dane flashed a smile of reassurance. "I'll square things with Aunt Ellen. Don't worry."

"When you gonna see Ira Hanley again?" Barry asked Lance.

Lance opened the door to his black Chevy pickup. "He's at Waldrop's most nights. I'll likely see him there tonight."

"Let me know," Barry said. "I'd be interested in what they're planning."

Dane leaned out the window of his truck. "Make that two of us."

# CHAPTER · 6

HILTON HEAD ISLAND, SOUTH CAROLINA

Standing alone on one of three large decks covering the ocean side of his expansive home, Grayson Locke watched a brown pelican skim the water, in search of its prey. The pelican drifted skyward, hovered for the briefest of moments, then dove straight down before crashing through the glistening surface. A second later, the bird flew out of the water, a squirming whiting firmly trapped in its beak.

Locke drew a deep breath of salt air. *Magnificent!* Each time he witnessed such an attack, he couldn't help feeling a kinship for the predator's instinctive need to overpower a weaker species.

As CEO of the Laramie Group, a Washington, D.C., political think tank, Locke reveled in his predatory reputation, an image he had worked hard to cultivate inside the Capitol Beltway, where preying on the weak had become an art form. His sprawling Tudor home, with four chimneys and wide picture windows, overlooked the Atlantic Ocean, the mouth of the Calibogue Sound, and the shadowy outline of nearby Daufuskie Island. The view was breathtaking, but Locke's gaze had deftly moved from the sea bird's search for food and now concentrated on a clutch of associates gathered in the gazebo perched above the pristine sands of Sea Pines Plantation.

A weathered plank walkway led from the gray stone patio beneath Locke to the gazebo, where six men—arguably among the most influential corporate power players in the United States—sipped brandy from their host's private stock. If the plan laid out before them bore fruit, they would soon be making policy for and controlling the resources of the most powerful nation in the world.

The important meeting was nearly postponed, due to the hurricane hovering off the South Carolina coast for the past few days. But when the killer storm veered north in the predawn hours of the previous day, sparing Savannah and Hilton Head, Locke wasted no time in summoning his guests.

Most flew in midmorning, after spending the previous afternoon checking on their holdings in the Charleston area. Two waited until late morning, arriving just an hour or so before the meeting was to begin, and one, Vice President Clark Randall, arrived before all of the others. He arrived early to meet with Locke, to ensure all who would be attending could be trusted to keep the guarded secret they were about to learn.

Locke had assured Randall that every man in attendance acknowledged the importance of the gathering, Locke perhaps more than the others. He stressed that all the men recognized time as a precious commodity. That was why, in the days leading up to the gathering, they had attended to personal business matters with the greatest expediency, before flying in their personal jets from scattered locales across the country.

Later, while people in Charleston, a hundred miles to the northeast, went about their cleanup and recovery, the Vice President, his host, and the guests dined on an exquisite cuisine of crab and lobster prepared by Locke's personal chef. Following the leisurely lunch, they held their meeting—one that could place each of the attendees on the president's cabinet and one that could put each in a position to shape the future of the entire world.

The men huddled in the gazebo, sipping a fine Napoleon brandy and smoking Cuban cigars, all compliments of Grayson Locke. These were the sharks of the corporate ocean. All had amassed their fortunes by being quick to size up struggling competitors and by being ruthless when they moved in for the kill. None understood mercy. In their world, survival of the fittest ruled. Nothing mattered but control—their control over everything.

From his deck, Locke tried to read the body language of each man as they discussed the offer he and the Vice President had presented to them over their midafternoon feast. He referred to the group as The Board, because their decisions had often directed the course of corporate America. Directives from Locke and his Board members could send the stock market into a death spiral or propel it to lofty profits. They controlled the flow of the nation's imports and exports. Their individual influences had often decided the fate of an election, not only through their capacities for being contributors of well-laundered campaign dollars, but also because of their willingness to do whatever necessary to guarantee the success of their candidates—even murder. Their collective desire was to shape world events, no matter the price.

Now they had been called together to listen to a plan to do that—and more. But even with all of their power, some outcomes couldn't be guaranteed. Locke knew his proposal no doubt created consternation among some in the group, despite their predatory instincts.

He knew he and the Vice President had steered the group into uncharted waters, a sea that could become turbulent and treacherous. During their early morning meeting, he had briefed the Vice President on each man. Some, Randall already knew about. He owed them for his current position.

One had used his extensive international holdings to construct a false trail of supposed illegal campaign contributions from the Middle East, creating the perception that the former Vice President's integrity had been compromised. Another used his publishing empire to expose the funding pipeline which led directly to Samuel Griffith's campaign chest. Still another called in markers from legislators who owed favors for his generous support of their campaigns. He had made sure his bought-and-paid-for lawmakers worked to rush the confirmation of Clark Randall as Flint's nominee for the new Vice President.

But Locke knew that even among this gathering of corporate hatchet men, some were stronger and more ruthless than others. His proposal stretched the laws of survival so tightly, each man had to fear the potential for a backlash that could leave them all floating facedown in an ocean of deceit. He needed the strongest to help him guide the others, because without their collective clout, the plan would certainly fail.

Locke glanced up at the pink striations in the evening sky. The Vice President had left and was well on his way back to the nation's capital. Deliberations had gone on long enough. As his pappy used to say, it was time to fish or cut bait. Now was the time to call for a vote.

Adam Cromwell stormed from the gazebo to meet Locke on the wooden walkway. Unlike his host, who stood six-foot-two, gaunt and bony despite a recent, albeit brief, flirtation with weight training, Cromwell stood only five-foot-six and weighed close to three hundred pounds. Neither man would ever be asked to model for *GQ Magazine*, unless of course they bought it, something either could do if desired.

Locke wore thick-rimmed glasses that he half joked made him look like Buddy Holly, but that was as far as the resemblance went. His oily dark hair, once combed back like the legendary rock-and-roll star, had thinned and grayed with age.

He had often bemoaned his physical shortcomings as a young man wanting to be seen in the company of the beautiful women of the world, but over the years he had learned that money could buy the necessary companionship, if not loyalty or love. These days, however, he didn't dwell on the flaws of his appearance. He had more important considerations—like world domination.

Locke cast a suspicious glance toward his short, heavyset guest. The man's round, ruddy face held beady eyes set so close together that one wondered if the man possessed any peripheral vision at all. Cromwell wasn't someone to disregard. He represented a ruthless, conscienceless force of influence on The Board, and he was a man who, Locke knew, had murdered just because he enjoyed the rush generated from watching a person draw his last breath.

The two men didn't like each other and made no secret of the fact, but Cromwell craved the kind of ultimate omnipotence his adversary could provide. Locke knew this and used a closely guarded secret of Cromwell's to harness control over his associate.

Cromwell had a private perversion, a merciless tendency to be overly rough with his women friends, most of whom, even Cromwell realized, bothered with him only because of his enormous wealth. One such affair had ended more violently than the rest, and except for the fact that Locke had learned of his misdeed, Cromwell would have felt no remorse. To him, women were expendable. Their only worth came when he could use them to manipulate and control the men who adored them.

Locke had used this special knowledge to turn the tables on Cromwell. He used it to control his old nemesis, and he knew Cromwell hated him for it.

Cromwell approached Locke. "The others want some guarantees." His tone hinted his distrust for the proposal offered earlier in the day.

Locke traced the tip of his finger along his eyebrow. "What sort of guarantees? You've each been promised key positions. Everything is evolving as we speak."

"We need to know to what extent our authority will be granted. We need to know that if we stick our necks—and wallets—out, there will be ample rewards for our risks. If we go along, everything we have rides on this one election, and I hear Hart has just gone ahead of Flint in the polls."

"We'll succeed. Plans are in motion to guarantee our success."

"What if something goes wrong?"

"I'm telling you, protections are in place, but"—Locke's eyes narrowed—"worst case, as always, each man handles his own damage control."

Cromwell's reddened face puffed like a blowfish. "From what I've heard so far, sounds like the rest of us are taking all the risk. I suspect, as usual, you've somehow insulated yourself."

"The risks are equal. I've got as much on the line as anyone—maybe more."

"That's not how we see it."

"We? Don't you mean you?" Locke looked to the others, who appeared to be content with their cigars and brandy, oblivious to the conversation on the walkway. "Why don't we all discuss this together?" He stepped past Cromwell toward the gazebo. "Gentlemen, the Vice President has gone, and I promised to have news for him by the time he reached Washington." He glanced at his watch. "Touchdown will be soon, so I need an answer. Events are in motion that will benefit us all, but only if we act now." He stared hard into each man's eyes. "So, shall we take a vote? Yea or nay. Henry, we'll start with you."

The forehead of a tall, stout man with a tanned, shaved head wrinkled. He sucked on his cigar, blew a plume of gray smoke into the air. The man looked at the others. His gaze lingered on Cromwell's scowl. "Yea."

Each man had watched the first closely. Once they heard his vote, each uttered the same word until it was Cromwell's turn. Cromwell grunted. He grimaced as he spoke. "I say yea, but only if we're kept informed of every detail. The risk we're taking demands it. What guarantee do we have that Randall will hold up his part of the bargain?"

A faint smile curved Locke's lips. "As the old saying goes, 'When you dance with the devil. . . .'" He regarded the group with his usual confident air. "Gentlemen, we are the devil. Even the leader of the free world isn't more powerful than we are when we act as one. The Vice President will uphold his part of the bargain."

# Chapter · 7

HISTORIC DISTRICT, CHARLESTON, SOUTH CAROLINA

A gruff-looking Charleston police sergeant stuck his perspiration-coated face in the door of the mobile command post. His scowl landed on Brock. "Hey, Elliot, your sweetheart reporter's outside asking for you. Don't mind tellin' you, she's worrying the snot out of us, so if you ain't interested in her no more, how 'bout makin' her disappear."

"Ha! There's as much chance of that as there is of snow starting to fall in the next thirty minutes," another officer quipped.

With everyone around him laughing at the joke, the sergeant didn't so much as hint at a smile. "Talk to her, Elliot. She's wantin' info on the senator, and when it comes to the press, none of us knows nothin'."

"Yeah, I'll talk to her." Brock's exasperation could be heard in his loud sigh. He spun around in his high-back swivel chair and watched the door as the sergeant slammed it shut.

Seeing Cassie again had rekindled his fire of longing for her, but in her reporter mode, she seemed to lack the necessary passion for romance. He had wanted to get with her the previous night, but she had been all business, disappearing with Jefferson to tape a live report before Brock could learn where they were staying.

He stared at the closed door, thinking about the blanket of superheated humidity waiting to suffocate him on the other side. He had just climbed into the command post minutes before, where cool air circulated inside the converted recreational camper. He wasn't anxious to go back outside, especially to get hit by a barrage of questions, even if they did come from Cassie.

His sweat-soaked green knit shirt, with SLED embroidered across his left breast, clung to his skin; the waistband and seat of his tan slacks felt like they had just come out of the washer. He knew that when he opened the door and stepped back outside into Mother Nature's sauna, he would be walking into ninety-eight degrees of heavy, heated air soaked with one hundred percent humidity. *Instant misery.* He moaned out loud as he pushed up from the chair and grabbed the door handle.

Outside the command post, hundreds of shirtless, sweaty carpenters hammered and sawed and drilled. Bulldozers clattered and rubble crashed as partially destroyed buildings were torn all the way down, to be later reconstructed. Charleston had become an anthill with thousands of workers scurrying around, eager to rebuild the destroyed city. Many volunteered their services or provided skilled labor at a reasonable rate. But opportunists arrived every day—some to scavenge, some to steal and defraud. All brought headaches for the police.

Not far down the street, beyond the police barricade that had been constructed during the night, Brock spotted Jefferson stretched out on a wide concrete wall near the Charleston Museum. The museum had weathered the storm better than most other buildings, although one wall had crumbled and was now covered with the same blue tarpaulin that covered roofs and other structural wounds all over the city. The replica of the Confederate submarine, the Hunley, that had marked one of the entrances to the museum had been tossed across Meeting Street, landing crumpled like an old beer can, in front of what was left of the Charleston Visitors Center.

Brock muttered as he approached Jefferson. "I hear her majesty's lookin' for me."

"Be careful. Somebody sho' crawled out of the wrong side of the bed this morning." Jefferson swung his feet around, bringing his long torso into a seated position on the wall. He pointed toward a row of green portable outhouses, each with the symbol of either a man or woman stenciled above the door. "Taking care of business."

"Guess when Mamma Nature beckons, you have to answer, no matter how driven you might be."

Jefferson nodded. "Truth."

A moment later the plastic door clattered, then swung open. Cassie stepped out, tucking in her pink-and-white-striped blouse and adjusting the belt of her blue shorts. When she saw Brock and Jefferson staring at her, she made an abrupt stop. Her cheeks flushed. "You two voyeurs getting your eyes full?"

"A beaten-down, answer-weary police sergeant told me you were looking for me," Brock replied. "You gotta quit harassing the local cops. They're just trying to do their job the best they know how, without having to stop and field questions from a pushy reporter."

As Cassie walked up to Brock, she wiped her hands on a piece of shredded toilet paper. "You know what I hate the most about those things?" She pointed at the row of plastic outhouses.

He looked at Jefferson, who shrugged his broad shoulders. "We give up," Brock said.

"Water to wash your hands. There's none, and now I feel dirty." She looked around at the closed businesses, the ones still standing. "I've got to find a place to clean my hands."

Brock chuckled. "You mean to tell me that you're standing in the middle of what is quite possibly the worst hurricane devastation in the history of the state and you're worried about finding a place to wash your hands?"

Cassie's eyes narrowed. "Men. Maybe if you weren't such a slob, we would still be togeth—" Recognition of the line she had just crossed pinched her facial features.

Brock looked as if he had been shot and was waiting to fall. His gaze swept the ground.

"Ouch!" Jefferson said, hopping off the wall. "I think I need to mosey up the street before I get slammed too. You two watch my camera." Taking exaggerated long strides, he hustled away from the couple.

Cassie's glare softened. "Brock, I . . . I'm sorry. I didn't mean—"

"No, forget it." He clenched his jaw and stared straight into her emerald eyes. "What was it you wanted me for?" His tone was all business.

She sidled up beside her crestfallen former beau. "I meant that collectively—not personally. I've been under a lot of pressure the past few days . . . weeks . . . months, for that matter. I love my job, but I really do miss you too. I've been a jerk, and you don't deserve that."

"No, I don't. Neither does anyone else. You've got to relax, Cas. You were always driven. But the person I've seen the past two days has been more than that. You're obsessed with the breaking news . . . the big events . . . like this destruction, the murder of the senator—"

"Murder?" Her voice grew shrill. "When did the senator's accidental death become a murder?"

He frowned. "See, that's what I mean."

On her tiptoes, Cassie leaned toward Brock and kissed his cheek. "If it makes any difference, you're still the man I dream about at night."

He couldn't hold in the laugh. "Please. I'm not that easy."

She kissed him again, this time on the lips, with her arms secured around his neck. "Want to bet? As soon as we're able to leave here, and things return to normal, I want you to come to Atlanta. I want us to spend some time together—just like before I left."

"When things return to normal? I'm not sure what that is anymore. I've seen you only a handful of times since you moved to Atlanta. And every time, I was the one who initiated the contact."

"We had fun, though, didn't we. Every time you came, we had a great time together . . . at least, I did."

"Yeah, but that's just it. Each time, I had to go to Atlanta. You wouldn't come back here."

"I had a new job. I just didn't feel I could leave."

"What about now?"

"We'll see. Tell me about the senator . . . please."

Brock sighed. "Yes, all indications are that the senator was murdered."

"How? Shot, stabbed, how?"

"I can't discuss method or possible motives."

"You have a motive?"

"No, not really."

Cassie's eyes probed. "What can you tell me, other than he was apparently murdered?"

"That's about it."

She blew a deep breath through her lips, then spotted Jefferson headed in their direction. "Will you say it on camera?"

"No. Charleston's PIO will, though."

"Public information officers always sound like they're reading from a script. Can't you do it? You'll lend credibility to the piece."

"Nope."

Cassie scowled, and Brock leered.

"Found you a sink with real running—" Jefferson began as he lumbered up beside Cassie. He looked at her, then Brock. "The North and South still at war?"

# CHAPTER · 8

UPSTATE SOUTH CAROLINA

Barry Lynch grabbed his jacket off the back of a dinette chair and hurried out the front door of his double-wide, pulling the door shut just as the second blast from a car horn rousted a barn owl out of a nearby hickory tree. He threw his hand up in the air. "Coming, I'm coming."

Lance Mackenzie waited behind the steering wheel of his wife's Chevrolet station wagon. Dane Everett was in the front passenger's seat, and Jimmy Joe, grinning like a kid at Christmas, sat behind him. Next to the other door in the backseat, Yates Arden percolated with excitement.

Barry stopped next to the car and peered in at the cramped space between Jimmy Joe and Yates. "If it'd be more comfortable, I'll follow behind in my truck."

"Won't work." Lance turned and talked across Dane's shoulder. "Ira said I could bring a few trusted friends. I told him what I'd be driving and how many folks I was bringing. We're supposed to drive to this out-of-the-way place—I have directions—then someone will take us to the meeting."

Barry looked at Jimmy Joe, whose big body took up nearly half the backseat. "I thought you said we were going to a church?" His gaze then roamed to Yates's impatient glare. "Never known a church to turn away potential converts."

Yates leaned forward, with his arms resting on the seatback between Dane and Lance. "This ain't no r-regular church," he said. "And these folks have g-got to be . . . be careful. They may be all we have left between us and outright tyranny."

Dane chuckled. He held up a pamphlet. In bold print across the front, it said BEANS, BOOTS, AND BULLETS. "Yates read this on the way over. He's psyched and ready to go to war."

"Yeah, who we fightin'?" Barry asked.

"Will you q-quit flappin' your gums and get in." Yates demanded.

Dane looked up at Barry. "You'd better come on and get in. Yates is likely to explode back there if you don't."

Barry shook his head and opened the door behind Dane. Jimmy Joe uncoiled and crawled out. Barry climbed in and slid over next to Yates, who sat drumming his fingers on the armrest of the door. Jimmy Joe slid back in, sandwiching Barry in the middle.

"How far is this place we're headin'?" Barry asked. "I feel like a piece of cheese between two slabs of sourdough."

Jimmy Joe laughed. Yates grunted.

"Nobody brought no guns, did they?" Lance glanced into his rearview mirror. "They don't allow no strangers bringing guns to their meetings."

Barry's forehead furrowed. "Are *they* gonna be armed?"

"Why we need guns at church?" Jimmy Joe asked.

Yates growled back at him. "Shut up, Jimmy Joe."

Lance steered the station wagon out onto the main road. "Ira said the members of the militia always wear their sidearms to the meetings, but until you get indoctrinated, you ain't allowed."

"What kind of sidearm?" Dane asked.

Lance shrugged. "Don't know. Some, like Ira, were in the military. They probably carry .45s."

Jimmy Joe's once-cheery expression evaporated into one of confusion. "Why do they have guns at church?"

Yates glared past Barry. He spoke through gritted teeth. "'Cause they're sick and t-tired of p-puttin' up with government assholes. Someday they gonna kick some ass, and I want to be there."

Jimmy Joe looked at Barry. "Kick whose ass?"

Releasing a loud sigh, Yates whirled around and stared out the side window.

"Nobody's tonight," Barry replied. "We're just gonna listen." He freed his arm to pat Jimmy Joe's shoulder. "Tonight will be sorta like church—I think."

Forty-five minutes later, Lance pointed out the windshield. "There's the sign." He slowed the car.

A large sheet of whitewashed plywood had been nailed to two posts. RIGHTEOUS SWORD AND HAND OF THE LORD had been hand-painted across the top in black, uneven letters. Below the words, an arrow pointed to a gravel road that disappeared into the forest. A crude Confederate flag was painted under the arrow.

Lance glanced around the car, then pointed down the gravel road. "Should be an old barn 'bout a mile down this road. That's where we'll meet up with our escorts."

The station wagon turned off the paved highway, onto the gravel road. As rocks bounced around in the wheel wells, sounding like shotgun pellets hitting the underside of the car, Lance angled his gaze across the front seat. "You know that hurricane that just hit Charleston?"

"Hell," Dane said, "I think the dead heard about that storm. I saw the pictures on the news last night. Looked like somebody dropped a bomb."

"Exactly. Ira asked me to ride down with him tomorrow. They're lettin' experienced carpenters in to start rebuilding. Payin' top dollar, too, from what I hear."

Yates perked up. He leaned forward near Lance's ear. "Ira Hanley asked you to go? How 'bout takin' me along."

Lance laughed. "What the hell you know about building anything?"

"Built my shed. Wired it too."

"Remind me not to go in there after dark," Barry said. "One flip of the switch, and Fluffy goes boom."

All except Yates were still laughing when the car rounded a curve. In the middle of the road stood two men waving flashlights, an obvious signal they wanted the station wagon to stop. Both men, tall with thick bodies and no necks, wore army fatigues and carried assault rifles strapped across their chests.

Lance glanced at Dane, then to the backseat. "Y'all keep your yaps shut. Let me do the talkin'."

The two men stepped to opposite sides of the road as Lance brought the station wagon to a standstill. One approached the driver-side window, and the other stood back from the car on the passenger side. He slid his assault rifle around to his front and cradled it in his arms.

"Ira Hanley invited us." Lance spoke before the man asked any questions.

"Your name?" The man's voice was deep. His piercing glare roamed the inside of the car.

"Lance Mackenzie." He moved his hand in a circular motion. "These are my friends. Ira's expecting them too."

The man pulled a walkie-talkie to his mouth. Following a short conversation, he leaned in the window. "Okay. Cut your headlights and pull into that driveway down there." He pointed beyond where the second man stood. "Park where you see the other cars. Don't get out until you're told to. Once you're on your way, follow instructions, lessen you're lookin' for trouble."

He nodded at his partner and motioned for Lance to drive forward.

"What'd he mean by that?" Dane asked.

Barry sat bolt upright in his seat as Lance turned onto the drive. Up ahead he saw an old barn and four cars parked beside it. "Looks like we ain't the only recruits."

Lance parked the car. Gripping the steering wheel with both hands, he stared out the windshield. "Reckon now we wait."

The wait was short. A dark van with dark-tinted windows pulled in behind Lance's station wagon. A loud command followed, telling everyone to exit the car. Yates was the first to jump out, then Lance and Dane.

Barry waited on Jimmy Joe. "You gettin' out?" he asked.

Jimmy Joe looked back at him with a sheepish expression. "I ain't sure at all 'bout this."

"It'll be okay. We'll all stick close together. Nothing will happen. Besides, I want to see where we're going."

When Jimmy Joe finally crawled out, with Barry behind him, the other three stood next to the van. Black hoods covered their heads. Lance was helped into the back of the van. Yates followed, then Dane. A man wearing the same uniform as the men on the road handed Barry and Jimmy Joe black hoods.

"Put these on and keep them on until you're told to remove them. If you take them off at any time during the trip, there'll be hell to pay. Understand?" The man's deep, gravelly voice exaggerated the harshness in his tone.

Jimmy Joe's hands shook so hard, he wasn't able to get the hood over his head.

"Here, let me help," Barry said as he held the hood open and slipped it down over Jimmy Joe's blond hair. Once Jimmy Joe was led away, Barry pulled his own hood down over his face.

Minutes later, he felt the van rumble over the rough drive before turning onto the gravel road. He listened as the rocks pelted the wheel well, then he relaxed back in his seat as the wheels began to hum on the asphalt.

Yates spoke out in an anxious tone. "How far we going? I can't wait to—"

"We'll tell you when we're there," the man with the gravelly voice replied. "Until then, don't talk."


"Okay, you can remove your hoods. But keep them, you'll need to put them back on when we leave."

Pulling his hood off, Barry glanced at his wristwatch. They had been on the road for nearly an hour, and his backside was stiff from the jostling.

They were now traversing a narrow dirt road surrounded by swampy terrain and a wall of forest on both sides.

The road soon opened into a clearing. A twelve-foot-high wooden fence with a wide gate stood at the end of the road. There was a tower with an armed uniformed man inside. Another man, also dressed in army fatigues and carrying an assault rifle, pulled open the thick log gate. He motioned the van through, and another man waved his flashlight toward a row of parked cars.

"Th-th-there's the church." Yates's voice cracked with excitement.

Dane peered out the window as the driver climbed out of the van and walked toward the back door. "Never seen a church steeple like that before," he said in a whisper.

Barry leaned across Yates for a peek. At the top of the church, a Confederate battle flag whipped in the night wind. Below it, at the base of the steeple, he spotted small, window-like openings, spaced about one foot apart. "What do you make of that?"

"Gunports?" Dane asked.

Lance craned his neck to see. "Yeah, that's what they look like to me."

Jimmy Joe had been quiet since his initial questions about the guns. "I ain't so sure I want to go in there. Why're all these men carryin' guns?"

"Geez," Yates said as he stepped out of the van's opened door. "Stay here if you want. As for me, I can't wait to find out how to join. These are my kind of folks."

Dane climbed out of the van, then looked back at Jimmy Joe, who stood stooped over in the doorway. "Come on. Stick close to me, and everything'll be all right. They invited us to come."

Jimmy Joe's eyes were round as saucers. "Okay, but I ain't at all sure 'bout this." He stepped out onto the gravel parking lot, and Barry hopped out behind him. At six-foot-six-inches tall and weighing close to three hundred pounds, Jimmy Joe was stouter and taller than Dane and Barry, but his height and girth didn't diminish his childlike hesitancy. The two men walked on each side of the bigger man, escorting him up to the front of the church building.

Lance led the way up the steps and through the open doors. Two men with handheld metal-detection wands met the group just inside the vestibule. Like the other uniformed guards they had encountered, both were stout and tall and looked like clones from Hitler's Aryan race. Both wore their blond hair short, cut high and tight above the ears, in military fashion. Barry thought he recognized one of the men from high school, but too many years had passed to be sure.

When Jimmy Joe's turn came to be searched, a shrill chirp rang out from the wand as it passed over his pocket. Those already inside turned and stared at the big man who had the face of a boy. Jimmy Joe's expression was that of a kid caught with his hand in the cookie jar.

"What's in your pocket?" asked the man holding the metal detector.

Jimmy Joe's massive body quaked. Moisture glistened in his eyes. He slid his quivering hand inside his jeans pocket and pulled out a closed fist. As he opened his hand, Yates's face flushed. Dane laughed, but Lance looked embarrassed as he stepped away and mixed into the crowd of onlookers. Barry moved closer, craned his neck to peer around Dane and see what seemed to have everyone's attention.

With a sheepish, sick look on his face, Jimmy Joe held his opened hand up for the other guard to see. Barry saw too. He smiled, stifling his laughter so as not to further humiliate Jimmy Joe, who had just revealed a miniature steel horseshoe and a rabbit's foot with a metal clasp and key chain on one end.

The solemn-faced guard didn't crack a smile. Shaking his head, he allowed Jimmy Joe to pass.

Inside the sanctuary—*if that's what you could call it*, Barry thought—the five men marched single file down the aisle and slid into the only available pew, where several other men and women were already seated. With his arms pinned on his right by Jimmy Joe and on his left by Dane, Barry shifted just to be able to breathe.

His gaze roamed the room as he listened to the low hum of conversations around him. Uniformed men stood in the corners, carrying rifles and wearing sidearms, confirming what Lance had earlier told the group. He continued to examine the small sanctuary, deciding it could comfortably accommodate about a hundred people. Oddly, no one sat in the chairs behind the pulpit—chairs normally reserved for a choir in a conventional church—but this was no ordinary house of worship.

Instead of a cross or stained-glass window behind the pulpit, an oversize Confederate battle flag, with a swastika in the center, hung from exposed rafters running across the inside of the peaked roof. Gun portals, like the ones beneath the steeple on top of the church, were visible in the boarded windows on each side of the sanctuary. The doors leading out of the vestibule and back to the parking lot were now shut and also appeared to have gun portals cut into them.

The place seemed to be fortified well enough to fend off a military assault, and it bore little resemblance to what Barry considered a house of worship. No one played organ music. No one passed out bulletins or spoke of members in the hospital or of families who had just lost a loved one. The members of the congregation—thinking of this assemblage as a congregation produced a smile on his face—looked more like the crowd found at a lynching than at a church service.

A cross did sit on a table in the front, alongside an elevated pulpit. Behind the table, Barry saw three large high-back chairs like ones the elders occupied during services he attended as a youth. He figured that at one time, the building probably had been a church, maybe one used by tenant farmers or sharecroppers who came and worked the cotton and tobacco fields that were once so prevalent all across both Carolinas. Who built the original church and where it was located were mysteries to Barry.

When all the attendees had been seated, the two men who had manned the metal detectors—*ushers*, he thought with a chuckle—stepped inside the sanctuary and closed the vestibule doors behind them. Within seconds, a side door opened. A man with flowing, pewter-gray hair and a full beard entered, followed by a dozen other men dressed in black T-shirts and black basic-duty utility pants with big pockets and the cuffs bloused into the top of their boots. The dozen took the seats normally occupied by a choir.

The first man looked like a frontier preacher. He wore a black suit and a collarless white shirt buttoned tight around his neck. He climbed the steps to the pulpit and faced his congregation.

*Must be Eustace Hanley,* Barry thought.

Black-pearl eyes glared from under bushy, gray eyebrows. The rumble of voices began to die as the man's silent glare cast a Svengali-like grip on everyone present.

Barry leaned over to Lance. "Eustace Hanley?" he asked in a muted voice.

Lance gave a quick nod of his head, as if he didn't want to get caught talking in church. His gaze remained fixed on the pulpit; he didn't speak.

No one moved. No one dared to make a sound. *You could hear a pin drop in this crowded room,* Barry thought. He felt a chill shudder his spine.

Two men—also dressed in black BDUs like those who had entered with Hanley—marched down the aisle and took positions on either side of the pulpit. When they arrived at their designated spots, they clicked the heels of their shin-high boots together and stood at parade rest. Both sported shaved heads and stern expressions; their penetrating scowls scoured the pews.

"Long live the Free Confederacy!" Eustace Hanley's voice boomed like a cannon shot.

Jimmy Joe jumped in his seat.

Hanley pointed to the flag hanging on the wall behind him. "And never forget your three Bs." His deep voice thundered as he spoke. "What are they?"

The crowd—all except Barry and the men who arrived with him, who had no idea what to say—called out in unison, "Beans, boots, and bullets!"

Barry spotted an elderly woman with sunken cheeks and short, snowy white hair sitting between two men who looked to be in their early twenties. She reminded him of a grandma out with her grandsons. But before he turned away, his maternal visage vanished as the woman thrust her bony fist into the air. "Beans, boots, and bullets!" she screamed in a raspy voice.

This time Barry heard Yates join in at the top of his lungs, too. "Beans, b-b-boots, and bullets!"

The crowd repeated the loud declaration six times, in thunderous voices, before growing silent. All the while, Barry eyed the group's leader, whose chest appeared to grow larger with pride on each recitation.

Hanley shouted from his pulpit. He pounded his fist against the wooden top. "Yes! Don't ever forget them. We are at war, and without them, we can't survive."

Barry glanced at Yates, sitting in rapt awe of the man railing in front of the church. Dane and Lance were attentive, and Jimmy Joe looked scared to death.

"We have to resist the jackbooted Waco and Ruby Ridge thugs of the New World Order. We are the true patriots, who must fight for our liberty from the blackhearted police state overseen by the United Nations. Their big black vultures roam our skies, spying on us, terrorizing our children, and labeling each and every one of us as surely as the Founding Fathers took branding irons to their cattle. They will stop at nothing to suppress us, and as free men, we must fight them and we must win."

As the wooden pew grew harder and harder against Barry's backside, and the discomfort of barely being able to breathe rose to where he didn't think he could bear it any longer, the speech mercifully ended.

Hanley concluded his tirade by declaring, "We are the sons and daughters of the Free Confederacy, and we must wake up and smell the tear gas of tyranny. Amass your beans, your boots, and your bullets. Show me you are ready to sacrifice. Show me you're ready to fight for your liberty."

With that call to arms, the sanctuary exploded into cheers and applause. Everyone leaped to their feet, although Barry, stunned and stiff, rose slower than the others. Yates had been the first of the newcomers to bounce up out of his seat. He clapped with a fervor. Barry even thought he heard a shrill whistle zip through the man's lips.

Jimmy Joe's visage was more of someone who had been punched in the gut. He stood dazed and reeling, a sight that brought a sympathetic pulse to Barry's heartbeat.

As the crowd started out of their pews, armed men stood in the aisles with straw-basket collection plates. Paper currency quickly piled inside each one. A few from the audience let loose a boisterous rebel yell, and when Barry glanced toward the pulpit, he saw that Hanley and his dozen myrmidons had disappeared out the side door.

Barry filed out with the crowd, his mind filled with the rhetoric of rebellion. If Hanley meant what he said—and there was no reason to doubt the leader's passion—when and where would the first battles be fought? And more importantly, exactly who would Hanley's army be fighting?

"The *sermon* lasted for almost an hour, and then came the testimonials from members of the *congregation,* who talked of actually witnessing the tyranny of the New World Order."

"Such as?" Bryson James sipped a bourbon on the rocks as he listened to the report from the Secret Service agent supervising and controlling the undercover agent known as Johnny Reb.

"According to Johnny Reb, one man claimed to have seen black helicopters hovering over Charlotte, North Carolina, late at night. He claimed he saw men dressed in dark clothing climbing down rope ladders, landing on the tops of buildings."

"This supposedly happened in Charlotte?" James thought for a minute. "Probably military maneuvers, if it happened at all. What was the spin of the witness?"

"The choppers were New World Order helicopters, and the soldiers were taking over the banks in downtown Charlotte. They were there to capture the financial assets and move them to the Zionist-controlled World Bank. That money would be used to finance further suppression of liberties and eventually bring the citizens of the United States under the control of the New World Order and its Zionist leaders."

"Damn. These folks are over the edge." James swirled his drink. "What did our UC think about the meeting?"

"He said he thought these people were dangerous. The leader, Eustace Hanley, seemed supremely confident, and his followers were mesmerized by what he told them. At times his speech alluded to something about to happen that would signal the start of the war."

"Now what?"

"Our UC is going to try to get close to Hanley. The only way to find out what or who the target is, is to gain Hanley's confidence."

"Agreed. When's the next contact?"

"Wednesday night."

"We're running out of time. Both candidates are scheduled to make their final Southern campaign swings later this month. I hope their target isn't one of them."

"I understand. I'll get him to press, but if he blows his cover. . . ."

James downed the remainder of his bourbon. He stared off into space. "Yes, I know. These folks don't take prisoners."

# Chapter · 9

WHITE POINT GARDENS, CHARLESTON, SOUTH CAROLINA

Sitting on a bench inside a white gazebo in White Point Gardens along Charleston's South Battery, Cassie watched as two gulls glided just above the harbor's shimmering surface. In the distance, she could see Fort Sumter. It still stood vigilant, overlooking the harbor as it had for so many years. Reports held that the old fort had survived the hurricane's onslaught, and from what she had heard after park personnel returned from the site, there seemed to be little, if any, damage.

Amazingly, the gardens where she now relaxed looked as if they, too, had a special dispensation from the cataclysmic event that occurred a few days before. The gazebo still stood intact, with only grime and chipped paint as a reminder that even Mother Nature's wrath yielded to the beauty of a pristine coastal garden.

Jefferson's white Bronco, with "Channel 4" painted on the doors, drove up Murray Boulevard and stopped near the park. As she watched him climb out of the SUV, Cassie recalled how their friendship had been formed when they both worked for Channel 11 in Columbia and how, together, they had uncovered a monumental conspiracy involving federal drug agents out to catch a Florida drug lord. Their coverage of that story earned her a chance with CNN and afforded Jefferson the opportunity to move back to his home near Charleston.

"Catchin' your breath?" he asked as he strode across the thick, coarse grass and stepped inside the gazebo.

"The network called. I've got another assignment," Cassie said, a hint of sadness in her voice. "Besides, the excitement's over here. Now it's on to rebuilding and cleanup."

"When you leavin'?"

"This afternoon. I need to do a wrap-up first."

"Want to shoot it here?" he asked. "Nice scenery. Doesn't look much like a storm hit, though."

"Let's ride back downtown and see if we can get in near the City Market. That area caught the brunt. We'll tape something there."

"Works for me." He grabbed her hand and pulled her to her feet. Side by side, they headed toward the Bronco.

As they neared the vehicle, Cassie took a deep breath and scanned the harbor a last time. Despite being from New Jersey, she had grown to appreciate the serenity of coastal South Carolina. Something relaxed her here, when she allowed it—which wasn't very often, she had to admit.

"Take East Bay," she said "I want to get a good dose of the water before I leave."

The Bronco rolled past piles of lumber and roofing shingles to be used during the city's revitalization. Seeing the myriad of people who had arrived to rebuild, Cassie drank in the ruin, wishing she'd taken the time to come and appreciate the area and its storied history before the storm. She had been in Charleston before, working on the drug-conspiracy story, but she hadn't taken the time to just soak up the beauty or appreciate the heritage that had made it a popular attraction. Brock had tried to get her to come and spend the weekend in one of the quaint bed-and-breakfasts, but she always seemed to have an excuse.

*Why do I always work to avoid relationships?* she thought. *Do I fear the commitment?*

"Well, I'll be. Will you look over there." Jefferson's observation disrupted Cassie's private pity party.

"Where?" she asked.

"There. Looks like our old friend Rowdy Dubois is out of SLED custody."

"Stop. I want to talk to her."

He grinned and winked. "Thought that might be the case." He pulled the Chevy next to the curb, in front of a stack of debris from a nearby vacant lot, where a landmark antebellum home once stood. All that was left now were piles of brick that once formed the foundation.

Before the car came to a complete stop, Cassie's feet hit the pavement. The street woman still wore the same dingy clothes she'd had on when Cassie and Jefferson first met her.

"Rowdy! Hold up, I want to talk to you."

The woman spun around. When she saw Cassie hurrying toward her, she looked like a squirrel trying to cross the road with a car coming. She darted one way first, then another. Before she could take evasive action and flee, the persistent reporter had caught up to her.

"What you want? I told you all I be knowing." Her eyes looked glassy, her pupils dilated.

Cassie had seen the look before, when she rode with Atlanta vice officers for a story about drug-related street crime on the south side of the city. "How about I get you something cold to drink?" She knew severe thirst was an ever-present aftereffect of heavy drug use.

"What you got?"

Cassie turned to holler at Jefferson, but he had already walked up behind her. She leaned back and whispered in his ear, "Got any cold juice or water in the cooler in your car?"

He nodded. "Gatorade."

"Perfect. She's stoned and, I'll bet, thirsty as hell. She must have gotten lit up as soon as Brock released her." Cassie turned to Rowdy. "How about some cool Gatorade?"

The woman rocked back and forth. Her distrustful gaze seemed as unsteady as her balance. "Why you bein' so nice?" Turning her attention to the bottles Jefferson pulled from the back of the Bronco, she licked her dry, cracked lips, and before Cassie could reply, Rowdy said, "Yeah, that'll be real good."

Cassie motioned to a tall live oak that had managed to avoid being uprooted or lose any of its broad, twisting limbs during the storm's onslaught. "Let's go over there, out of the sun."

Rowdy looked around as if she were searching for the refreshing drink. She smacked her lips, then staggered toward the tree. One of its big thick branches swooped down low to the ground and formed a natural railing, making a perfect place to lean.

With Rowdy leaning against the branch, Cassie eased alongside of her and began talking like an old friend. "I know you've spoken to Lieutenant Elliott already, but I wondered if you'd tell me a little more about what you saw the other night during the storm."

"You and him got somethin' goin'?"

Carrying three bottles of Gatorade, Jefferson joined the two women. He snickered at the slurred question.

"We did once."

"Not now?"

Cassie tossed a harsh glare at Jefferson, who struggled to hold back his laughter. "I guess not."

"Good." The woman raked her fingers through her uneven hair. "'Cause I think he's a real hunk."

This time Cassie almost laughed, but she caught herself just in time. "Tell you what. If you'll help me out a little by telling us what you saw, the next time I see him, I'll drop a hint that you like him."

"Would ya?"

"Sure." Cassie bit her lip as she answered. She really did hope she would have an opportunity to see Brock before she left, but she didn't plan on talking about Rowdy. "So, what did you see the night the hurricane hit?"

Obviously stoned out of her head, but somehow managing to recall the events a few nights before, Rowdy looked around surreptitiously before answering. She leaned closer to Cassie, as if she might be about to reveal a secret. "If they sees me talkin' to ya, they'll kill me."

For the first time, Cassie caught a whiff of the woman's body odor, and her eyes burned. She fought to keep from gagging. "Who . . . who'll kill you?" She leaned back, away from Rowdy.

"Good ole boys."

Cassie turned her head, drew a breath of fresher air, then leaned closer, despite the stench. "Pardon? What did you say?"

"I seen this truck. Funny looking thing, sorta squashed down and mashed out. It pulled up to the church, and these two good ole boys hopped out."

Jefferson had walked around to the other side of Rowdy for a better listen. He handed her one of the bottles of Gatorade. "How you know they were good ole boys?" he asked.

She flashed a knowing grin. "I knows a redneck good ole boy when I sees one. One wore bib overalls. And they had a rebel flag in their back window."

"Yep, sounds like good ole boys to me." Jefferson chuckled as he spoke.

Cassie's harsh glare hit him again. She leaned back toward the woman, but not as close as before. "What else do you remember?"

Rowdy struggled to open her Gatorade bottle. Her face flushed red as she strained to turn the cap.

"Here, let me help," Jefferson offered as he took the bottle and twisted off the top. He handed the opened drink back to Rowdy.

She took a long guzzle from the widemouthed bottle, then wiped her arm across her lips. "Mmmm. Hits the spot." She dragged her forearm across her forehead. "Damn, sure is hot, ain't it?"

Cassie's impatience began to bubble to the surface. "Yeah, yeah, it's hot. What else did you see?"

Rowdy glared at her. "Don't have to get snooty. I'll tell you."

Jefferson grinned.

Cassie sneered at him behind Rowdy's back. "I'm sorry. Whenever you're ready."

"Them boys pulled this long, rolled-up something out of the back of that truck and carried it toward the cemetery." She measured Jefferson's reaction first, then Cassie's. "Guess now we know what they had was that senator. What's his name?" She poured down some more of her drink.

"Laney," Cassie said.

"Yeah, Laney. Anyhow, he was likely dead before the storm came. That long rolled-up thing they carried didn't wiggle none."

Cassie asked, "Did you get a look at their faces? Could you identify them if you saw them again?"

"That good-looking detective friend of yours asked that question too. Nope. Too dark. Besides, I think they might've been wearing masks. It looked like something covered their faces." She emptied the bottle.

"Anything else?" Jefferson handed Rowdy another Gatorade.

"Thanky. You're nice . . . for a colored. Uh . . . you prefer to be called black? I know you don't like to be called a nigger. Do you?"

"Nah, guess not," Jefferson replied, noticing Cassie's smile, despite her frustration.

"Tell you what, honey." Rowdy leaned forward and winked at Cassie. "Your hunk cop. He ain't as nice as your colored friend here. He tried to get me to tell more, when all I wanted was to leave and get a fix. But y'all been nice today. Nicer than before." She grinned with missing front teeth. "Since you're nice to me, I'm gonna be nice to you and give you what he'd got if he'd helped me get my fix." Rowdy nodded at Jefferson as she reached in the back pocket of her jeans and pulled out a folded pamphlet. "Found this after the truck left. Must've fallen out and blew across near where I was stayin'."

Jefferson took the pamphlet. "Thank you, Ms. Dubois. Here's another bottle if you get thirsty later on."

Rowdy giggled. "Thanks, but now I've had so much, I gotta go find a place to pee."

Jefferson straightened up. "Please, don't let us stop you."

"Don't tell the detective what I showed you." Rowdy winked at Cassie and pushed away from the tree branch. "He'll get madder than an ole gator."

"Don't worry. We won't say anything," Cassie said, trying to read the pamphlet Jefferson was holding.

As the woman stumbled down the littered sidewalk, she stopped and turned on unsteady legs. She put her finger to her lips. "Don't tell nobody else where you got that, neither. Don't want the cops and the good ole boys wantin' to kill me."

"We promise." Jefferson waited until Rowdy had staggered away, then he opened up the pamphlet. "Beans, boots and bullets? What the hell?"

# Chapter · 10

SECRET SERVICE HEADQUARTERS, WASHINGTON, D.C.

Senator Jeff Hart, candidate for president of the United States, stepped into Finley Sawyer's finely appointed office, accompanied by a tall, slender woman with hair the color and texture of fresh corn silk. Hart's steady gaze roamed the dark-paneled walls, the photos of Sawyer with past presidents on one side, Bob Timberlake's paintings of rural Southern settings on another. Impressive sculptures and curios sat on end tables and shelves. One large vase with Oriental markings stood on a wooden pedestal. A glass dome covered the expensive-looking museum piece.

"I need to check your budget allotment for furnishings," Hart said as he sat down in one of the leather wing chairs in front of Sawyer's desk. The blonde sat beside him. "This is my assistant, Creighton Lansford."

Sawyer stepped around his desk and took the hand of the woman. He nodded with a slight bow at the waist. "Welcome."

Lansford's cold, blue eyes never left the director's. "Thank you."

Sawyer looked back at Hart. "You'll find that much of what you see are my personal furnishings, bought with my money, not the taxpayers'."

Hart smirked. "I've already checked, and I admire someone in your position saving taxpayer dollars." He pointed to the wall of photos. "Hopefully, we'll have the opportunity to add a picture of us after November."

Ever the diplomat when talking to presidential candidates, Sawyer nodded. "That's possible."

Lansford's hand swept across the right leg of her lime-green, silk pantsuit. "I doubt you invited Senator Hart over to show off your taste in interior decorating or to talk about his inauguration plans just yet."

Sawyer returned to his desk and sat down behind it. "I understand you're scheduled to swing through the South in a couple of weeks."

Lansford again responded before Hart could answer. "Raleigh, Charlotte, and Columbia on the first day. Charleston, Savannah, then on to Atlanta the next. So on and so on for six days."

Hart smiled with closed lips, causing his tanned cheeks to dimple. "No rest for the weary until after the election." His eyebrow raised. "But your folks already know all that. They're in each city, days before I arrive. Is something up?"

Sawyer leaned forward in his chair and studied Hart's youthful face. "You ever heard of a group called the Free Confederacy?"

Jeff Hart was in his second six-year term as U.S. Senator from Tennessee. The 53-year-old attorney had made a personal fortune suing corporations and insurance companies for everything from black lung in the Kentucky and Pennsylvania coal mines to wrongful death accidents, usually claiming a minimum of one third on the multimillion-dollar settlements. Raking his fingers through his mousy brown hair, he blinked with just a hint of concern. "No, can't say that I have."

Sawyer crossed his right leg over his left, looked at Lansford. "We have information that leads us to believe this Free Confederacy might be planning to disrupt our political process by attempting attacks on both the senator and President Flint."

"Both of us, huh?" Hart smiled, revealing cosmetically enhanced white teeth. "A bipartisan attack, I guess you'd call it."

Sawyer didn't smile. "These people are very capable of carrying out a threat. Their leader is U.S. Army trained, and just the other night he preached a doctrine of anarchy and revolution to a hundred very enthusiastic followers. You need to consider these threats as serious. They're very, very real."

Lansford glared at Sawyer. Her voice grew indignant. "And just what is he supposed to do, carry out the rest of his campaign over the phone? I can assure you that Flint won't slow down his personal appearances. Clark Randall won't allow it."

Hart looked at his assistant, then Sawyer. He flashed a conspiratorial glint. "In fact, as far as I'm concerned, Flint has more to fear from his own vice president than from some fringe group espousing the overthrow of the American government. You ought to be talking to Flint, warning him that Randall would love nothing more than to see him felled by some psychotic sniper." He wiped at the corner of his mouth, as if in an attempt to conceal the smirk he wore. "Of course, Randall would be better served for that event to occur after the election; then the job would certainly be his."

Sawyer didn't respond. He glanced at Lansford. Hidden beneath her movie-star good looks, he suspected an equal to Clark Randall's ruthlessness lurked. Intelligent and quick-witted, she no doubt was skilled in using her attributes; and, he would wager, she possessed the poisonous demeanor of a black widow spider. *Does Hart have as much to fear as Flint?*

Sawyer directed his comments to Lansford. "I don't expect you to slow down your campaign. I do expect you to listen to my agents, however, when they approach you about specific security concerns. To ignore them could cost you a lot more than the election."

Hart glanced at his assistant. She, in turn, looked at Sawyer. "Is that all?"

Hart pushed his lean, five-foot-ten-inch frame out of the chair. Lansford rose beside him, standing as tall and decidedly more elegant.

"That's all," Sawyer said as he, too, stood from his chair. "I hope you understand the necessity of this meeting?"

Hart extended his hand. "I realize you have a job to do, but I faced formidable threats back in Nam too. And those came every hour of every day. I survived those and I'll survive these. I plan to be on your wall over there, and nothing will stop me—especially not some band of misguided yokels called . . . what was it, the Free Confederates?"

"Free Confederacy," Sawyer replied. He shook Lansford's hand a final time and echoed his warning. "But don't underestimate their potential for violence."

"Fair enough." Hart adjusted his navy silk tie, then held the door for his assistant.

Sawyer escorted them to the outer hallway, then returned to his office, closed the door, and pushed the intercom on his desk. "Come in here."

Moments later, Bryson James entered the director's office through the same door Hart had exited. Sawyer stood at the window, silently overlooking the streets of Washington and the Capitol dome in the distance.

"Well, what do you think?" James asked.

Sawyer spoke without turning around. "Our work's cut out for us. Both have as much to fear from inside their organizations as they do outside. I take it we're not going to be able to get in to talk to the President."

James glanced at his watch. "Doesn't look like it. His campaign secretary called just before Hart arrived. I explained the situation, but the President was en route to Air Force One when we talked. The message conveyed was Flint had a full campaign schedule until the election. He won't alter it, and he expects us to take care of any unforeseen problems."

"Try to contact Johnny Reb. See if he can speed up his timetable."

\* \* \*

"What do you make of this?" Cassie asked Jefferson as she studied the pamphlet Rowdy had given them.

Jefferson swigged Gatorade from another bottle he had retrieved from the cooler in the back of his Bronco. He wiped his mouth with a swipe of his arm. "What do I make of it? I spend a hundred dollars and get jack; but give the crazy bitch something cold to drink when she's stoned, and she comes across with the ranting of some white-supremacy nut group. Wished I'd known what she wanted the other day. You can buy a passel of sports drink with a hundred dollars."

Cassie partially ignored Jefferson as she read. "What's with this beans, boots, and bullets BS?"

"You might say the three Bs is a guy thing, a testosterone-based rallying cry for some of these nut groups. Most are outdoorsmen who believe you can exist just fine with the basic staples of beans to eat, a good pair of boots to wear, and ammunition to fight anybody who tries to tell you what to do. Most are several bricks shy of a load."

"And there're groups like this here in South Carolina?"

"Some say the Carolinas have the largest concentration of right-wing nut cases of any region in the country. Even more than the Midwest. Of course, it don't matter where you are, you'll always find a group of malcontents who ain't happy with the good ole US of A."

"What makes you think they're white supremacists?"

"You see that swastika in the middle of the rebel flag? Neither symbol favors blacks, Jews, or anybody else, for that matter, that ain't lily white." He smirked. "Ain't real sure they cotton to the Irish, either."

Cassie glared at Jefferson, then the pamphlet. "In that case, I need to find out more about them. Maybe they did have something to do with killing the senator. After all, this thing claims their members don't have to pay taxes or abide by any federal law. They need only answer to their own courts and leaders. As members of the Free Confederacy, they claim to answer only to God." She looked over at Jefferson. "Pretty scary, actually."

"Yep, you got that right." He turned the key in the ignition. The engine revved as he pumped the accelerator like a race-car driver. "You still got time to go to the City Market?"

Cassie glanced at her watch. "Yeah, just, then I'll need to get to the airport. But I want to keep in touch. If I can convince my editors, I'll be back to try and track down some of these Free Confederacy dudes."

"Dudes? You ain't talkin' dudes here. You're talkin' about good ole boys on hate-induced natural steroids. They're the type who play for keeps, and they don't have no sense of humor." Jefferson worked the knobs on the radio until a jazz trumpet blared. He glanced at Cassie, his eyebrow lifted. "They may very well be involved with the senator's death, but he ain't likely the only person they've sent to the hereafter on an early admission plan. I personally wouldn't want to cross the assholes."

"So you're not interested in being my cameraman if I can pull off the assignment? The story could turn out to be huge."

Jefferson stared at her and sighed. He hated it when she played him, and right now he felt like an old banjo. "Yeah, call me if you get somethin'. Somebody's gotta keep that pretty head of yours from gettin' blown off."

"Thanks. I'll need you for this one." Cassie leaned across the seat and pecked a kiss on his cheek. "Oh, and if we don't see Brock before I have to leave, tell him I'll call first chance I get."

# Chapter · 11

ONE WEEK LATER, AT A CONSTRUCTION SITE IN CHARLESTON, SOUTH CAROLINA

Ira Hanley wiped the sweat from his forehead with a red bandanna he had picked up from a local street vendor. "Got any more nails?" he asked Lance Mackenzie, who was standing on the scaffolding next to him.

"Catch." Lance hurled a tall cardboard box in Ira's direction.

The two men had been in Charleston two days and had already earned over eight hundred dollars apiece. Work had fallen into their laps from the minute they arrived. First they had been asked to help out with the main sanctuary reconstruction of the old Blessed Redeemer AME Zion Church on Calhoun Street. Then they were pulled off that job to help with a historical bed-and-breakfast on Meeting Street, where they were working now. Who knew where they would be sent next. The days were long, the nights filled with beer, raw oysters, and little sleep, but the money was plentiful.

"Hey, Ira, climb down here. I got somebody you need to meet."

Ira looked over his shoulder at one of his father's friends from Sumter, who belonged to the Free Confederacy. Lester Sease, a man Ira trusted, headed up one of the construction crews, and he had talked Ira into coming to Charleston for a few weeks.

"It'll be like going to California during the gold rush," Lester had said shortly after the hurricane hit. "People will pay whatever we ask, just to get their homes and businesses rebuilt. You can be on my crew. Bring along a few more good workers if you want, but make sure they're coming to work."

Ira eased back onto the ladder extending from the scaffolding where he was perched. Skipping several rungs at a time, he shinnied the twelve feet to the ground.

"Ira Hanley, this here's Bo," Lester said. "Bo's a supporter. He seen something the other night I thought you might want to pass on to your pappy."

Ira nodded at the man wearing bib overalls, no shirt, and a soiled, straw cowboy hat. "What you seen?"

The man took off his hat and wiped his arm across his forehead. "I was stacking shingling out behind the Peanut Shack on Calhoun the other night, and I heard this woman braggin' to friends 'bout seein' who killed that senator they found in the cemetery on Church. She was stoned out of her gourd and talked loud, but I think she really did see something."

Ira glared at Bo. "Why should I care about some old woman's lies and exaggerations?" He took a step toward the man, leaned into his face. "You think I got something to do with killing the son of a bitch?"

Bo didn't flinch. His jaw set rock hard, his eyes narrowed. "I ain't accusing nobody of nothing. You want to hear what I got to say, or not?"

"Let him finish," Lester said.

Ira stepped back. "Go ahead. Finish."

"Her friends started raggin' her 'bout makin' things up. That's when she told 'em about the black military-style truck and the piece of paper she found."

"What paper?" Ira asked.

"She said it fell out of the truck when the men took the body out."

"She actually seen them totin' a body?" Ira asked. Concern rose in his voice.

"Claimed she did. Said after the truck left, she ran over and seen the paper. Claimed she planned on seein' what they dropped off, but the storm hit before she could. Now she claims she knows it was that senator."

"This woman got a name?"

"I asked around. Folks call her Rowdy. She's a doper, lives on the street. Way she described it, that paper she found was one of your pappy's handouts."

Ira pulled off his work gloves, then took his bandanna out of the back pocket of his jeans. He wiped his mouth and forehead. "You told anybody else 'bout this?"

"Nope, but when one of her friends asked her to show them the paper, I heard her tell him she gave it to a reporter."

"A reporter." Ira rubbed the back of his neck. He looked at Lester. "I gotta go get up with Daddy. Ain't sure if I'll be back or not."

"Understood," Lester said. "Tell Eustace, if he needs anything, to just call."

Ira looked at Bo. "Thanks." He turned and climbed back up the ladder to get his tool belt. When he got back up on the scaffolding, he motioned to Lance. "Come on, our work here is done, but we may have another job—a more important one—to take care of after I talk to my daddy."

* * *

Jefferson checked the gear in his tackle box. *Fishing hooks, line, wire cutters, first-aid kit. What's missing? Flashlight batteries. Can't forget those.* He grabbed a new pack of D-cells out of a drawer in his utility room, then walked over to his workbench and surveyed the items he had laid out for one of his favorite nighttime activities.

His cousin, Tree Calhoun, had called earlier in the day. They were going frog gigging, and with any luck at all, they would soon be dining on one of the finest delicacies the Lowcountry had to offer—deep-fried frog legs.

*Looks like everything's here.* He grabbed the aluminum pole with the barbed gig affixed to one end, then picked up his high-intensity, four-cell flashlight. He flipped the switch and shined the beam against the wall. *Awfully dim.*

Opening a pack of the batteries, he looked over at his shiny black Lexus, a perk from his NFL days. *'Bout time to trade the flash for the practical.* What he needed now was a car like his station's Bronco, with its four-wheel drive. Fortunately, Tree, who owned a Jeep, had offered to drive this time, but sooner or later Jefferson knew his increasing interest in hunting and fishing and the like would dictate the need to abandon the luxury for a go-anywhere-type vehicle.

Jefferson and Tree, a narcotics agent with SLED, had always been close, but over the past few months they had grown closer than ever. Every chance they got, they hunted and fished and did the kinds of things they had done as young boys living in the Lowcountry.

Tree had nearly died the year before, after being shot during a drug raid in Charleston. That experience helped bring focus into both men's lives. Now they appreciated each day together more than either one ever had.

Jefferson glanced at his watch, then out the window. Clouds covered the moon, making the night darker than usual. *Anytime now, Cuz. Them frogs are waitin'.*

His cell phone rang. Usually, only the assignment editor at his station called him on his mobile phone at night. Everybody else called him at home. He glared at the tiny phone resting next to his tackle box. *Not now.*

He glanced at the number on the caller ID, recognized it as Tree's cell phone number. "Yo, Cuz. We're burnin' moonlight. Where are you?"

"Bad news." Tree's deep voice paused.

Jefferson could hear the wail of a siren. "Don't tell me."

"Homicide. They just called. Looks like it's drug related, and I'm the only narc available."

Disappointment didn't dull Jefferson's journalistic instincts. "Where's the body?"

"Found her in an alley off Bee Street, near the Medical University. First officers on scene say it's probably a drug deal gone bad."

"You got a name yet?"

"Nope. They think she's one of the homeless souls, though."

Rowdy's face flashed in Jefferson's mind. Only a week earlier, he and Cassie had pumped her full of Gatorade to get her to talk about what she had seen the night the senator died. He recalled how nervous the woman had been about being caught talking to them, and how she had commented that if the good ole boys saw her with them, they'd kill her.

"You know a street regular named Rowdy Dubois?" Jefferson asked.

Tree chuckled. "Everybody knows Rowdy. She's a crackhead, but deep down a pretty good ole gal. Why?"

"Just wondering. Think your victim could be her?"

"Possible, I suppose. Ain't heard a name yet, though."

"When you get there, if it's her, will you call me back?"

"What's up with you and Rowdy?"

"Maybe nothin'. Maybe something. Call me. If it's her, I'll fill you in on a conversation I had with her a week or so ago."

"Will do, but if I tell you, keep it to yourself until we can locate a next of kin. Chief gets real bent out of shape when the media puts victims' names out before we're able to contact the family."

"Gotcha. I just need to know."

A light drizzle fell as Jefferson parked his Lexus and stepped out onto a busier-than-normal Bee Street. Tree had called back. Rowdy was dead.

Red and blue lights bounced off nearby buildings. Police dispatchers' voices echoed in the night air from loudspeakers attached to the light bars of nearby patrol cars. Strobes from cameras flashed in an alley a half block up from where he had parked. *Rowdy's last stand?*

Jefferson pulled his waterproof parka tight around his chest and headed for the commotion. He hadn't gotten far when a high-pitched male voice challenged him.

"Hold it right there. You ain't got no business here, so move on away. This here's a police crime scene." The young officer, who wore a bright, reflective orange rain suit over his uniform, was the same one Jefferson and Cassie had encountered after they discovered Senator Laney's corpse in the churchyard.

"Don't you ever sleep?" Jefferson asked with a half grin.

The officer flashed a quizzical look. "I know you?" His question revealed a tentative tone, as if he feared he had misspoken to some ranking officer.

"No. We met a week or so ago, that's all. I need to see Tree Calhoun. He called me."

"You are. . . ?"

"His cousin. He'll explain. Just find him."

The officer's condescending glare was beginning to irritate Jefferson. He watched as the youthful cop pulled his radio to his mouth.

"Somebody here's claiming to be Agent Calhoun's cousin. He want to see him?" The squelch on the radio crackled. He turned back to Jefferson and said, "He's on his way." The officer looked almost disappointed.

A couple minutes later, Jefferson spotted Tree's towering physique striding out of the darkness toward him. The letters SLED glowed a luminescent yellow across the chest of the dark jacket he wore.

John Calhoun had been tagged with the nickname "Tree" after lifting a fallen tree trunk off another one of his cousins while they were on a hunting trip in a swampy wetland on the Georgia and South Carolina border. At the time, Tree was only twelve, the cousin thirteen. Lean and tall in the dark mist, Tree looked just like a hardwood that had suddenly come to life in the middle of Bee Street.

"You got here in a hurry," Tree said as he escorted Jefferson beyond the yellow tape marking the outside perimeter of the crime scene.

"Sure did hate to hear it was Rowdy. But thanks for the call back."

"Why don't you tell me about Rowdy Dubois and why you're so concerned about her."

Jefferson told Tree about his and Cassie's first encounter with the woman. Pointing toward the rookie policeman guarding the scene, he recounted the argument he had witnessed when Rowdy tried to get inside the churchyard to talk to a detective. He ended his recollection with the last time he had seen the woman and the pamphlet she had given Cassie.

"You said she seemed to be scared that some of these militia guys might want to kill her?" Tree asked.

"Pretty much. Still, she offered up the information without too much hesitation."

Tree scratched his shaven head. "And Brock Elliott had talked to her, but she didn't tell him about finding the pamphlet?"

"Said she didn't."

"Curious. Still, everything here looks like she got killed over some crack rocks. Leastwise, that's the theory the PD's going on. Little packages of crack are scattered all over the ground around her."

"If the killer was a seller or user, would he have left the dope behind?" Jefferson asked.

"Good question. I wondered that myself, but Charleston PD's treating it as a bad drug deal, and I don't see nothing compelling to argue any different."

A second ribbon of yellow tape cordoned off the actual murder scene and the corpse from everyone except crime-scene technicians and the primary investigators. Jefferson stretched up on tiptoes to get a glimpse. He saw Rowdy, facedown on the wet pavement.

"You still got that pamphlet?" Tree asked.

"No. Cassie took it with her. She said she wanted to look into doing a story on right-wing extremist groups."

"She'd better be careful, if she does. Those boys have a mean streak about 'em." He pointed toward Rowdy's corpse. "And if your theory's right, they won't have much of a sense of humor when it comes to dealing with snooping reporters."

"I told her the same thing before she left. If she comes back here to work on a story, she'll call me. Maybe I can keep her out of trouble."

Tree glared. "You'd better be careful, too. Them boys especially don't care much for our kind."

Jefferson twisted his lips, nodded his understanding. "If it's okay, I'm gonna call her and tell her about Rowdy. I don't think they'll run anything about her death, but Cassie would want to know, since she helped us."

Tree nodded. "Yeah, okay. Just tell her not to run the name for a day or so. After that, the lid will come off, notification of next of kin or not."

# Chapter · 12

CONGAREE SWAMP NEAR COLUMBIA, SOUTH CAROLINA

The black Humvee traversed the pothole-laden, long-abandoned logging road as easily as if it were riding down a nearby freeway. In the back, Lance, Barry, and Dane bounced on a steel bench—blindfolded.

Barry leaned toward Lance and whispered, "Is this really necessary? This is the second time we've had to go in blind."

"Shhh! They want to protect the location of their training camp," Lance said.

From the front seat, Ira hollered over the roar of the diesel engine. "We're almost there. You can remove your blindfolds."

Barry pulled his off and looked out the side window. This time the trip was in daylight, revealing more of what actually surrounded the secluded base camp for the Free Confederacy. On both sides of the road he saw the forest and swampy wetland, but now he could discern more. Cypress trees poked out of water the color of black-bean soup. Many of the trees were heavy with vines and Spanish moss. But that was all—no sign of houses or civilization. All he could see on either side of the gravel road was swamp and forest.

"Just around the next bend," Ira said.

The words no sooner escaped his lips than the men in the Humvee heard the retort of automatic weapons off in the distance. An explosion followed.

"What was that?" Dane asked. Concern laced his voice.

"Just some of the boys practicin'," Ira explained. "Ain't nothin' to worry 'bout. They're over yonder, away from the cabins." He pointed across the wetland to their right.

All Barry could see were streaks of sunlight filtering through the dense foliage. "What cabins? They in the swamp?"

Ira laughed. "The training ground, where we conduct maneuvers, is on a peninsula out in the swamp. We like to pick rough conditions for our training. Anticipate the worst, hope for the best. That's Daddy's philosophy."

"Any gators out there?" Lance asked.

"Mostly cottonmouths and rattlers. Ain't seen no gators around these parts."

Dane leaned toward Barry. "I'd rather deal with the gators than the snakes."

Barry nodded and looked at his watch. They had been on the road for over an hour, and he had felt every tortuous mile in his backside, even worse than when he was brought here in the van. At least the van's seats had cushions. Riding in the built-for-off-road military vehicle wasn't exactly like riding in a limousine.

As he leaned forward, partly to stretch his back and partly to peer out the windshield to see what was up ahead, he guessed they were somewhere in the Congaree Swamp near Columbia. Where in the over 22,000 acres of rotting tree stumps and murky, smelly water they were was anybody's guess, but there weren't that many swamps of size around the upstate area. *Has to be the Congaree.*

Lance had called the night after he returned from Charleston, with news that they had been invited back to the headquarters compound of the Free Confederacy. He stressed that only the three of them were invited on this first trip. He didn't want Yates or Jimmy Joe coming. "I want Ira to get to know you and Dane," he had told Barry. "Then we can talk about the others. First impressions are important. Let's get to know these folks before inviting anybody else along."

Barry didn't have a problem leaving the others behind. Jimmy Joe probably would prefer to be left out, anyway, especially after the way he had acted during the previous trip. And Yates—he was just plain crazy and way too dangerous. Barry had wanted to put some distance between that nut case and the group after hearing some of his comments at the church. *Maybe this is the time to cut the ties completely.*

The Humvee rounded a turn, and the land area widened. The tall wooden fence came into view. In the daylight the top of the tower was clearly visible. Two uniformed men holding what looked like AR-15 assault rifles watched the Humvee approach.

As the thick log gate opened, Barry glimpsed the church with the gunports in the steeple. There were more vehicles—regular ones, like Toyotas and Hondas—sprinkled amid the tall pine trees. Four olive-green Army jeeps were parked side by side on the other side of the camp. Beyond them, he saw two canvas-covered trucks, the kind used to haul troops in every World

War II movie he had ever seen.

Off to the right, he noticed three log cabins he hadn't seen in the darkness the first time. A front porch ran the full length of the largest one, which even had rocking chairs, just like a normal home in an ordinary neighborhood.

Ira parked and turned around in his seat. "Well, folks, this is it. Base camp for the army of the Free Confederacy. Welcome to God's country."

The three men in the back of the Humvee looked at each other. Lance's face glowed with anticipation, and he gave a thumbs-up. Dane and Barry remained silent as they exited the vehicle.

Men and women, most wearing camouflage or olive-drab uniforms, and all carrying automatic weapons of one type or another, stopped their activities to see who was arriving. Once the people in the compound had taken long looks at the newcomers, they returned to their previous activities.

One man and woman inspected an opened box of hand grenades sitting in the back of a jeep with US ARMY stenciled on the side. Several others marched in a close-order drill a few hundred yards away. At the far end of the camp, another group of men and women, even a few children, practiced kickboxing and other martial arts.

"Busy place," Dane said as Ira escorted the three men to the main cabin.

Unlike the others in the compound, Ira wore faded blue jeans and a black T-shirt. "Wait here," he said, stopping at the foot of the steps leading to the front porch. He pointed to the rockers. "Make yourselves comfortable. Daddy will be out directly to talk to you. I'm going to change."

As Ira walked away, Barry, Lance, and Dane stared at each other. "I don't know 'bout you two," Lance said as he started up the steps, "but I'm for doing just exactly as he said."

Barry watched Ira disappear into the cabin next door before he followed Lance and Dane up the steps. On the porch, he stood and looked out at all of the activity. *Preparations for war?*

"Pretty impressive, ain't it?" Eustace Hanley opened the screen door and stepped out onto the porch. He wore a black BDU uniform, with a replica of the same flag they had seen at the church sewn above his right breast—a Confederate battle flag with a swastika in the center.

"Very," Lance replied.

Hanley nodded. "Understand you helped Ira carry out a special assignment down in Charleston."

Lance's face flushed, and he glanced around at Dane and Barry, as if he hoped they hadn't heard Hanley's comment. "Yes, sir. Yes, I did."

"Good job." He patted Lance on the back. "We're not strong in numbers yet, but we're picking up new members every day. What we lack in bodies, we make up for in grit and determination." Hanley propped his large hands against the porch railing as he surveyed his troops. "So, you boys want to be soldiers in the Free Confederacy." He turned and glared at the three men. "Why?"

The direct question stunned Barry, who glanced at his two friends.

"Freedom from tyranny." Lance spoke first. "I, for one, am sick and tired of being told what I can and can't do. We have to take our country back from the Gestapo of the New World Order."

Hanley nodded as he pulled a pipe from his pants pocket. "You've already shown you're worthy. What about you two?" Holding the bowl of the pipe like the grip of a pistol, he pointed at Barry and Dane with the stem. "Why y'all come?"

Barry looked around the compound, avoiding eye contact with the man, reflecting on his reasons for coming. He wondered what assignment Lance had helped Ira carry out. His friend had spouted off the same rhetoric that the men had heard spoken by Hanley at the church, but Barry realized Lance's actions, not his words, were what pleased Hanley. Besides, Barry didn't want to sound like a robot.

Dane spoke before Barry had a chance. "My home's in Iowa. Born and raised there, and my brother farmed the family land there. The bank loaned him money but made the terms impossible for him to be able to pay back the loan. He lost his farm and his pride. Ashamed to face his family and friends, he took his own life. I believe the bankers of the New World Order killed him with their greed and oppression. Just the same as pulling the trigger themselves, far as I'm concerned."

Hanley's face grew solemn. "Bless you, son. You're the kind of oppressed American we want. I only wish that your brother had lived to see his day of atonement."

Barry watched as Dane's eyes swept the gray wooden floor. *Jimmy Joe had said Dane came from Georgia.* Barry realized he didn't know much about Dane—where he really came from or anything else. All he had known was that he was Jimmy Joe's cousin from Georgia and that he'd been around for about a month. Before that, Barry had never heard of him. He looked over at Lance, who didn't seem to pick up on the contradiction.

Hanley's gaze landed on Barry. "What about you, son? You have a history?"

Barry swallowed hard. "No, sir. I only want to be able to own my own land, keep my own guns, and live a life without some jackbooted bureaucrat telling me what I can and can't do."

"Amen to you, too, son. You boys are exactly what we're lookin' for, but I already knew all about you."

"How's that?" Lance asked.

"We have our—"

Automatic weapons fire erupted from the tower guarding the entrance to the compound. The loud, rapid blasts flushed a flock of white birds from a tall tree out in the swamp.

Three men rushed out of the camp through the gate, their rifles held level across their chests. Hanley bounced out of his chair and rushed to the porch railing. He leaned forward, craning his neck toward the gate opening.

"Halt!" screamed a voice out of sight, beyond the fence. Another burst of gunfire spit live rounds from the tower, shredding the branches of smaller trees and shrubs beneath it. "Freeze right there! Down, down on the ground." The guard with the loud, harsh voice sounded like he meant business.

As quick as the commotion occurred, silence fell over the encampment. Men and women stood frozen. Those who had rifles nearby had pulled them to their shoulders, and now they stood aiming them toward the opening at the entrance gate.

Ira bolted through the front door of the cabin he had gone into earlier. Having changed clothes, he now wore the same black BDU uniform as his father. He grabbed an AR-15 resting against the cabin's siding and ran across the compound.

When he reached the gate, the three men who ran out earlier appeared in the opened entrance. They were dragging a fourth man, a man dripping swamp water and covered in muck.

As the soldiers drew closer with their captive, Lance stammered, "What th—"

"Yates!" Barry said.

"You know this feller?" the elder Hanley asked Barry. He scowled at all three visitors.

"Know him, don't claim him," Lance said, before Barry could reply. Disgust clung to his words. "He must have followed us. We didn't know."

"We know him," Barry said. "But Lance is right. We didn't bring him."

Yates rubbed his jaw against his shoulder.

Ira poked the end of his rifle barrel into Yates's back. "Hold still. Don't be tryin' nothing foolish."

Eustace Hanley nodded at his son. "Okay." He looked at all the others, their rifles trained on Yates. "Lower your weapons. He ain't gonna try nothin' now." He glared at Yates. "What you out here for, boy?"

— 70 —

"I . . . I'm a s-soldier. I want to j-join."

Hanley stared with an incredulous look. He walked down the porch steps and over to where Yates stood cowering. Hanley raked wet gunk off of Yates's head with his hand, held it up to show the others, then slung it to the ground. "You look more like an old hog what's been wallowing in the mud than any soldier I ever seen."

The men and women in the compound broke into hysterical laughter. Yates's injured look told Barry he was anything but amused.

"I want to join. I want to fight the t-tyranny."

"Fight t-t-tyranny," Ira said, mocking the prisoner. He laughed. "You look like you're afraid of your own shadow. We don't need the likes of you here."

Yates looked to Barry, then Dane, and finally Lance. "Tell 'em I'd be a good soldier. Tell 'em," he pleaded, his pointed chin quivering.

None of the three spoke a word in Yates's favor. They looked back and forth at each other.

Lance shook his head. "We didn't bring him here," he repeated to Hanley. "We want to stay, to fight alongside of you."

Hanley stared at his son for several seconds, then glanced over at Barry. "Okay, the three of you can stay." His glare bore down on Yates. "As for you, I want you to leave. And if you tell anybody anything about what you found out here today, I'll see to it that those will be the last words you ever utter. You hear what I'm sayin'?"

Yates shook. "But—"

"You don't hear good, do you, boy? On second thought. . . ." Hanley pointed a long bony finger toward the gate. "Get him out of here. Take him into the swamp and leave him for the snakes."

Barry stepped forward. "Don't kill him. He'll keep quiet. Won't you, Yates?"

Yates cowered. "I w-won't say nothin'. I p-promise."

Hanley's gaze pierced Yates's forehead. "Put him in whatever he came in, and make sure he leaves. If I ever see you again or hear so much as a peep out of you after today, you won't be able to find a place to hide." He drew in a deep breath, then released it. "Get him out of here."

"Hey, Lieutenant, call for you. Long distance from Atlanta."

Brock stopped in front of the receptionist's desk in the lobby of the SLED headquarters building in Columbia, South Carolina. He reached out for the pink slip of paper the woman held. "When?"

"It's there on the top. 'Bout twenty minutes ago, give or take." The heavyset brunette winked and smiled, revealing lipstick stains on her teeth. "Rekindling an old flame?"

"Humph." Brock grabbed the handle of the door leading into the secured office hallway of the building. He swiped his ID card through the slot mounted on the wall, glanced back at the receptionist's sardonic smile while he waited for the familiar electronic hum, and then pulled open the door.

He read the note as he walked. *Cassie O'Connor. Number isn't her apartment or her cell phone,* he thought. *Must be at work.*

He recalled how he had looked all over for her the day she left Charleston. He had found Jefferson late that afternoon, working with another reporter on a story for the Charleston station. Jefferson told him Cassie had flown out earlier that day, that she looked around for him before she left but finally had to go.

Brock hadn't heard from her in over a week. He patted his cell phone. *She's got my number. Why didn't she call?* He dialed the number left on the note by his receptionist.

On the third ring, a woman answered. "CNN news desk."

"Cassie O'Connor, please."

"Just a minute."

Brock studied the ceiling tiles in his office. Several were water stained and needed replacing.

"O'Connor." Her voice sounded anxious.

Leaning back in his chair, his feet propped on his desk, Brock stared at a stain on a tile directly above his desk. "You forget my cell number?" He didn't identify himself, hoped he didn't have to.

There was a brief silence. "Brock. No, just didn't want to interrupt if you were interviewing someone."

*Plausible,* he thought, *but since when did the famous Cassie O'Connor mind if she interrupted an interview.* "What about since you flew back to Atlanta? You could've at least called to say you arrived home okay."

"Sorry. You know me. I've been wide open ever since I arrived. That's why I called. I'm working on this story, and I need your help."

Brock rolled his eyes. *Figures.* "Wazzup?"

"With the election right around the corner, we're doing a piece on organizations who oppose the government. You know, like those militia groups, the ones who throw out all those conspiracy theories about a New World Order."

"Yeah. We've got a few like that around these parts."

"More than a few, from what I've heard. You ever hear of a group called the Free Confederacy?"

Brock remained silent. This was the second time in two days someone had mentioned the Free Confederacy. The last time, it was agents from the United States Secret Service, sitting right here in his office, talking about possible threats against the presidential candidates when they're in the state. His gaze slid around the room. *She got my office bugged?*

"Yeah, I've heard of 'em. They're a freemen militia group. Sparse membership. No reported acts of violence, just indignant disregard for our laws. They don't cotton to much the government has to offer."

"You consider them dangerous?"

He thought about what the Secret Service agents had said at their briefing. "Can be, I suppose. Some of their members have been suspected in a couple of arsons of government buildings—nothing substantiated. Mostly, though, they just refuse to comply with our registration laws, like use of any government-issued documents—driver's licenses, vehicle registrations, honoring subpoenas, that sort of stuff. Claim they only recognize God as their governing power. About a year ago, one got his car impounded because his homemade license tag read 'Kingdom of Heaven' instead of 'South Carolina.' Why you ask?"

"Any chance I can meet one of their leaders and interview him?"

"You're asking me? I can't set up something like that for you. Wouldn't if I could. I'm the enemy, hon. When we have need to go talk to one of them boys, we take along plenty of firepower. I'd work on another angle, were I you."

"What if I think they've already murdered somebody?"

"Who?" Brock pulled his feet off his desk and sat up straight in his chair. His question was met with silence, and his mind wandered back to when Cassie had covered the hurricane. "You're not referring to Senator Laney, are you?"

"Not necessarily, but let's use him as an example. Would he be someone they would target?"

Reflecting on some of what Rowdy Dubois had told him before she got mad and clammed up, he wondered if the men she had seen were part of a group like the Free Confederacy. Then he thought about Tree Calhoun's call, telling him Rowdy had been found dead. "I know you too well, darlin'. What's got you runnin' this rabbit?"

"Nothing. Listen, I've gotta go. I'll call again. Soon. I promise."

Before Brock could stop her, the line went dead. *Laney and the Free Confederacy? How did Cassie get that group tied to Laney? Does she know about Rowdy's death?*

He picked up the phone and dialed the extension for SLED's intelligence unit. They kept tabs on fringe groups, motorcycle gangs, the Klan, and any other gatherings that might present a threat. He needed to find out as much as he could about the Free Confederacy, and he needed to find out quick. If he knew Ms. Cassie O'Connor, she'd be back in the state before long, up to her pretty little neck in trouble.

# Chapter · 13

DOWNTOWN ATLANTA

Two days after his return from Charleston and the attempt by an intruder to gain entry into the Free Confederacy compound, Ira Hanley found himself standing in a canyon of skyscrapers in downtown Atlanta, staring at the imposing building before him. It wasn't as tall as the other structures surrounding it. It didn't have a covered crosswalk linking it to another tower, or an elevator slipping up and down its inky outside skin of glass and steel. This decidedly smaller building stretched up only fifteen stories, its unlit upper floors disappearing in the night sky.

Despite its smaller size and lack of amenities in relation to the other buildings, it stood as a monument to intimidation for Ira as he glared at the black glass and saw only the reflection of the lights from the surrounding city.

A six-foot-high fence of black iron surrounded strips of manicured green grass just outside the building, and high-voltage warning signs cautioned passersby to stay away. Full of trepidation on this, his first visit to the building, Ira shuffled toward the main gate and pushed his finger against a dimly lit button on a black call box. As he waited for a response, he almost expected to hear Darth Vader's breathy voice answer. Instead, he heard a sharp, military-type retort.

"State your business."

He swallowed hard. "Ira Hanley to see Colonel Thornton."

"Punch the code you were given on the pad next to the box, then step back and wait for the gate to open."

Ira pulled a torn piece of paper from the pocket of his slacks and held it close to the lit button. He pressed the numbers on the pad, then stepped back as he had been instructed. Inside his chest, he felt his heart quivering.

A motor whirred, and the black iron gate began to roll open. When it stopped, Ira glanced over his shoulder. A surge of energy ran through his body. He felt like one of those secret agents he had seen in the movies. He drew a deep breath and walked toward the building.

As he neared the front door, he looked up and saw what looked like the bottom of a black glass bowl mounted in the ceiling of the portico. He knew someone was watching him.

The voice from the gate returned. "Stop right there and look into the window beside the door."

Doing as he was told, Ira stared into the dark wall of glass and saw only himself. A loud click sounded to his left, and a door swung open.

"Proceed inside. Wait in the lobby for someone to come and escort you."

Again, Ira followed the instructions. Once inside, he found himself surrounded by walls of black marble. Standing in front of a gleaming black elevator door, he watched his own reflection glare back at him. The lobby reminded him of being deep in a foreboding cavern, encircled by stone-cold silence. The only break in his inky environment came from the stainless-steel door he had entered through and the dim ribbon of lights snaking along the edges of the ceiling.

The ding of the elevator startled Ira, causing him to jump. Anger flashed in his mind. *Get a grip*, he scolded himself. *Don't be so damn jumpy.* Despite his attempt at self-calming, he felt his legs weaken.

The doors slid open. A muscular man wearing a coal-black suit over a black shirt and tie stepped forward and filled the opening to the elevator. He glared with eyes as dark as the clothing he wore.

"You carrying any weapons?"

Ira could feel the sting of the man's steely glare. "No, no weapons. I'm unarmed."

"Raise your arms out from your sides."

The man's tone and obvious distrust caused Ira's jaw to tighten. He wanted to buck, to not comply, but the man was stronger and no doubt well trained to handle dissenters. There were also the cameras, four that he could see from where he stood. Others were watching—he was sure of it— and he knew they would come if he resisted. Ira extended his arms as the man began patting him down.

When the search was complete, the man motioned for Ira to board the elevator. Inside, the guard pushed the button for the fourteenth floor. The elevator shot up as if it had been mounted on the nose of a rocket. Ira stumbled and felt like his stomach had been left on the ground floor. He glanced at the man in the suit, who stood at parade rest. Neither man said a word.

When the elevator stopped, the doors opened into a large, dimly lit office. Across the room, like an island in a vast ocean of empty space, stood a desk with two straight-back chairs positioned in front. A soft light glowed from a single lamp. Behind the desk, Ira could see the lights of Atlanta through the dark glass. He saw no one in the room, but as he stepped from the elevator, he could hear the soft whoosh of air flowing through the ventilation system. He realized the only other sound was his own labored breathing.

"Wait here," the guard said, without exiting the elevator.

The doors closed, leaving Ira alone in the dim room. As his eyes adjusted to the darkness, he noticed television screens mounted in the walls. There were three in the wall nearest the desk. Overhead, in the center of the ceiling, he spotted another dark globe. *Nowhere to hide.*

He walked to the windows, careful to avoid the appearance he might be snooping around the desk, and looked out at the city. Despite the breathtaking view, his thoughts were on why his father had insisted on sending him here to meet the colonel in person. Thornton had given the Hanleys a secure phone, one that couldn't be tapped or traced. Why the insistence on a face-to-face encounter? Why him instead of his father?

"Are your troops ready for battle?"

Startled by Ambrose Thornton's deep resonant voice, Ira spun around. The colonel was no more than a few feet away, and Ira hadn't heard a sound. If the older man had been an assassin, Ira knew he would be dead. The thrill of being a secret agent faded; a trembling feeling returned to his legs.

"We're . . . ready . . . I think."

"You *think*?" Thornton's voice bellowed. "Your daddy assured me you boys would be ready when the time came. Are you ready or not? There will be no margin for error in this operation."

Ira hadn't been told a great deal by his father, which bothered him a lot. *Does my own father distrust me?* "My men are loyal," he said, his tone sounding more defensive than the confident one he had intended. "They'll be ready." He wiped his fingers across his dry lips, cleared his throat. "Am I here to receive our orders? Nobody's briefed us on our mission."

Eustace Hanley had served with Colonel Thornton in Desert Storm. Ira's father had never spoken in detail about his time overseas, but he talked proudly of Thornton and his leadership. Ira didn't know much about the colonel, but he knew his father would follow the man to hell and back, and that was good enough for him. What little Ira did know was that Thornton's Ranger unit had been an elite group who'd been given special assignments, usually covert. He suspected, although his father had never confirmed those suspicions, the unit had engaged in assassinations of key enemy leaders.

He remembered back to when his father first returned from the war. The old man had groused about how they could have taken out Iraq's leadership. The older Hanley had blamed the "pantywaists" in Washington for pulling the unit out just as they were preparing to strike, even after one of their unit, a personal friend of Hanley's, had been captured. They were forced to leave him there. Three months later, a CIA operative told Hanley that his comrade had been tortured and slowly killed days after they departed, and if his unit had been allowed to remain, they would have been close enough to have heard his friend screaming. Eustace Hanley had never forgiven the politicians for their decision.

"You were sent here because I told your father to send you. I wanted to see for myself if you were up to the task."

As Ira studied the colonel—his shaved head and square jaw, a scar above his right cheek—the legend became more human. Ira's confidence began to return. "I've proven my worth."

Thornton grinned. "Can you kill a man without remorse?"

Ira thought back to the disturbance at the compound, when the stranger, a friend of the new recruits, showed up uninvited. Ira had wanted to kill the intruder that day. He wanted to silence him, to keep him from causing future problems, but his father had ordered him to let the man go. He had obeyed that order, but he hadn't wanted to.

"Yes, I can kill a man."

"What about a woman . . . or a child? Can you kill them too?"

Ira glared at the man his father had spoken of in almost deified reverence. He thought about the question. He thought about the braggart street woman in Charleston. He wondered if Thornton knew about her. "If they are the enemy—yes I can kill a woman, even a child."

Thornton's steely stare locked on his visitor. Ira watched the man's eyes. They didn't blink.

*How does he do that?* He tried in vain to outlast Thornton's mesmerizing stare, but he couldn't. By now Ira had grown tired of the colonel's games of intimidation. He was able to view the man before him as just that—a man—instead of a god or mythical being with supernatural powers.

"Let's cut to the chase," Ira said in an attempt to let Thornton know he wasn't just another Army grunt to be pushed around. "Who are you wanting killed, and when do you want the job done?"

Thornton turned to leave. "You can go now."

"Wait a damn minute." Ira stepped after the colonel.

Before he could reach him, Thornton disappeared through a door Ira hadn't even seen. When it closed, it blended into the wall as if it didn't even exist.

Ira glared at the wall. "Asshole."

The doors to the elevator slid open, and the guard stepped out. He motioned for Ira to enter. "You're to leave now."

Ira shrugged his shoulders and shook his head. He decided not to argue with the man who reminded him of the Hulk. Instead, he stepped into the elevator and stared silently as the floor seemed to drop out from under him. When he arrived in the lobby, he quietly stepped out of the elevator and continued out the front door into Atlanta's night.

Outside the iron gate, he turned and stared back up toward the floor where he had been. He tried to pick out the faint glow of the desk lamp, but nothing penetrated the darkness in the walls.

*What does Thornton want from me? Did he believe me when I said I could kill? Man, woman, or even a child? If he didn't, he need only check around to find out how wrong he could be.*

# Chapter · 14

CAROLINA COLISEUM, COLUMBIA, SOUTH CAROLINA

Grayson Locke felt like a cow being herded into a pen at the Chicago stockyards. Admittedly, the people crushing around him weren't being corralled to await their slaughter, but beyond that sole distinction, he noted few differences to his plight and that of one of the ruminant mammals awaiting its fate in Chicago.

Locke didn't like crowds. In fact, he despised them. His obsession had begun on a snowy February morning in the fifth grade, when a school fire alarm drew him and the rest of the student body out into the hallway. They were supposed to move in orderly lines down the hall and out of the building, but when the first student smelled the smoke, order was abandoned. Girls and boys became a stampeding herd, crushing and shoving against one another, most screaming at the top of their lungs. In the chaos, one stocky kid rammed into Locke.

He fell, but no one stopped to help him. His hands and legs were stomped, his head kicked, and he wasn't able to get back to his feet until the last student had passed by, leaving him to whatever fate awaited. The behavior had been typical of how other children always treated him. He was the school geek, the kid who didn't play sports but who excelled at every academic subject. Girls wouldn't have anything to do with him. Boys teased and bullied him.

He never forgot that cold winter day. The alarm had been for a small fire in a trash can that was quickly extinguished, but no one knew at the time, and no one cared about the misfit sprawled in the middle of the hallway floor.

Years later, he returned to the school for his twenty-fifth reunion, a millionaire hundreds of times over with a New York model on his arm as his wife. On that night he no longer was the geek. He wasn't ignored, nor was he mistreated.

He smiled, recalling how all of his former classmates had flocked around to remind him how they had been good friends back in school. Locke knew better. After all, he had been born with photographic recall, so he forgot very little, especially the fire drill and how he had been run over like some stray dog loose on the freeway.

Now, despite his severe distaste for crowds, Locke had allowed himself to become packed into a small area, waiting with a bunch of other two-legged bovines for the arrival of their candidate for president of the United States.

The decision to go through with carrying out his assignment hadn't been an easy one, knowing what he would surely encounter inside the Carolina Coliseum, located on the campus of the University of South Carolina in downtown Columbia. *For the good of the cause*, he had reminded himself on the way down Assembly Street. *Only for the cause.*

As he stood in the lobby of the facility's special-events center, he felt his patience begin to wane and his anger grow as people all around him shoved their way toward the closed doors leading into the large Gamecock Club dining hall.

An elbow punched his rib cage. Someone stepped on his patent-leather shoes, mashing his toes together. Locke grimaced. Memories of that cold February morning filled his head.

Through a hostile glare, he watched the faces around him. *One grenade would get them all*, he mused.

Formally dressed in black tie and tails, he had arrived early like everyone else for the thousand-dollars-a-plate dinner. Soon presidential candidate Jeffrey Hart would be escorted inside, and his guests, blue bloods of South Carolina, would pour into the room to eat cold potato soup, Cornish hen, and chilled asparagus. They would hear their candidate regale his many accomplishments as senator, then springboard into what he planned to do if elected president. Many of the too rich and gullible had paid an extra thousand dollars for the opportunity to be photographed with the man they hoped would be the future president.

He wondered why they would humiliate themselves in such a fashion. He'd rather just hand over the cash—after Hart groveled a little to get his hands on it. Locke grinned at the notion.

He would eat the dinner, but he hadn't come to hear Hart. He knew what the man had to say; he had heard it all before. Locke had come to observe.

The candidate required dozens of United States Secret Service agents surveilling the crowds, checking out potential threats, and ensuring an orderly and safe appearance. Security was tight, just as if Hart were already elected president. The assignment Locke had given himself was to see if there was any difference in the amount of security provided for a roomful of supposed friendly admirers versus that provided out in the general public. This had been the first part of the plan outlined to the Board at his Hilton Head home two weeks before.

As he inched along amid the wave of humanity, Locke recognized several faces in the crowd, and he suspected a few might even recognize him—though none had indicated as much, which suited him just fine. His day would come. There would be the right time and the right place for him to become known all across America—even the world. That was also part of the plan. But for now, his goal was to blend in, not draw any attention to his presence. He was just an observer.

The room buzzed with busy conversations. "Have you ever actually met him?" a woman nearby asked in an excited voice.

The woman beside her answered, "No, but I hear he is perfectly charming. A real Southern gentleman."

Locke rolled his eyes. *Southern gentleman, my ass.* Memories of his classmates came rushing back, how truly stupid they all had been. He grimaced as he listened to more conversations, each sounding like a bunch of drugged teenagers anxious to see a rock star.

No longer able to stand the closeness and the reeking perfume drifting up his nostrils, Locke glanced at his watch, then pushed and maneuvered his way to an unmanned door leading to a back hallway. Why an agent hadn't been posted there like at every other exit both puzzled and delighted him. He made a mental note, one he knew he wouldn't forget.

Reaching the door, he scoped the crowd, then took hold of the knob. It turned. *Unlocked. A sign of good fortune or lax security?*

He had to escape the horde, if only for a few minutes. Slipping through unchallenged, he walked about thirty feet before realizing security had not been derelict, after all.

"Sorry, sir. You can't come back here." In the dimly lit hallway, he saw the Secret Service agent, a black man the size and build of an NFL linebacker, standing between the door Locke had entered and a back door leading to the specially prepared dining room.

"I know you. Don't you recognize me?" Locke had seen the same agent working the White House detail on visits with both the President and Vice President.

"Yes, sir. I know who you are, Mr. Locke," the agent responded with a glowering expression. "That doesn't change anything, though. You can't be back here."

Pleased he had been recognized, Locke nodded to the door. "Just trying to catch a breath of air without inhaling a snoot full of perfume."

The agent's right eyebrow raised. "Yes, sir. I understand." He pushed his index finger against the hearing device in his ear. "You better go on back out. They've just entered the building."

"How many agents are with the candidate?"

The agent frowned. "Sorry, sir. You know I can't divulge security details."

"Of course. I don't know what I was thinking." Locke drew a deep breath, nodded to the agent, then returned to the jammed lobby just as the doors to the dining room swung open, revealing row after row of tables covered with white linen tablecloths and black linen napkins. The silver sparkled and the crystal glistened. Waiters stood with bottles of French wine ready to be served.

The agent had been more helpful than he had realized. Only one in the back hallway. Two more outside the ballroom. That meant the rest of the entourage was with the candidate. Another mental note locked in his memory.

He figured they followed a similar pattern with President Flint. All he had to do to get the exact numbers was make a call, but he enjoyed seeing for himself, adding a little intrigue to his life.

As the throng of Columbia's aristocracy wedged their ample torsos through the openings leading to the spacious room, Locke hung back. He watched the last of the invited guests present their handwritten invitations to the tuxedoed Secret Service agents guarding the entrance to the dining room. Soon he would pull his from his inside pocket and join the others, but first he would step outside and take care of business.

"I don't think this is such a good idea," Jimmy Joe said as Yates pulled his dented, faded silver Ford Crown Victoria into a deserted alley a few blocks away from the Carolina Coliseum.

"It's perfect," Yates said. He pulled the handle and leaned hard to unstick the door of his recent acquisition.

Jimmy Joe fumbled with the pamphlet Yates had given him to read. He had been studying on it the best he could since they had left home more than an hour before. He didn't understand what beans and boots had to do with bullets. And he sure didn't understand all of the stuff about tyranny and the New World Order written inside, but he understood enough to know he didn't like what he was seeing—or hearing—from his friend. "This ain't right. You're gonna get us in all kinds of trouble."

"We ain't gettin' in no trouble. I've got everything planned out. I even bought this old cruiser at the Highway Patrol auction. Paid cash and used a made-up name. It ain't much to look at, but it still runs good, and nobody's gonna link it to us."

"I don't like it. We should've talked to Dane first."

"If you don't like it, then get out and go home. Dane sold me out, j-just like all the rest did. To hell with him and to hell with all them other rednecks out in the swamp. I ain't got n-no use for none of 'em. I'm gonna show 'em, though. They'll see I'm one hell of a soldier. After tonight, they'll be beggin' me to join 'em." He stepped out, looked into the litter-strewn alley.

"What you gonna do now?"

"Come on out and see. M-maybe you'll learn something 'bout guerrilla warfare."

Jimmy Joe crawled out of the car. He stuffed the pamphlet into the pocket of his overalls and crouched low as he eased toward the back of the Ford, where Yates had opened the trunk. Jimmy Joe whispered as he glanced toward the street. "I don't like this none at all. What's monkeys fighting have to do with why we're here, anyhow?"

"Monkeys?"

"You said you're going to teach me gorilla—"

"Sh-shut up and follow me. You're a simpleton, you know." Yates pulled a green duffel bag out of the trunk, shoved it toward Jimmy Joe. "Here, carry this." He slammed the trunk closed.

"What're *you* carryin'?" Jimmy Joe asked, noticing that Yates had left the trunk empty-handed.

Yates opened the back door of the Crown Vic. He reached inside and pulled out a small rifle. "This. Just in case there's trouble."

Jimmy Joe cringed. "You're not gonna shoot nobody are you?"

"Not lessen I have to. This here's just security."

Jimmy Joe swallowed hard. He knew he should never have let his friend talk him into coming along, but lately he hadn't had anyone to hang out with. Dane and Lance and Barry had been gone for several days. Yates had told him they were probably in the swamp, training with folks there; he'd called them numb nuts and didn't seem to like them near as much as he had the night they all went to that church and listened to that preacher talk about killing people.

Jimmy Joe was pretty sure he didn't want any part of what that crowd was up to, but he sure did miss hanging out with his friends, especially his cousin Dane, who had just come to live with him and his mamma a little over a month before. Jimmy Joe liked Dane, and for a while he thought Dane liked him, too, but lately he wasn't so sure.

Soon after the trip to that church where everybody carried guns and hollered about how bad America had been to them, Dane started spending more time with Barry and Lance. He even told Jimmy Joe not to come along on the trips they took to somewhere out in the swamp. Jimmy Joe hadn't wanted to, anyway, so he stayed home, but he sure did miss hanging out with the guys. Besides, Yates worried him; he had a real bad temper sometimes, and lately he seemed to be mad at everyone—including Jimmy Joe.

"Come on, we got to move," Yates said, sprinting toward the end of the alley where it opened up onto Devine Street.

With the full duffel bag hoisted over his right shoulder, Jimmy Joe loped along behind Yates as they darted across the street and into the shadows of a tall building.

"Stay close to the wall," Yates said. "Stay in the shadows."

"Why we got to sneak around? What you plannin' on doin'?"

"You'll know in just a few minutes. We're a couple of blocks away. As soon as we get close enough, I'll take the duffel. You keep a lookout for cops."

"Cops?! I don't want no trouble with the police. You're gettin' ready to do something bad, aren't you?"

Yates glared over his shoulder at Jimmy Joe. "Shush up."

A few minutes later, after one ducking beneath a bus-stop bench and the other beside a trash receptacle when a car turned onto the street behind them, Yates and Jimmy Joe arrived in the alleyway at the back of a brick building.

"We're here."

"We're where?" Jimmy Joe asked.

"This is the South Carolina Election Commission office. They're the folks who handle all of the elections in the state."

"We ain't votin' this time of night. What you got planned?"

"You ask too many damn questions. Just sit here and keep an eye out. If anybody comes, you call me on this." Yates handed him a small walkie-talkie.

"It's awful dark out here. You gonna be long?" Jimmy Joe's voice filled with trepidation.

"Not long. Quit worryin' 'bout being in the dark. You're bigger than anything you'll see in this alley."

Jimmy Joe stared into the darkness. "I ain't worried 'bout big things, just them creepy crawly ones. Them's what boogers me."

Ignoring Jimmy Joe's last comment, Yates grabbed the duffel bag. "I'll be back in a few minutes."

Jimmy Joe watched his friend disappear into the night. Sitting in the darkness, every sound around him became magnified. Somewhere behind him he could hear water splashing into a puddle and dripping onto the metal top of a Dumpster. He heard scratching noises too, hoped they weren't from rats. He hated the nasty things.

A shiver ran down his spine. *Dirty, furry, vicious creatures with big sharp teeth and mean eyes.* His throat constricted.

Once, he chanced a glance back into the inky pitch deep in the alley. He thought he saw two beady red glows staring back out at him, but when he blinked, they were gone. He stood up, moved around, not wanting to be crouching low where something could jump up and grab his throat in its teeth.

Jimmy Joe looked toward the end of the alley. *Where's Yates? He ought to be back by now.* He inched his way to the corner of the building and looked out in the direction he had last seen his friend going. No one in sight. No cars coming, either. *Thank goodness.*

Spit wouldn't form in his mouth. He tried to whistle. He reasoned that whistling "Jesus Loves Me" might ease his concern, but he couldn't get any sound to come out from between his lips. *Where's Yates?*

The bright flash came first, turning the night sky into daylight for just an instant. The thunderous noise stunned him. Jimmy Joe barely heard the explosion before it ripped bricks and glass above his head, showering them down on top of him. He tried to dive out of the way, but something heavy hit the back of his head. The darkness all around him turned white. A high-pitched ringing deafened him. A dark blanket of total silence enveloped him.

Jeffrey Hart, candidate for president of the United States of America, had just approached the podium when the tremor hit. Two sentences into his speech, the interior walls of the Coliseum shook. A crystal pitcher tumbled off a cart and shattered. Silverware spilled from the tables, clattering onto the concrete floor. A muffled rumble rolled through the crowded room, and then everything grew very still.

*What the hell?* Locke shot out of his chair near the back of the room. He bolted toward the doors, with dozens following him outside.

Up front, near the dais, dumbstruck Secret Service agents surrounded the candidate. Their bodies formed a human cocoon around the senator as they rushed him off the stage into the back hallway.

When Locke arrived at the glass doors leading to the outside, he saw broken glass covering the lobby area. In the distance, a few blocks away, he could see flames shooting through a rooftop, climbing toward the sky. Car alarms whooped. Sirens wailed and air horns honked. He could see students pouring out onto the sidewalk from the nearby University of South Carolina Law Library. Surrounding dorms full of more students quickly emptied. Some ran toward the fire; some stood in stunned silence with their hands covering their mouths.

The night air bore the distinct scent of explosives. Locke had smelled it before, and the odor was unmistakable.

Off to his left, he spotted the candidate's motorcade speeding away from the arena. Bemusement sculpted his features. He couldn't explain the sense of excitement and expectation that swirled inside of him. "Welcome to South Carolina, Senator. The fun is just beginning."

# CHAPTER · 15

ELECTION COMMISSION OFFICE, COLUMBIA, SOUTH CAROLINA

Brock Elliott's cell phone rang as he stepped out of the bombed-out shell of what used to be the South Carolina Election Commission office building. "Elliot," he said, pulling the phone to his ear. He pressed the heel of his left palm against his other ear to block out the commotion from the workers surrounding him.

"Are the reports I'm hearing true? Did someone try to kill Senator Hart tonight?"

Brock stopped. He held the phone in front of his face and stared at the number in the illuminated window. "Who . . . Cassie, is that you?"

"Exactly how many other women have your cell phone number and call you this time of night? We just got an anonymous tip that someone tried to kill Senator Hart there tonight."

Stepping over broken brick and smoldering boards, Brock walked across Divine street, out of earshot of the police officers and fire personnel scurrying around the scene. He glanced at his watch. *A little after midnight.* "You got a bogus tip."

"Nobody tried to kill the senator?"

"You sound disappointed."

"You know what I mean. Nothing happened there tonight?"

Brock kicked at some of the rubble that had been blown across the street, then noticed a twisted signpost. It looked like a steel pretzel. "I wouldn't exactly say *nothing* happened."

There was a moment of silence, followed by an exasperated sigh. "Coming from you, that kind of a comment could mean World War III just broke out. What is it?"

"An explosion."

"Near the senator?" Cassie's voice rose an octave.

Brock looked toward the coliseum. "Oh, I'd say several blocks or so."

"That close, huh? Anybody hurt?"

"It's a little early to tell. We did find one guy buried under some rubble. He's alive, but barely."

"Any idea what happened?"

"Some, but nothing for public consumption just yet."

"You didn't say what blew up. Was it a manufacturing plant? Did they store hazardous materials there?"

"South Carolina Election Commission."

Silence rained through the phone. "Did you just say someone blew up the headquarters for the South Carolina Election Commission?"

"Yeah, you heard right." Brock closed his eyes. *Here we go.*

"Damn, Brock. Don't be so coy. That's big news—especially when it happens mere blocks away from where a candidate for president of the United States is speaking. Any idea who did it?"

"Too early." He looked at the pamphlet he had found in the pocket of the man found under the rubble.

"Nobody claimed credit?"

"Doubt anybody will, unless you know something I don't. What did your tipster tell you?"

"Not much. He just asked if we had heard about the near-death experience the presidential candidate had in Columbia."

"He?"

"Definitely a male voice."

"Could you tell anything else about him?"

Cassie's lengthy pause roused Brock's curiosity. "Maybe a bit on the country side," she said, "but aren't you all."

"Cute. Somehow I get the feeling you're holding something back. What else did your caller say?"

Cassie's tone didn't alleviate Brock's suspicions. "Nothing. Nothing else."

"Have it your way. Oh, yeah, just in case you're interested, several have my number."

"What?"

"You asked if I had given my cell number to other women. You didn't expect me to spend the rest of my life waiting on you to call, did you?"

"Cute, yourself. Twenty thousand comedians out of work, and you want to be funny. I'm coming to Columbia, even if I have to do it on my own time."

"Why?"

"Pardon the pun, but you're sitting on a powder keg of a story. What if the explosion was part of that militia group's plan to cause trouble?"

Brock looked at the pamphlet again. *Damn.* "I suppose anything's possible. Hate to see you come all the way here on a wild-goose chase, though." As bad as he wanted to see Cassie again, he wanted her coming for the right reason—to see him. The last thing he needed was to have to deal with her digging around, screwing up his investigation.

"You wouldn't be glad to see me?"

"I didn't say that. Fact is, you've been gone so long now, I'm not sure I'd know how to act."

She laughed. "You'd know. You haven't changed that much over the past year."

"You know what I mean. I'd rather you be coming here on my account, not for some news story."

Cassie didn't respond.

Brock cleared his throat. "Okay, so much for that thought. Y'all going to run anything on this tonight?"

"Probably just a mention—especially since Senator Hart was in town when it occurred. I'll be following up with the local stations to see what their folks turn up. Can I count on you to call if anything significant develops?"

"You know I can't talk about an ongoing investigation."

"We'll see about that." Cassie imitated the accent of a German spy she had recently seen in a movie. "We have our vays to make you talk." The line went dead.

Brock stared at the phone. *Yes, you do.*

The middle-of-the-night telephone call jostled Jefferson Lee out of a deep sleep. He pulled his pillow tight over his head, but the incessant ringing wouldn't stop.

At last, the merciful recording on his answering machine kicked in. "J-Man can't catch the phone. Chill if you will, don't if you won't. Hate it for you, but I ain't home."

"Jefferson! Jefferson, I know you're there. Pick up the phone, it's important."

He moaned. The voice on the machine was all too familiar. Rolling over in his bed, he grabbed the clock off the bedside table. He stared at the luminous numbers until they began to come into focus, then he coughed to clear the clabber out of his throat. The groggy cameraman snatched the phone receiver from its cradle. "Who is this?"

"Don't play games. You know very well who this is."

"Don't be so sure. I don't recognize my own mother's voice at one-thirty in the morning."

"Have you heard what happened in Columbia tonight?"

"I'm in Charleston. What the hell do I care what happened in Columbia?" He paused. "Don't you ever sleep?"

"I talked to Brock about an hour ago. He's at the scene."

"Scene of what? You know, some folks do sleep at night. Vampires and werewolves are the ones who roam the dark. Have you been tested to see which you are?"

"Funny. Everybody wants to be a comedian tonight. Wake up enough to listen, okay?"

Jefferson's head had fallen back onto his pillow. With his eyes closed, his consciousness faded. The receiver still rested against his ear.

"Jefferson, you still with me?"

His eyelids fluttered, then cracked open. "Yeah." He cleared his throat again. "Yeah, I'm with you. What?"

"I've been thinking about all of this since I heard about the explosion."

"What blew up?"

"Election Commission building in Columbia."

Jefferson's eyes opened wider. He stared into the darkness. "Yeah?"

"Yeah. Think about it. Someone driving a military-looking vehicle kills Senator Laney. Rowdy Dubois witnesses them carrying Laney's body into the cemetery. Then somebody kills Rowdy and tries to make it look like a drug deal gone bad—"

"Could've been, you know."

"Yeah, and the Tooth Fairy's going into business with the Easter Bunny. Rowdy got killed because she saw and knew too much. That pamphlet she showed us says it all. If the Free Confederacy wants to overthrow the United States Government, what better way to do it than by disrupting the most basic form of democracy—our elections?"

"You think the Free Confederacy blew up the building?" he asked.

"I'd stake my career on it."

Jefferson didn't respond.

"You still there. Don't drift off on me now."

"I'm here. How can you be so certain?"

"Let's just say a birdie told me. I'll fill you in when I get there."

"So what do you have in mind? I hope you didn't wake me out of a sound sleep to bounce conspiracy theories around. I was dreaming I called Halle

Berry, asked her out, and she said yes. Do you have any idea how much I would have enjoyed going out with that gorgeous—"

"By the time we're finished with this story, you'll be famous. Halle Berry will be calling *you* for a date."

"Ha. Since when did the cameraman get any credit for a story? You'll be the one on the cover of *Time* magazine. Don't try conning me. I know you. I'm wise to your ways."

Cassie's voice softened, the way it always did when she wanted something. "Will you help me? I need your knowledge of the area. I'll have my producer call your news director. Just like I did for the hurricane coverage."

Jefferson picked out objects floating in the darkness. "Yeah, yeah. Your people will call my people. This network stardom's startin' to affect your brain. I told you before, I'd help. And I will. But you've got to let me get some sleep right now. I've got to be at the newsroom early. Hart will be in Charleston in a couple of days, and we've got a strategy session to plan our coverage."

"Don't stress too much over that meeting. You'll be with me by the time the good senator arrives, if I have anything to say about it. Get some sleep. You'll hear from me tomorrow."

Now wide awake, Jefferson leaned over and dropped the phone back to its cradle. *Got to get back to sleep. Something tells me it'll come at a premium over the next few days.*

# Chapter · 16

RICHLAND MEMORIAL HOSPITAL, COLUMBIA, SOUTH CAROLINA

The morning after his sleepless night at the scene of the bombing, Brock pushed open the wooden doors leading into the intensive care unit of the Richland Memorial Hospital in Columbia. Greeted by beeping monitors and the smell of disinfectant, he looked around the room of cubicles cordoned off by green curtains, wondering which one concealed the victim of the explosion. His fingers raked the damp strands of his thick brown hair.

A light drizzle had begun falling that morning around four o'clock, making processing the site of the blast all the more tedious. By the time the crime-scene technicians had finished their arduous tasks, the low gray morning skies had begun to brighten, so he decided to come straight to the hospital to learn if his only witness was dead or alive.

Brock glanced at his watch. This day would be another where sleep would become a sought-after stranger.

A silver-haired nurse, dressed in her traditional white uniform, stepped away from the nurses station and hurried toward him. Her eyes held a stern, protective glare. "May I help you?"

"I'm here to see James Joseph Harden." He flashed a haggard, disarming smile.

"Are you family?" she asked in a raspy, smoker's voice.

He pulled his credentials from the inside pocket of his tan-and-brown-plaid sports coat that smelled of smoke and wet wool. "I'm with SLED," he said as he opened the wallet and showed his badge and identification to her.

The glower on the woman's face didn't flicker. "Only family's allowed."

Brock's cheeks flushed. "I'm not here to question him. I just want to see how he's doin'." His gaze fell on long gray and black hairs growing from a mole on the woman's chin.

"Just as well. He's still unconscious. Don't know yet if he'll come out of it." She pointed up at the round clock on the wall behind the nurses station. "Doctor won't be back around for at least an hour. You'll need his okay to disturb the patient since you're not family."

"Can I at least have a look?"

"Why?" With her eyes studying Brock's, she ran her finger across her chin. She stopped on the mole. Her scowl intensified.

The nurse reminded him of his seventh-grade math teacher. He nearly flunked math that year and didn't carry much regard for the teacher. "I'm just doin' my job," he said. "I'll take a quick look and leave. You can stand right beside me if you want."

"Don't think I won't. Someone's in with him right now, though." She inadvertently glanced toward the third curtain on the right. Then, as if she realized her error, she looked back at Brock with a sheepish frown. "When they come out, you can take a quick look. God only knows why you need to, though."

"Who's in with him?"

"Family."

Lack of sleep eroded his patience. "Yeah, I figured that much. You know who?"

She shook her head, released a long, protracted sigh. "I've got to check on another patient. Don't move until I get back. I'll need to be with you when you go in."

Brock leaned against the wall, his hands stuck in the back pockets of his denim jeans. He watched as the nurse strutted with broad shoulders and bowed legs, like an old bulldog, toward the opposite end of the room. She stopped beside another curtained-off area, looked back, and hit Brock with a scolding glare, as if reiterating her previous order for him to stay put. Then she pulled back the curtain and disappeared inside.

Brock didn't hesitate. He pushed away from the wall and hurried toward the third blue curtain on the right. Just as he began to pull back the cloth, a tall man with dark hair stepped out. Both men recoiled, startled expressions on their faces.

With a suspicious look, Dane recovered first. "Can I help you?"

"I'm Brock Elliott—SLED." He held up his identification.

"Dane Everett. I'm Jimmy Joe's cousin." He offered his hand and shook Brock's. "I'm afraid he's not up to answering questions. He's still unconscious."

Brock peered over Dane's shoulder into the dimly lit area. Jimmy Joe, whose face and features were obscured by massive swelling, lay on his back, with tubes running into his nose and arms. An electronic monitor beeped a quiet tone as green numbers registered the patient's heartbeat and blood pressure on one side of the screen, and a green line of peaks and valleys streaked across the middle, revealing other vital information. "What are the doctors saying?"

"They're not. I think they're all surprised he's still alive. He's strong. If anybody can pull through this, Jimmy Joe can."

Brock glanced around the immediate area. "No other family here?"

"His mother's on her way. I called her and told her he was here."

Brock's eyebrow raised. "How'd you find out?"

Dane looked away, as if he didn't want to make eye contact. His explanation came slow, causing Brock to wonder if he was making it up on the fly. "I went by Jimmy Joe's house. A deputy sheriff pulled up behind me as I arrived, told me what had happened." He looked back at Brock and released a heavy sigh. "I didn't go in and tell his mother. I wanted to make sure he was okay before I called her."

Brock studied Dane's expression. Checking with the county sheriff to verify the story would be easy enough. Even so, there was that uneasiness in the explanation that bothered Brock. "You don't—"

"I thought I told you to wait over there." The raspy tone was unmistakable.

Without turning around, Brock said, "Dane Everett, meet the Wicked Witch of the West." He turned and sneered as the nurse approached.

She glowered. "I suppose you've seen what you came to see. Now you need to leave."

Brock turned back to Dane. "You might be able to clear up a few things about Jimmy Joe. You have a few minutes to talk?" He noticed the woman's unrelenting glare and added, "Out in the hallway."

As the two men pushed open the wooden doors, Brock looked back at the watchful nurse. Her balled fists were planted on her ample hips; her fleshy, pink cheeks puffed.

"You know how they say folks resemble their pets?" he said to Dane, loud enough for the nurse to hear. "I bet she owns a mean old bulldog."

The doors closed behind them.

Jefferson eased his television station's white Bronco out of the parking space at Charleston International Airport. He glanced at Cassie leaning back in her seat with her eyes closed. Seeing her this still and quiet was not a common scene.

Earlier in the morning, his assignment editor and news director had called him into the news director's office. Their tones were almost apologetic when they told him he was to be working with Cassie O'Connor on another special assignment. *If they only knew*, Jefferson remembered having thought at the time.

"For how long?" he had asked, acting surprised.

"For as long as it takes," his news director replied. "We're told this is a big story, and we've negotiated the rights to a local exclusive that will tie in with the national piece."

"Let me get this straight. You're trading me for a big story. This sounds like the NFL," Jefferson said with a feigned grimace.

"No, not at all."

Jeannie, his assignment editor, had been quick to assure him they weren't using staff as barter for exclusive rights to a story. "CNN will be paying your salary, but only temporarily. You still work for us." She said this with a tone of genuine pride, which Jefferson appreciated. Then a quizzical expression draped her face. "They insisted that you had to be the cameraman. You were the key to the story being a success. I'm not sure why, but you are the reason we got the local exclusive."

Jefferson had almost broken out with laughter. The determination of Cassie O'Connor was not to be underestimated. He had actually enjoyed the meeting, watching his two bosses try to understand his importance to the story, if not the international broadcast station, while he acted put-upon for the assignment. In reality, what he really wanted to know was how Cassie had managed to convince her bosses and how she had put the details together so fast.

"Why do you want to go to Columbia?" he asked Cassie as he pulled onto the ramp to head northwest on Interstate 26, toward South Carolina's capital city. "Hart will be in Charleston in a couple of days, and I hear the President is coming soon after that."

"Answers," she said without opening her eyes. "If everything works out, we'll be back in Charleston in time to see Hart and the President."

"What sort of answers?"

"Who would want to blow up the election office, for one? And was the explosion really a precursor of things to come?"

"Who's going to know those answers?"

"I'll check with Brock first. I know he's investigating the explosion. Maybe he's learned something he'll share."

"Yeah, right. And if he *hasn't* learned anything he's willing to share with you?"

"Then I'll visit that little birdie I told you about. He's agreed to meet me. I told him where we would be staying tonight."

Cassie sat up in her seat, pulled on the collar of her green cotton blouse. "But don't breathe a word to Brock. I don't want him knowing that I've turned an informant." She shivered and rubbed her hands along her upper arms. "Now, can you turn the air conditioner down. I feel like I'm riding in a meat locker."

Jefferson reached over and adjusted the thermostat setting. He recalled another secret meeting Cassie attended, one with a local stripper turned informant. And although he didn't go with her that night, he recalled hearing how when Cassie arrived, she interrupted a murder in progress—the stripper's. "If I recollect, the last time you went out to a clandestine meeting with an informant, you nearly got your pretty self killed. You sufferin' from short-term memory loss?"

She leaned back and closed her eyes again. "Not now . . . please. I didn't get much sleep last night, then I had to catch a plane before sunrise. In another couple of hours, we'll be in Columbia, where possibly the biggest story of this year's election is unfolding." She tilted her head and smiled at Jefferson. "So, for now, just drive."

"Yes'm. I'll mind my tongue while I'm driving Miss Cassie."

"Don't start," she said, almost under her breath.

Jefferson snickered as he reached over and turned up the soft jazz on the radio. *The next few days are going to really be something*, he thought.

Deep in a dense stand of timber, mixed with towering pines and thick hardwoods, near the Santee Dam south of Manning, South Carolina, a black Lincoln Navigator pulled off a dirt road onto the sandy, pine-needle-carpeted forest floor. Moments later, a black Humvee pulled in behind it. Eustace Hanley climbed down out of the Humvee and walked to the rear passenger door of the SUV. The tinted windows blocked any view inside the vehicle, but he knew who waited there. He opened the door and crawled into the backseat.

"What happened in Columbia?" Colonel Ambrose Thornton asked before Hanley could settle into his seat.

The Lincoln drove off, bouncing across potholes and crushing small tree limbs dotting the old roadway. Once the Navigator had driven out of sight, the Humvee followed, maintaining a secure distance between the two vehicles in case either car had been tailed to the secluded meeting site.

Hanley fidgeted. "The explosion?"

"At the election office. Yes. Now Hart's security detail is heightened, and you can bet your ass they won't be lettin' anybody or anything escape their scrutiny. Did you authorize that fiasco?"

Hanley's face showed surprise. "Hell, no! What kind o' fool do you take me for? Far as I know, none of my boys were involved. They wouldn't just go out on their own. They know better. We only carry out missions with a purpose. Blowing up that office served no purpose."

"Who would do it, then?"

Hanley recalled the rumor his son had relayed to him just that morning. "Word is that this might have been carried out by a loner. If that's true, he's not likely to be botherin' nobody else. I heard they found him buried under rubble and he's in bad shape. I assure you he weren't one of us."

"Any idea who he might be?"

"An idea, yeah. I have men checking now. If it's who we think, and if he manages to survive, we'll make sure he's blown up his last building."

Thornton grew quiet. "There's another matter, and the two may be related." He glared at Hanley from under a furrowed brow.

Hanley braced for the unknown. Despite having fought alongside Thornton, he feared him, and for good reason. The colonel was impulsive and conscienceless, two traits that had served the hardened military man well in wartime. He considered everyone expendable, and the leader of the Free Confederacy worried that the renegade bomber, whoever he was, had caused Thornton to lose faith in Hanley's ability to control the fringe elements of his organization.

"My sources in the government tell me you may have a spy infiltrating your group."

Hanley stared with incredulity. "Impossible."

"Nothing's impossible. The bombing could have been a ploy to disrupt our mission. If they have infiltrated your ranks, we have to find them, and find them quick. Send me the files you have on your people, and I'll have them checked by people who are very good at ferreting out imposters."

"You think the UN and those New World Order pantywaists have infiltrated my flock?"

"Likely federal agents. FBI, ATF, Secret Service, even military intelligence, but they amount to the same mentality. They're all capable of creating havoc, and their presence could compromise the success of our mission." His glare hardened. "That won't be tolerated."

"I'll get you the rosters, and we'll conduct our own investigation. If the cowardly bastards are in our midst, we'll find them and deal with them."

Thornton motioned for the driver of the Lincoln to pull over. Less than a minute later, the Humvee pulled in behind it and Hanley got out. As he walked back to the off-road vehicle, the black Navigator pulled away.

"Take me to the compound," Hanley ordered as he opened the door and climbed back into the Humvee. "We have to find the traitor in our camp, or Thornton will consider us expendable."

# Chapter · 17

SLED HEADQUARTERS, COLUMBIA, SOUTH CAROLINA

Brock had just arrived back in his office from the hospital when his cell phone rang. He flipped it open, looked at the caller ID. *Cassie.*

"Good morning," he said. "You calling this time of day is highly unusual. What's up?"

"Good morning, yourself. How about lunch? I'm starved."

Brock couldn't believe what he was hearing. "Lunch? Where are you?"

"In about five minutes we'll be pulling into the SLED parking lot."

"We?"

"Jefferson and I. We're in his station's Bronco."

He groaned. No matter where they went for lunch, Brock knew he would be the one grilled. "I take it you've decided to do a story on the bombing."

"Not exactly. I'll explain while we eat. Meet us in the parking lot. We'll need to take your car. The Bronco's loaded with equipment and luggage."

He shook his head. "Yes, dear. Anything else, dear?"

Brock had been pleasantly surprised. From the time Cassie and Jefferson pulled into the SLED parking lot, piled into his Crown Victoria, and drove to a nearby pizza parlor, Cassie hadn't mentioned the bombing or asked about his investigation. Now, as they sat across from each other in a booth near the back of the restaurant, he stared at her intently and wished only the two of them were there, late at night, enjoying a bottle of Chianti and listening to soft violin music. "I'm glad you came," he said, really meaning it. "How long can you stay?"

Cassie propped her elbows on the table's red-checkered cloth and rested her chin in her open palms. She smirked. "As long as it takes."

With those words, the fantasy of their togetherness vanished, disintegrating like a soap bubble floating into the thorns of a rosebush. Brock knew better than to ask the next question, but he blurted it out instinctively. "As long as what takes?"

He noticed Jefferson's uncomfortable shift on the bench seat. The former football player shook his head.

Cassie sat up straight. "I believe there's some type of conspiracy brewing amid all this political backslapping and Southern hospitality. One that might be aimed at the President or Senator Hart. So I'm here until all hell breaks loose or Flint and Hart have finished campaigning in the state. Whichever comes first."

Brock's forehead furrowed. "A conspiracy? Someone blowing up an office building near where a candidate was speaking is a far cry from a conspiracy to kill the President or his opponent."

"There's more," she said, glancing around, checking out the other booths. No one else was seated nearby. "If you take the death of Senator Laney, and couple it with the murder of Rowdy Dubois, things begin to look suspicious. Factor in somebody blowing up the state's election office building near where Senator Hart is speaking, and I think you have the makings of a conspiracy."

Brock leaned back against the booth. He looked at Jefferson. "What's she talking about? I'm missing something, something to connect all of these events together."

Jefferson shrugged. He looked at Cassie. "Tell him about the pamphlet."

Cassie hit her cameraman with a harsh glare. She didn't say anything.

"He's on our side. He's a cop. He needs to know about the pamphlet."

Brock's interest heightened. "What kind of pamphlet?"

Before his answer came, the pizza they had ordered arrived. The young waiter set it on the table. "One pepperoni and sausage with onions and mushrooms. Can I get you anything else?"

"We're fine, thanks," Brock said in a hurried tone. He paused until the waiter left, then leaned across the table and whispered, "What pamphlet is he talking about?"

Cassie shot another unpleasant look at Jefferson. She pulled her purse up to the table and fished out a folded and soiled piece of paper.

As soon as Brock saw it, he recognized it as the same kind of pamphlet he had found in Jimmy Joe Harden's pocket after they found him buried in the rubble from the explosion. He took the folded paper from Cassie and opened it. "Where did you get this?"

"From Rowdy Dubois," she replied. "She gave it to us a few days before she was found murdered."

"She say where she got it?"

Cassie and Jefferson exchanged glances. Jefferson responded this time. "She found it near the entrance to the cemetery where they found Laney. Near where the truck had stopped and where she saw two men take a body out of the back."

"She didn't say anything about this when I talked to her."

"Maybe you didn't ask the right question." Cassie's tone hinted of sarcasm. "Maybe you didn't treat her right."

"Humph." Brock read the same words he had read at the scene of the explosion. He decided downplaying a connection to Rowdy's death and the senator's was in his best interest. "Well, it may not mean anything. From the looks of it, it could have been blown from halfway across Charleston during the storm." He slid it back to Cassie.

She shrugged. "You can keep it. I made a copy."

"So tell me, how do *you* connect that pamphlet to the explosion here?"

"I think it's pretty obvious if you read their message. Members of the Free Confederacy are the most likely suspects in the election office bombing."

"That's a reach," Brock said.

"Have you been able to talk to the survivor? The one you told me you found under the rubble."

"No. He's still in a coma." Brock picked up a wedge of pizza and folded it, taking a big bite. As he chewed, he studied Cassie's features, the dimples in her cheeks. "Tell me about this fellow who called you after the bombing," he said after swallowing.

"Not much to tell." She lifted a piece of the pizza and laid it in her plate. "Southern sounding—backwoods Southern. He told me he was part of a group who wanted to free all citizens from the tyranny—especially his brothers living in the South." Using the edge of her fork, she cut a section of pizza. She stabbed the bite with the fork's prongs and lifted it to her mouth.

Brock watched Cassie, then sucked the sauce from his fingers. Over the years he had learned to tell when she was holding something back. "There's more. What is it?"

Jefferson, his mouth full of pizza, glanced at Cassie.

She shook her head. "If I turn up anything that might be pertinent to your investigation, I promise I'll let you know."

Revealing a muddled expression, Brock looked at the cameraman he had known longer than he had known Cassie. "Tell me. What's she up to?"

Jefferson wiped his hands and mouth with a napkin. He shook his head and held the palms of his big hands up in front of him. "Not me. I figure she's more dangerous than any ten Free Confederates."

Brock sighed. "Don't count on it." He tossed a hard look at Cassie. "Don't you go pullin' another boneheaded move like you did the night you tried to meet Juney and almost got yourself killed."

"Boneheaded?" Cassie said, revealing a dark scowl. She threw down her napkin. "Boneheaded?"

"Yes, boneheaded." He looked back at Jefferson. "Don't let her out of your sight."

"Yeah, right," Jefferson said with a chuckle. "Why don't you tell me to go fetch the Holy Grail? That would be easier."

Back in the SLED parking lot, Brock tried one more time to learn more about Cassie's plans in Columbia. "Can we get together tonight?"

"Can't tonight. Maybe in a day or two. I've got a bunch of leads to look into while we're here. Besides, the President begins his last swing through the South in a few days, right here in Columbia, and I hope to set up an interview."

"Yes, I know. We've been meeting with the Secret Service to discuss the particulars."

"Any particulars you care to share?" she asked.

He knew she expected the you've-got-to-be-kidding look he flashed in response. "No."

As if his reply didn't matter, she said, "Anyway, we have to get back to Charleston before Hart arrives." She hugged Brock—not hard or rememberable, but more in a gentle way—then she pecked a kiss on his cheek. "Definitely before I go back to Atlanta. I really do want to spend some time with you."

That night, just after Cassie had showered, brushed her teeth, and climbed into bed, her cell phone rang. *Not tonight, Brock.* She looked at the number on the caller ID but didn't recognize it. "Hello."

"This O'Connor?" The words of the caller revealed a tell-tale drawl, one with a familiar twang.

Cassie sat bolt upright in her bed. "Yes, yes, this is O'Connor." She grabbed a pad and pen off the bedside table.

"We need to talk. Tonight."

She glanced at the clock. "It's almost midnight. Can't we set a time tomorrow, maybe in the afternoon?"

"Tonight. And come alone."

Cassie looked out the hotel window into the darkness. Streetlights reflected on the damp streets. "Where?"

"You know the Farmers Market near the fairgrounds?"

"Yes, I know it," she said, recalling an assignment to cover a garden show held there a couple of years before. "When?"

"Make it an hour from now. Remember, I'll be watching you, and if you're not alone, our discussions are over. I've got a war to wage and won't have time to mess with you after tonight."

"What kind of war? What—"

"Your questions will be answered when we meet."

She heard the distinctive click. The phone went silent.

"Hello. Hello."

# CHAPTER · 18

DOWNTOWN COLUMBIA, SOUTH CAROLINA

Cassie's taxi waited as she stepped out the front door of the hotel. A misty rain fell, and the temperature had dropped to the low forties. She shivered, pulling her green parka tight around her shoulders as she remembered another night, another clandestine meeting—Brock had referred to it earlier in the day—the night she agreed to meet an informant named Juney in the parking lot of the Riverbanks Zoo.

That night had been foggy and damp, too. She'd witnessed a murder on that evening, almost becoming a victim herself. As she opened the back door of the cab, she hoped this meeting would go smoother. If it did, she should be back in her warm bed in a little over an hour.

"Farmers Market," Cassie said as she slid into the back of the taxi. The artificial and sickening aroma of sweet gardenias assaulted her senses. Looking around the dark interior, she spotted the culprit, a cardboard deodorizer that hung from the rearview mirror along with a plastic crucifix.

"*Tarde noche*," the Hispanic driver rattled off in Spanish, but in a way she could tell he wanted her to understand.

Cassie's high school Spanish had mostly faded from her memory, but she recalled *tarde* meant late. The man must have been stating the obvious. "Yes, I know it's late and the place is closed, but take me there anyway. How much?"

She saw the man's brown eyes fill with concern as they stared at her through the mirror. He held up eight fingers. "*Ocho dólares.*"

She fished a ten from her purse and handed it across the back of the front seat. "Keep the change."

As the taxi pulled away from the curb, Cassie wrote down the number posted on the dash. "If I call you in, say, an hour, would you pick me up where you drop me off?"

He looked up at the rearview mirror, nodded his head, and smiled. "*Sí.*"

Cassie exhaled. The man obviously understood English but didn't speak it well. "*Gracias,*" she said.

Glancing back over her shoulder as the hotel lights faded behind her, she was glad she had left a note with the night clerk for Jefferson. Right after she hung up the phone from talking to her informant, she started to call Jefferson's room but decided against it, afraid he would follow her and blow the meeting. The note explained why she hadn't let him in on the meeting. It also told him where she was going and to come looking for her if she wasn't back by breakfast.

She had instructed the night clerk to hold the message and not deliver it until daybreak. That way, she could retrieve it if she got back before Jefferson woke up, something she fully planned on doing.

She released another deep breath as she stared out onto the nearly deserted streets. *At least if anything goes wrong, someone will know enough to come looking for me.*

A short time later, the taxi pulled up next to a chain blocking traffic from entering the parking lot of the closed Farmers Market. Cassie stepped out onto the damp asphalt and stared into total darkness. She looked back inside the cab. The concern in the driver's eyes deepened. She wanted him to stay, to provide a quick getaway if needed, but she knew he had to leave. Her caller wouldn't dare approach her if he saw anyone else around.

"I'll be all right," she said, forcing a smile.

"You . . . sure?" he said in a slow cadence, carefully choosing the right words to speak.

"*Sí,*" Cassie said as she patted the front fender of the car. "*Adiós.*"

She watched the red taillights of the taxi disappear into the dark morning, then she started across the parking lot toward a distant row of buildings. Looking up the street, she saw the shadowy outline of Williams-Brice Stadium, where the University of South Carolina Gamecocks played their football games. She had once been assigned to cover the opening game of the season there, a public-interest piece on how many hot dogs and hamburgers, pretzels and popcorn were sold on a typical game day. Boring, meaningless drivel that she had been required to report on before she got her big break and moved to the network. With apprehension constricting her throat, making breathing difficult, she tried to relive that boring day, to take her mind off what she feared might be waiting in the darkness ahead.

No matter how hard she tried, the chilling sting of the evening rain, the occasional howl from a distant dog, or the shriek of a cat plundering a nearby garbage can managed to keep her imagination fertile for what dangers lurked around her. Brock's calling her a bonehead echoed in her mind.

As she continued toward the nearest building, she tried to concentrate on what her future might hold following a successful encounter with the informant. If any of her suspicions bore fruit, this story might launch her higher up the broadcast-news food chain. That is, if her source showed up and if he really had the kind of information she hoped for.

She might even get the chance to host her own prime-time TV show, just like those women reporters knocking down million-dollar-plus salaries. *Time for one of them to pass the torch to someone younger, anyway*, she thought through a nervous chuckle, desperate to keep her mind off her spooky surroundings.

She reached the building and pushed close under the roof overhang to keep out of the rain, which had begun to fall harder. *A flashlight would have been a good idea. How could this fringe lunatic find anybody in all this rain and darkness?* Her words ricocheted in her head. *Fringe lunatic?*

"Y-y-you O'Connor?" The stuttering voice came out of the pitch black that surrounded her.

Cassie's heart leaped up her throat. By the time she turned to face the sound, the pounding in her chest beat so hard and fast, she thought she was about to pass out. She hadn't heard anyone approach. "Yes. Where are you?"

A rail-thin man wearing a ball cap and a dark jacket stepped out of the darkness and walked toward her. She clutched her purse, prepared to swing it if necessary. She figured the recorder inside might be hard enough to at least stagger the man if he tried anything.

As he drew closer, the rain began to blow under the eaves. Water slid down the back of her neck. She shivered, as much from nerves as from the cold dampness soaking through her poncho.

"I . . . I'm freezing," she said. "Do you have a place we can go talk that's out of this monsoon?"

He stared hard, then looked around. "You alone?"

"Yes, dammit, I'm alone. But if I die of pneumonia from being out here, I won't do either of us much good."

"My car's over yonder." He pointed across the lot. "Come on, follow me."

He began to jog, but Cassie noticed he did so with a pronounced limp. She followed, wishing he would go faster. They reached the end of the Farmers Market lot and ran down the edge of the roadway, careful to stay on the asphalt and out of the roadside mud. He turned down a side street. Cassie stayed close behind, wondering how much farther they would have to go. Up ahead, off the road, she spotted what looked like an old police car rescued from a demolition derby.

"There it is," the man said. He ran to the driver's door, unlocked it, and climbed in.

As Cassie rounded the back of the car, she could see him reach across the seat and unlock her door. He didn't open it.

*So much for chivalry.* She tugged on the door. It didn't budge. "It's stuck," she yelled, giving a big pull.

Her hands slipped from the handle, and her feet shot out from under her. The next thing she knew, she was sitting in a patch of wet grass and mud. She glared up at the still-closed door. *No interview is worth this hassle*, she decided.

Cursing, the man jumped from the car and ran around the front. He stopped and stared down at Cassie. "Y-y-you got to give it some hip." He grabbed the door handle, yanked it, and slammed his hip into it, all in one motion. The metal moaned, and the door creaked as it swung open. "Come on. Someone's liable to hear all the commotion. We gotta go." He ran back around the car, leaving her sprawled on the wet ground.

"You bastard!" Cassie pushed her wet bottom up and grabbed the open door. Her soaked and muddy denim jeans clinging to her skin, she pulled herself into the front seat, a sullen look sculpted on her face. "What you have to tell me better be damn good or I'll—"

"Shut up and get in."

The man's vitriolic tone caused Cassie to hesitate. The words *fringe lunatic* resurfaced in her head. *What have I done?*

She eased her head back out of the car, her eyes never leaving the man seated behind the steering wheel. She glanced up the dark road, then at the hazy, gray sky. The rain pelted her face; rivulets of water streamed down her back.

"God help me," she said just above a whisper, then climbed in and plopped down on the vinyl seat.

# Chapter · 19

RURAL COUNTRYSIDE OUTSIDE COLUMBIA, SOUTH CAROLINA

"Where are we going?" Cassie asked as the man pulled the Ford into a nearby driveway, backed out, and turned back toward the Farmers Market.

"My plan is to ride and talk." He glanced into the rearview mirror. "You weren't followed, were you?"

"No." Cassie now wished she had told Jefferson before she left, instead of just leaving him a note he wouldn't even get until morning. If she had, they at least could have set a time for her return. If she didn't get back by then, she would know someone was out looking for her. "What's your name?"

The man, whose face looked even more gaunt up close, glared at her. "Why you w-w-want to know that for?"

"It's just easier. Look, I'm a reporter. You're my source. We don't burn our sources; we'd lose credibility." Questioning the man, focusing on learning all she could about what made him tick, helped her relax a little, despite feeling like she had just climbed from a cold mud bath. "Heater work?"

"Nope."

"Great. Don't suppose you have any towels or anything like that in here—something to dry off with."

"Some stuff in the back." He nodded toward the rear of the car.

Cassie leaned over the seat. She spotted a pile of rags in the floorboard. Grabbing a fistful, she straightened up, then sat back down and fastened her seat belt. Wiping her face and hair, she thought she detected a faint scent of gasoline or something similar. "So, tell me about this war you're wanting to wage, Mr. . . ."

"Just call me Yates."

"Well, Yates, what's your story?"

"Ain't got no story. I'm j-just like a lot of other folk who're sick and tired of being pushed around. Time's come for us to take a stand."

Cassie's eyes narrowed. "Are you the one who blew up the election building the other night?"

A faint smile crept across his face. "What if I did? What w-would you think of that?" His prideful tone answered Cassie's question.

"I'd think that's a pretty dangerous thing to do. You could've gotten killed or seriously injured."

His smile faded. He rubbed his right leg, the one Cassie had noted he favored when he ran. "Had to be done. No one wanted to take me serious. I had to prove my worth."

"What about the other person, the one in the hospital? Was he with you? Did you know him, or did he just happen to be in the wrong place?"

Yates shook his head. His voice saddened. "Reckon you could say both. Didn't mean for him to go and get hurt. He rode along with me, but he weren't no part of the bombing. He's a little slow in the head. You know what I mean?"

Cassie nodded.

"He had no idea what was about to happen." Contrition veiled his face. "You heared how he's doin'?"

"Not good. But he's still alive." She looked out the windshield, watched and listened as the wipers streaked the water across the glass. They were speeding along a deserted road away from Columbia, and she hadn't seen another car since they pulled out onto the highway.

"You said you had to prove your worth. To whom?"

"To the soldiers of the Free Confederacy. They're the ones who'll fight the war. I just want to be a part."

"And you figure by blowing up the election building, you'll be invited to join?"

"Hope so. Ain't heared nothin' from 'em yet, though."

"Do they know how to get in touch with you?"

"Oh, yeah. They know. Some friends. . . ." His features fell. "Used to be friends, anyway. They know how to find me."

"Tell me about this Free Confederacy. Where are they located? Who's their leader? Are there many of them?"

"Most of what you're askin' is classified information. You know, top-secret stuff. I don't even know the answer to some of it. I'll tell you what I can, though."

"Well," Cassie said, relieved that maybe the misery she had endured up to this point would yield some reward. "Just tell me the parts you know."

"The leader's an old man named Eustace Hanley. He's sort of like a preacher, but he's also the Free Confederacy army's general."

"Preacher? How can you be a preacher and lead an army to fight your own country?"

"That's just it, it ain't our country no more. It's been invaded. Reason I called you is that we need someone to spread the word. Let others know that we gotta stand up and fight."

Cassie stared at Yates. His hands squeezed the steering wheel so hard, his knuckles were white.

"I don't think I understand," she said. "Invaded by whom?"

"The army of the New World Order. They're seizing our farms and land, stealing our money from our banks. They're even spying on us with helicopters and listening devices."

Cassie recalled reading some of this in the pamphlet Rowdy had given her. "Who's leading this New World Order? Is it another country?"

"United Nations. You ever heared of the World Bank?"

"Yes."

"There you go. It's part of the conspiracy, too. I've heared of them black helicopters hovering over the bank buildings up in Charlotte, landing their soldiers on the roofs at night, breaking into the vaults, stealing all of the money and taking it back to the World Bank. They're stealing our money and using it to control us all."

"Do you really believe that?"

His foot slammed the brake pedal. The car went into a skid, throwing Cassie to the dashboard despite the seat belt she wore. The Ford slid off the pavement onto the shoulder of the road, spun around in the sandy soil, and rocked hard before stopping.

Dazed, Cassie looked over at Yates. "Are you crazy?" She regretted the question as soon as she asked it.

His eyes blazed, his nostrils flared. "Hell, no, I ain't crazy." An edge of impatience crept into his voice. "I'm not stupid, neither, and that's what you're thinking right now, ain't it? You're just like all the rest. You believe that UN propaganda out of Washington. By the time you and the others realize folks like me have been right all along, it'll be too damn late."

Yates jumped out of the car and stormed toward the back. He stopped at the trunk, jerked it open, then shouted at Cassie, who was peering out through the rear window. "Come here."

She looked out the side window, then out the windshield. Nothing but forest and highway surrounded her and the crazy lunatic she had chosen to ride with. *Damn fool.* Brock had been right when he accused her of being boneheaded, and she wished she could tell him so.

"I-I-I s-said come here." Yates's stutter grew more pronounced as the anger in his voice intensified.

Cassie pulled on the handle and pushed her shoulder into the door. It opened with a loud groan.

Outside, she walked with hesitant strides toward the back of the Ford. The rain had stopped, but she barely noticed. Her gaze locked on Yates, who stood with his bony arm propped on the opened trunk lid. A smug grin masked his face.

"Look here," he said.

Cassie eased around and peered into the trunk. "What the hell?"

"How is it they say on your news? Them's what you call instruments of war."

She counted four assault rifles, seven ammunition clips, a box of ammunition, and a crate marked "grenades."

"Are those really hand grenades?" she asked, her voice quivering.

Yates reached into the box and pulled out one of the small metal objects. He looked at her, excitement dancing in his eyes. "They call this one a M26. Friend sold me a case he smuggled out of Fort Jackson." He laughed. "Some folks call 'em pineapples, 'cause that's what they were called back in World War II. These are better than them old ones, though. Bet this one would really spice up your fruit basket." He cackled as he tossed the grenade up in the air and caught it on its way back down. "Want to chunk it?" He sounded like a kid inviting her to play with his most treasured toy.

When Cassie didn't reach for the grenade, Yates thrust it toward her. She jumped back, raising her hands.

"No. No, thank you."

Once again he tossed the grenade up in the air and caught it like a baseball. "Got more of these in my secret armory." He pulled the pin out with his teeth, spit it onto the ground. "I seen John Wayne do that once in a movie."

Cassie's fearful glare never left the grenade.

Yates shook the explosive in her face. "Watch this," he said as he leaned back with his arm cocked. He heaved the grenade into the nearby tree line.

Cassie ducked, with her arms across her face. Her hands covered her head.

Seconds later, a loud blast ripped the quiet night, filling the air with dirt and splintered wood. Cassie stumbled back against the car.

*Someone had to hear the explosion. Maybe they'll call the police.* She looked toward the highway but saw no houses or cars.

"Ain't no need to worry. Nobody lives for miles around here." He pointed toward the trees. "Not far beyond those woods is the beginnings of the Congaree Swamp. Ever been there?"

Still wet and cold, Cassie crossed her chest with her arms. She tried in vain to keep her voice steady and unshaken. "Look, I need to get back. I'll do your story, let people know the treachery of the New World Order. I promise." She stared at the man's feral grin. "Can we go back now?"

Yates looked up at the sky. "Weren't for the clouds, I'd be able to tell how late it was."

Cassie glanced at her watch. "It's two-thirty. Can we go now?"

He grimaced. "Ain't no need to be afeared. I ain't gonna hurt you. You're our source for the news to be spread." He closed the trunk, released a loud exaggerated sigh. "Come on, I'll take you back into town."

As Yates stomped toward the driver's door, Cassie drew a deep breath, let it out slowly. Before getting inside, she looked toward the heavens. *Thank you, God.*

After pulling back onto the highway to turn around, Yates's surplus patrol car sat crossways in the road when Cassie heard the mind-numbing roar and saw the bright headlights bearing down on her side. "Oh, shit!"

Her scream startled Yates, who stopped his turn to stare out the side window. "Son of a—" He threw the gearshift in reverse, mashed the accelerator. The Ford lurched backwards, but not fast enough for the front end to miss the oncoming truck.

Cassie's second scream froze in her throat. She couldn't move. Bright headlights blinded her. Debris and metal shards exploded from the front of the Crown Vic. The windshield caved in on the front seat. The roof buckled.

A sharp pain shot through Cassie's shoulder. She felt her body rise and go airborne as darkness enveloped her in a quiet cocoon.

# CHAPTER · 20

FARMERS MARKET, COLUMBIA, SOUTH CAROLINA

"Wazzup, Cuz?" Tree Calhoun's cheery deep voice bellowed over Jefferson's cell phone. "Ain't like you to be callin' at the crack of dawn."

Jefferson felt anything but cheery as he stood next to his Bronco, watching a rosy-colored sun rising over the stands of nearby Williams-Brice Stadium. "Cassie O'Connor's gone, and I can't get hold of Elliott. I have no idea where she is, who's she with, even if she went of her own accord. I need help, man. Something's wrong. She left this note about how she went—"

"Whoa, mule. Slow down. You're talkin' crazy, and I ain't hangin' with ya. What's up with the girl?"

"You remember me tellin' you she's wantin' to do a story on that militia group."

"Yeah, I know, you told me that the night Rowdy Dubois got killed. I'm with ya so far."

"Well, apparently, last night she goes out of the hotel—"

"What hotel? Where are you?"

"We're in Columbia. She wanted to follow up on the bombing at the election office up here, and then we're headin' back to Charleston." Jefferson leaned back against the door of the Bronco. "Anyway, sometime last night, Cassie must have gotten a call from this informant she has, and she went out to meet him. She never came back." He drew a deep breath.

"Any idea who this informant is, where they met, how she got there?"

"Not much on the who. She told me about getting this call after the bombing, said it was a man, but that's it. She thinks he's an insider with the Free Confederacy. I'm not sure she had any idea who she was dealin' with."

"And she went out to meet him without backup. That's dumb. Even I don't pull that kind of crazy stunt."

"You've got to know Cassie. . . ." Jefferson stared skyward, shook his head. "Anyway, she left me a note that basically said for me to come lookin' for her if she wasn't back by this morning. I had the hotel manager check her room. She's not back."

"Where are you now?" Tree asked.

"Standing smack in the middle of the Farmers Market parking lot near the football stadium. There's a bunch of folks 'round here, but Cassie ain't one of 'em. Far as I can tell, nobody's seen anyone matching her description, either."

"That where the note says she was to meet the informant?"

"Pretty much, yeah."

"You said you tried to call Brock?"

"Yeah, I was hopin' if she got in some kind of a jam, she would have called him. But according to his office, he won't be back until tomorrow. Said he had to go somewhere in the western part of the state on an assignment. I didn't leave a message, so he doesn't know."

"I'll check with headquarters, see if I can get up with him. Meantime, why don't you call around to the taxi companies, see if one of their drivers picked her up. She had to get out there somehow—unless she walked."

Jefferson smiled. "Trust me, I know this gal. She didn't walk. It's more than a couple of miles from our hotel to the Farmers Market, and she wouldn't walk on a bright sunny day, much less in the dead of night, alone."

"Then, she either took a cab or the informant picked her up. I'm bettin' on the cab, 'cause the snitch probably didn't want to be identified by anyone but her."

"Okay, I'll check the taxis. Then what?"

"I'm coming up there, but it'll take a while. Meet me back out at the Farmers Market around noon."

"Thanks, Cuz. I owe ya."

Grayson Locke paused in front of the Franklin Roosevelt Memorial, near the area known as the Tidal Basin, in Washington, D.C. He clasped his hands behind his back and stared in near reverence at the lifelike rendering of the former president and his dog, who sat beside the master. "You sly bastard," he said, talking to the statue. "You snatched your fame right out of the jaws of the Depression."

He smirked. "If everything goes accordingly, maybe someday there will be a monument to me, here somewhere." He looked across the water, then back at the seated statue of President Roosevelt. "Maybe on the other side, nearer to the Washington Monument, where more people would notice. Just like in the real estate market, old boy, location is everything."

He glanced at his watch. Ten after ten. Adam Cromwell was late. Locke had been reluctant to grant Cromwell's request to meet. He didn't like being seen together, but he had given in to the impertinent man's insistence after their fierce discussion over the phone grew annoying. The son of a bitch had been like an irritating rock in Locke's shoe for years, but since their meeting on Hilton Head, Cromwell had become an even greater pain in the ass.

A cool breeze sifted through nearby trees, but the sun shone brightly, keeping the air temperature pleasant and mild. Locke pulled off his suit coat, loosened his tie, and walked to a nearby bench. He had just settled on the bench when Cromwell arrived and sat beside him.

"That bombing had to be more than a coincidence," Cromwell said as he unzipped his jacket and pulled out a pipe from an inside pocket. "Too damn close to the senator to be just a coincidence, and too damn sloppy. That how you're ensuring Flint stays in the White House?"

"You're putting too much stock in the propaganda that Hart's spin doctors are distributing. I was there. The explosion happened several blocks away, and I have no idea who did it."

"No idea, huh? Trying to kill off the opposition has your fingerprints all over it, Locke. We agreed to finance your plan, based on your word, without knowing exactly what was going to happen and to whom. We agreed to stick out our necks and risk our fortunes for the promise of key cabinet positions. We didn't agree to go to prison for some stupid—"

"I told you, our people had nothing to do with the bombing." Locke felt the muscles in his neck tighten.

"Yeah?! I'm not convinced. I haven't seen a damn thing on the news about how our investments are helping the President. Everything is about how Hart is gaining in the polls." Cromwell looked down as he tapped the pipe, hard, on the side of the bench. Ashes, along with loose, charred tobacco, fell onto the ground. He looked Locke dead in the eye. "I want out of this insanity, and I want my investment back."

"Your investment has already been put to work. And don't insult me with your sudden concern for human life. We both know you don't want me to go there." Locke sighed. "Our plan is sound—trust me."

"Trust you!" Mock laughter rose from Cromwell's throat. "You think I'm the only person who suspects operatives close to the President's campaign for that bombing? Randall's own party leaders would sooner see Hart win than to have Randall as their next president. The man's a pariah. The folks on the Hill hate the bastard for the way he weaseled his way into the vice presidency. Mark my words, if anything happens to Flint, the Capitol Hill power players will find a way to appoint someone else, and everything we've invested in will be up in smoke." He looked away as he pulled a tobacco pouch out of his coat pocket and refilled the pipe.

Locke watched. Cromwell might be bluffing, but if he wasn't, he had finally handed Locke the opportunity he had been waiting for. If Cromwell wanted enough rope to hang himself, Locke was more than willing to oblige. Inside, he laughed at the insolent bastard; outside, he glowered.

As a puff of aromatic smoke drifted past him, Locke said, "If you want out, then get out. I'll make good your meager investment until now."

Cromwell's forehead furrowed, and he squinted. "You don't think I'll walk, do you? Hart would love to have my financial backing, and the way things look, he'll be the one in a position to make me a major player."

Locke kept the challenge alive. "You're crazy. You won't get close to him."

Cromwell's lips curled. "Money talks. I'll make a contribution big enough to get his attention. In fact, look for me to be standing with him at the rest of his appearances. You'll see just how close I can get."

Locke wanted to cheer the bastard on, encourage him to join Hart. That would make the job of dealing with him that much easier. But he also wanted to make sure Cromwell kept his mouth shut. "You want to throw everything down the toilet, go ahead. But don't leave thinking you can sell the rest of our asses down the river. You have a lot of baggage that the police would like to know about. A dead senator, for one. The late Vice President of the United States, for another."

Cromwell glanced around. "Don't lay Griffith's death at my doorstep. Play your games with someone else."

"If you recall, it was your Arab friend who moved the money into accounts in the Vice President's name, then leaked the scandal to the press. And trust me, this is no game. It's very serious—deadly serious."

"We all had a role. What's your point?"

"You know what I'm saying. If you back out of our deal now, don't try using our past associations and dealings to better yourself, or you'll tumble much harder than the rest of us."

"That works both ways, old boy." Cromwell's tone dripped with sarcasm. He glanced at his watch. "Hart will be in Charleston tonight. He speaks at a fund-raising dinner, then on the campus of the College of Charleston tomorrow afternoon. I already have someone working on an introduction. If I use my contacts—and checkbook—I can be a close personal friend by morning."

He sucked his pipe, blew smoke out the corner of his mouth. "I understand his campaign chief is a real beauty. Enjoying her favors will be an added benefit."

Locke grimaced. Cromwell's sardonic expression worried him. Did Cromwell know about him and Hart's campaign chief, Creighton Lansford? If he did, what did he know? What could he know?

Locke had met her a year before, a chance meeting at a Capitol Hill reception. Lansford had accidentally spilled champagne on his dinner jacket, and her apology led to the two of them retreating to a balcony away from the gathering. There he learned they both shared a loathing of crowds.

In time, he found that not only was she physically attractive, she also possessed a sharp wit and an intellectual cunning that complemented his own predatory instincts. The latter quality was the one he most admired.

They had seemed to be drawn to each other from the second they met. He had never had another woman care for him like she did, indifferent to his wealth, appearing to be interested only in him as a person.

They shared laughs about their political polarity. "Hart's closest advisor involved with one of the President's major contributors—what would everyone think?" she had joked after one memorable night, early in their courtship.

Inwardly, Locke smiled at the recollection. To her, he was only a contributor, with a differing political agenda, nothing else. That was all she knew, all she could know. He hoped she would still care for him after he ascended to power, regardless of the circumstances surrounding his ascension.

Cromwell's remark bothered him. If Cromwell knew, who else knew? How could he? As a couple, Locke and Lansford had been careful. Besides, since the convention, they hadn't had a chance to see each other even one time.

"I hear she's ruthless," Locke said to Cromwell. "Do you think you can conquer her like. . . ." He flashed a sinister grin. "You know."

"I love a challenge." Cromwell feigned a smile.

Locke cursed to himself. Cromwell was to the women of powerful men what a pedophile was to a fair-skinned child; he couldn't help himself. But this time Locke believed the man would meet his match. Still, Cromwell's self-aggrandizing attitude had gotten to him, but Locke would never give the man the satisfaction of knowing.

He remembered how a friend, a senator, had fallen victim to Cromwell's wrath and ended up dead. The time had come for Locke to turn the tables on the bastard—a payback for his old friend, a security move for himself.

"I've never questioned your resourcefulness," Locke said, shrugging his shoulders. He decided to toss out a dare, like a kid would to a playground friend. "I just think teaming with Hart at this late date will be your ruin. You have too much to overcome in a short time."

Cromwell laughed. "We'll just see about that. By the way, word is that Hart and his sexy chief keep the campaign trail steamy. It'll be fun trying to lure her away from him."

Locke didn't react, but he knew Cromwell was baiting him. He was sure now his nemesis knew about his relationship with Lansford. Still, he refused to be cajoled into reacting. "Interesting," he said without emotion. "The only thing I've heard is that she is very protective, but he's too focused on the campaign to be involved."

Cromwell nodded, his eyes holding a faraway gaze as he smoked his pipe. The tiniest of grins creased his lips. "I wonder who's right?"

Jefferson stepped out of his Bronco when he saw Tree's oversize body uncoil from a blue Thunderbird with shiny chrome trim. "Nice ride, Cuz. You must be doin' all right. When did you pick this one up?"

"Belongs to the department, courtesy of a local drug dealer. You know—seized assets, fruits of our labor." Tree chuckled. "We get to use it for undercover ops, so I figured I'd break it in today. Any word on O'Connor?"

"Not a peep, and I'm starting to get serious about my worry. I've tried her cell phone, off and on, since I called you this morning. No answer."

Tree straightened the creases out of his leather pants. "I finally got up with Brock. He ain't happy."

"Hope he doesn't blame me. He's really hot for this li'l gal."

"Truth. But bad as he might want to, he can't leave to come home, though. There was a shooting over near Calhoun Falls last night. They pulled him off the bombing to head up that investigation. He had just arrived when I got up with him, so he asked me to find her. I promised I'd do everything I could."

"So, where to first?" Jefferson asked.

"You check with the cabbies?"

"Yeah, found the one who dropped her off, but he wasn't much help. Hardly speaks any English. Best I could get, by using his dispatcher as a translator, is that Cassie had planned to call him to come back and pick her up. He's off now, and yet to hear from her."

Tree frowned. "He see anybody around here last night when he let her out?"

"Nope. He said it was dark and rainy. He saw no one."

"Brock mentioned this guy they found after the bombing. Apparently he's out of his coma, so we'll start at the hospital and see if he can help."

"Sounds like a plan," Jefferson said. "Your ride or mine?"

"Let's style a while on the state's dime. We'll take mine."

"Righteous." Jefferson locked his Bronco and slid into the front seat of the specially equipped car. He looked around the interior of dark wood and leather. "Truly righteous."

Tree turned the key in the ignition. The engine roared. "Runs like a scalded dog." He reached over to the CD player. "Six-disk changer in the dash, Bose speakers everywhere. Listen to this." He punched a button, filling the car with music from a blues guitar. "My man Stevie Ray. As the commercials say, it don't get no better than this."

"Don't you know," Jefferson yelled above the music, "whoever owned this was truly bummed when y'all took it from him."

Tree pulled out onto the highway. "Her. We took it from a her, and you might say she was lethal in how she displayed her displeasure. She tried to emphasize her resentment by grabbing a loaded fully automatic assault rifle. She never got to use it, though. Now she's waitin' trial on federal charges, and I suspect by the time she gets out of prison, they might have hovercraft floating above the highways instead of cars driving on them."

# CHAPTER · 21

RICHLAND MEMORIAL HOSPITAL, COLUMBIA, SOUTH CAROLINA

Twenty minutes later, Jefferson and Tree walked through the sliding glass doors leading into the lobby of the Richland Memorial Hospital. They stopped at the front desk, obtained the room number for Jimmy Joe Harden, then proceeded toward the bank of elevators leading to the upper floors. An elderly man in a blue uniform, with HOSPITAL SECURITY written on the white patches of each arm, rose from his seat behind a counter. He approached the two men as they waited on an elevator.

Tree and Jefferson exchanged glances as the guard stepped between them and the elevator doors. His yellowed white hair had been combed into a lopsided pile on the side of his head, and his ruddy, fleshy face looked dry and scaly.

"You fellows visitin' a friend?" The man hooked his thumbs on a black belt that disappeared under his extended belly. His glare signaled a challenge as he looked back and forth between Jefferson and Tree.

Tree read the metal nametag over the man's right breast pocket, then replied with a hint of disdain. "Not exactly, Allen. But we *are* here to see a patient."

As if he hadn't heard a word, the guard's eyes roamed Tree from head to toe, pausing on the wide lapels of the open collar of his black silk shirt, then the silver buttons on his leather vest. He glared up at the matter-of-fact expression on Tree's wide face, then looked down at the officer's black leather pants and basketball shoes. "You boys can't just be roamin' the corridors without business here."

"That so?" Tree said as he fished out the gold chain, hanging around his neck, from under his shirt. He held up the SLED badge attached to the end. "We're not your 'boys.' If you're finished trying to hassle us, then we'll be gettin' on with our business."

The elevator doors slid open, and the guard cast a hard look at the shield. He shot a glance at Jefferson, then back at Tree. His voice grew less confrontational, even though a hint of contempt remained. "Guess you can go ahead, but y'all don't look much like cops to me."

Tree and Jefferson stepped around the man, into the waiting elevator. As the doors closed on the security guard's probing stare, Tree spoke with a deadpan expression. "Funny. To me, he looks just like a rent-a-cop."

On the fourth floor, Tree pulled open the door to room 4014. Inside, he saw a pale-complexioned, young, blond-haired man lying on his back. His body stretched the length of the steel-framed bed. Tubes ran into thick muscular arms from IV bags that hung from hooks on each side of the bed. The curtains covering the window were pulled closed, and a single lamp in one corner lit the room. A monitor's periodic beep revealed blood pressure and heartbeat, producing an intermittent break in the room's church-like silence.

As Tree and Jefferson entered, a woman rose from a chair near the lamp and stepped to the foot of the bed. She straightened her black dress and stroked her pewter-colored hair where it was pulled into a bun behind her head. She approached the two men while projecting a mixture of fear and suspicion. "May . . . may I help you?" she asked, her voice soft and wilting.

Tree pulled out his badge for the woman to inspect. "I'm agent Calhoun with SLED. This is Jefferson Lee. If it's okay, I'd like to speak with Mr. Harden for just a minute."

Her pale features drooped. "I'm his mother. Jimmy's a good boy. I just can't believe he'd have had anything to do with that explosion." The woman studied her son's prone body covered by a white sheet and pale blue spread. She rubbed her hands together. "Of course, I can't explain how he ended up under all that rubble, neither." She shook her head. "It truly mystifies me."

"Ma'am, we're hopin' Jimmy can help us identify any others who might have been with him that night," Tree explained. "There's a woman missin', and we believe whoever blew up that building knows where she is."

Moisture built in the middle-aged woman's pale blue eyes. "Jimmy wouldn't hurt no woman. He's a mite slow on learnin', but he's a good boy."

"Yes, ma'am. We know Jimmy didn't have anything to do with the woman's disappearance. We're just hopin' he might know who did and where they might be."

"Is it okay if I stay here while you talk to him? He's scared of strangers as a rule. . . ." She looked back and forth between the two men. "I hope you understand what I'm sayin', 'cause I ain't meanin' to be hurtful, but Jimmy don't know many coloreds. He. . . ."

"Yes'm, I understand." Tree smiled. "And we don't take offense. If your stayin' will make Jimmy more comfortable around us, you're more than welcome."

He stepped beside the bed and sat in a straight-back chair next to Jimmy Joe's head. Jefferson leaned back against the wall to observe.

"Jimmy." Tree spoke in a whispered voice. "Jimmy, can you hear me?"

Jimmy Joe's eyelids fluttered.

"Jimmy, I'm Agent Calhoun. I'm with SLED, and I want to ask you about the men you were with the night the building blew up and fell on you. Do you feel up to talkin'?"

Jimmy Joe's eyelids fluttered again. This time they eased open. He rolled his head toward where Tree sat. When he saw the big black man, fear crept into his expression. "Who . . . who are you?" His voice sounded scratchy.

Tree picked up a glass of water from a bedside stand. He held the straw and guided it toward Jimmy Joe's parched, cracked lips. "Drink. It'll help your throat."

With the look of a deer caught in a spotlight, Jimmy Joe allowed Tree to slip the straw between his lips. He sipped the water, but his gaze remained locked on his visitor.

"I'm an agent with SLED, a police officer. I'm not here to get you in trouble; I'm here to find out who you were with the night you got hurt." Tree talked to Jimmy Joe the same way he questioned juveniles. From what Brock had told him, all confirmed by the man's mother, Jimmy Joe's mental acuity wasn't much more than that of a 12- or 13-year-old boy.

"You don't look like a policeman."

Tree couldn't conceal his amusement. He glanced at Jefferson, whose wide grin told him he wasn't alone. "Yes, I've heard that already today." He pulled his badge out and held it close for Jimmy Joe to see. "Here's my badge. I work undercover, so I'm not supposed to look like a policeman."

"I seen a show on TV one time with a man dressed something like you. He was a policeman, too, and he sure got in a lot of fights and shootouts."

Tree grinned. "I'm pretty lucky. I don't get in that many fights." He held the straw for Jimmy Joe to take another sip of water. "Now that you know I'm really a policeman, will you tell me who the men were who got you hurt?"

Jimmy Joe's gaze shot over to where his mother stood at the foot of his bed. Tree glanced back at her, saw her nod her approval.

"There was only one man. He wanted to show our friends he could be like them. I didn't know he was going to blow up that building. Honest."

"I believe you, Jimmy. Who's this friend of yours?"

Jimmy Joe rubbed the bruises on his face. He looked back at his mother. "Mamma said we couldn't be friends no more. She's afraid he'll get me hurt again, ain't you, Mamma?"

Her cheeks flushed, the woman nodded again. "I guess I'm overly protective, but he's all I got, and I don't want none of these fools gettin' him killed."

"No need to be ashamed, ma'am," Tree said. "Don't blame you a bit. He's lucky to be here, after what happened." He looked back at the young patient. "What's this man's name, Jimmy?"

"Yates. Yates Arden."

Tree jotted the name on a pad he had pulled from his vest pocket. "You said there were other friends that Yates wanted to impress. Who are they?"

Jimmy Joe looked back at his mother.

"One's Jimmy's cousin, Dane Everett," she answered for her son. "He's a third cousin—branch kin, some call it. He showed up a few months back. We put him up, gave him a place to sleep and eat, but not anymore. He's done gone and got with the wrong crowd, far as I'm concerned."

"When did you last see him?"

"He called me about Jimmy, even came to the hospital the day after Jimmy got hurt. But I ain't seen him since." Her eyes held a resentful glare. "Good riddance, too."

Tree wrote the name on his pad. "Who else, Jimmy?"

Jimmy Joe drew a deep breath, then let it out. "There's Barry. I like Barry; he's nice to me. And there's Lance. Lance is the one who took us to the church where they had guns. I didn't like that at all."

Jefferson pushed away from the wall and stepped to the foot of the bed. He stood beside Jimmy Joe's mother, with a look of curiosity.

Tree exchanged glances with his cousin before turning to the woman. "You know these two, Barry and Lance?"

"Yes," she replied, projecting a tone of disapproval. "They're like Dane—too dadgum preoccupied with guns and fighting. Barry Lynch has come by the house on occasion. More often, since Dane got here. Don't know much about him, though. Jimmy Joe met him where a lot of local folks go to hang out."

"Where's that?"

"Carter's General Store. Men who ain't got nothing better to do go up there to swap lies. They chew tobacco, take the Lord's name in vain, and mostly talk 'bout the way things used to be and how they ought to be now. Pure waste of time, if you ask me. I tried to keep Jimmy from going, but he has to be around folks other than me. There ain't many options in our neck of the woods."

"And this Lance . . . what's his last name?"

"Mackenzie. Never have trusted that boy. I knew his mamma. Daddy too. He grew up without much supervision, if you ask me. Since they passed, he's grown wilder than a young stallion. He's married, but not so's you'd notice. Spends too much time down at Waldrop's."

"Waldrop's?" Jefferson said.

"A bar near us. Local den of sin, where troublemakers go to get drunk. I hear there's drugs in that place. And the women who go there are rumored to be pretty loose." She blushed. "Jimmy ain't allowed to be there."

Tree turned his attention back to Jimmy Joe. "You feelin' okay enough for me to ask a few more questions?"

"Suppose so." Despite his willingness to go on, the man-child's eyes looked weak.

Tree decided to learn what he could about the location of the Free Confederacy's encampment, then call it a day. "Tell me about this church, the one where everyone carried guns. Know where it is?"

"No. When we went, we had to wear hoods over our heads so we couldn't see. They didn't take the hoods off till we got to the church. Weren't no Bibles or song books in the pews, neither. I like our church lots better." He smiled at his mother.

"Who put the hoods on you?" Tree asked.

"Friend of Lance. I forget his name, but his daddy was the preacher."

"You recall if this church had a name?"

Jimmy Joe's eyes narrowed. He raked his teeth across his lower lip. Finally he shook his head. "Nope. Somethin' 'bout a sword of God. Somethin like that. It was surrounded by this wooden fence, and I overheard Dane and Barry talkin' something 'bout gunports in the steeple."

Tree's eyebrows lifted as he stood up. He patted the younger man's hand. "You've been a big help, Jimmy." He nodded at the mother. "Thank you. I hope Jimmy gets to feelin' better real soon. Meantime, we're going to try and find out why his friends are wantin' to blow up buildings and hang out at a church with guns instead of Bibles."

Jefferson walked to the door and pushed it open. Tree followed.

Out in the hallway, Tree grabbed Jefferson's shoulder. "Things might get a little dicey as I go about tracking down this church. You get paid to report the news, not make it, so this might be the time for you—"

"Forget it, Cuz," Jefferson interrupted. "I'm in this for Cassie—maybe even a tiny bit for ole Rowdy. Cassie can be a pain in the ass at times, but I've kind of grown accustomed to her stubbornness."

"Have it your way. Don't say I didn't warn you, though."

Jefferson pushed the button for the elevator. "So, now what?"

"I think I know this Waldrop's," Tree said. "It's smack in the middle of the redneck capital of South Carolina, but I know a regular there. Couple of years back, I busted this guy on a marijuana charge. He rolled on his dealer, who got five years for his troubles. They hung out at Waldrop's. That's where he bought his dope." Tree winked. "Once you get a guy to roll on another, you own him for life. If there's a connection to that church and this Free Confederacy bunch, I'll know it before the sun comes up tomorrow."

"While you're working your source," Jefferson said, "I'm going back to my old station here in Columbia. They may have something in their files on this crowd. Cassie and I had planned on checking with them before heading back to Charleston, anyway. I'll see what I can find and meet back up with you tonight."

"Sounds like a plan. I'll take you back to your ride, then look under a few rocks for my snitch. I'll swing by your hotel and pick you up when I'm done."

# Chapter · 22

A LOCAL BAR IN UPSTATE SOUTH CAROLINA

The odor of stale beer and sweat assaulted Barry's nostrils as he walked through the door into Waldrop's Do-Drop-In. Wrapped in the eerie red glow from a neon beer sign in the front window, he looked around the crowded one-room tavern. His gaze picked through the throng of men—and a few women—gathered in booths and sitting on stools lining the bar.

"Barry, over here." Lance's voice rose above the conversations in the room.

Barry looked to his left. Lance sat at the end of the bar, waving a mug of beer as if it were a lantern. Barry nodded, gave a thumbs-up to show he saw him, and then stepped around a couple headed out into the cool night. The man, skinny as a pipe cleaner, staggered as he tried to avoid bumping into Barry.

His sharp elbow caught Barry's ribs. "Sorry, partner. My wheels got a little wobbly on me." He sounded like he had a mouthful of mush.

"Sorry," the short woman with a bowling-ball figure added. She flashed a toothless smile as she guided her drunk friend through the doorway.

Barry rubbed his side and continued on toward the end of the bar, where Lance sat downing the last of his mug of beer.

"Where's Dane?" Lance asked, sliding off the stool.

"No idea. Thought he might be with you."

Lance shook his head. "Nope."

Two men stood to leave, and Lance motioned toward their corner booth. "Let's sit there. I've got some shit to tell you that you won't believe, and we don't need no one overhearing."

His words slurred just enough for Barry to realize that the beer his friend had just finished hadn't been his first.

"How long you been here?"

"Couple hours. Since sometime after lunch." He glanced at his watch, laughed, and shrugged his shoulders. "Hell, I don't know. Want a beer? I'm buyin'."

"Sure, but I'll get it." Barry gestured at a middle-aged waitress with dyed black hair and a weather-wrinkled face. "Two Buds," he said when she came over. He handed her a ten-dollar bill.

The woman showed a flirtatious smile. Her eyes fixed on his, held for a moment. "Be right back, honey."

Barry waited until she walked away, then he turned back to Lance. "So, what's got you so excited?"

"It's going to happen real soon. I think tomorrow. It's finally going to really happen." Lance's dilated pupils elevated his excited expression.

"What's going to happen? What're you talking about?"

"The first shots of the war . . . the new civil war. We're gonna show 'em all. Those bastards at the United Nations are gonna be—"

Barry motioned for Lance to lower his voice. "What the hell are you sayin'?" He glanced around to see who else might be listening. "What war? Where?"

"Ira wants me to go with him," Lance said in a quieter voice. "He ain't said where yet, but he said we'd shock the world, just like the Confederates did when they attacked Fort Sumter."

Barry opened his mouth to ask another question, but he hesitated when the waitress walked up.

She set the beers and Barry's change on the table. "Anything else?"

"No, thanks." He slid a dollar bill to the edge of the table.

The woman grabbed it, forced it down into the front pocket of her tight jeans. "Thanks, honey. Let me know if you want anything else." She winked. "And I do mean *anything*."

Barry tossed her a quick nod, then turned his attention back to Lance. "You told Dane about this?"

"Ain't told nobody but you so far, and you have to keep it a secret." This time Lance spoke in a whisper.

"I thought we were all in this together," Barry said. "You sure you can trust Ira?"

Lance's tone grew indignant. "Ira's a friend. Weren't for him, none of us would have ever gotten to join up." His features relaxed, his voice softened. "Look, I'll get Ira to include you and Dane. The war's just startin'. There'll be more targets."

"Lance!"

The loud voice startled Barry. He looked up to see Ira Hanley, red-faced and dressed in green fatigues.

The color drained from Lance's cheeks. "Ira." He tried to recover his composure, but his expression revealed his alarm. "We're just havin' a beer."

Ira scorched Barry with his glare. "What's he told you?"

Lance recoiled as Barry sprang from his seat and made an aggressive move that put him chin-to-chin with Ira.

"About what?" Barry's angry tone caused the surprised younger Hanley to backpedal. "Don't come in here flashing no attitude when I'm drinking a beer with my friend." He sneered. "What exactly is your problem?"

Ira didn't speak at first. He glared at Barry, the intensity slowly fading until he finally diverted his gaze and glanced at Lance. "We've got a busy day tomorrow, Lynch. That's all. He don't need to be drinking to where he'll run his mouth."

"He ain't runnin' his mouth. We've been talkin' 'bout another paint war," Barry said as he stepped back and relaxed his fierce posture. "What's so all-fired important about tomorrow that you've got yourself all bent out of shape, anyway?" He motioned to the seat next to Lance.

Ira looked around the room. Several bar patrons had turned to watch the two men argue. He slid into the booth beside Lance. "I'm okay. I just—"

"Want to join us?" Barry asked.

Ira's forehead furrowed.

"In a paint war. We've got extra guns, pellets, and goggles. Maybe you'd like to take Yates Arden's place in our little battle."

"Yeah," Lance said, still with a hint of nervousness in his voice. "We ain't heard from that bastard since you and the others tossed him out of camp. Guess he's gone from these parts for good and won't be a problem for us again."

Ira chewed on his lower lip as he stared at both men. "Nope, he won't be a problem. That, I'll guarantee."

Barry had just turned up his Budweiser to take a drink. He stopped; the skin above his nose pinched tight. "You sound awfully sure."

"Count on it." Ira's arrogant tone returned. He craned his head and peered around the noisy tavern.

Barry looked around too. No one was paying them any attention anymore. "They lost interest once they figured we weren't gonna fight."

"I guess," Ira said, his gaze still unsettled. "Listen, we need to get out of here. There's a big meeting tonight. I came to get Lance, but since y'all are together, both of you might as well come on back to the camp with me."

"Meeting?" Lance said. "Tonight? What's happening?"

Ira nodded. "Yeah, we've had a development and may need you to help us dispose of another problem."

"Like Charleston?" Lance said in a sheepish tone, then swigged his beer.

Ira flashed an angry glare, shook his head as if to silence Lance. He leaned across the table and spoke in a low voice. "Tonight's meeting is about the operation. You don't won't to miss it."

Lance looked at Barry and shrugged. "I'm ready. Let's do it." A touch of his earlier excitement reappeared.

"Can't," Barry said.

"Why not?" Disappointment fell across Lance's face.

"Yeah, why not?" Ira's tone was one of suspicion.

Barry leaned across the table. "Don't get me wrong. I want to go. I just can't up and leave right this minute. I've got a few things to do back home."

"Like what?"

"The way you're talkin', we might be gone several days. I left a heater burning in my trailer. I'd hate like hell to burn down the place. I also have to check on my dog, out back. Feed him, that sort of stuff."

"When, then?" Ira asked, still talking just above a whisper. His impatience hung on his words.

Barry shrugged. "Hour or so. Maybe two. No more than that. Why don't y'all go on ahead? Give me directions, and I'll come as soon as I can."

Lance looked at Ira as a soldier would, awaiting a decision from a superior officer. He didn't speak.

Ira's suspicious look became more pronounced. He shook his head. "I've got a few things to do myself." He glanced at his watch. "I'll pick you up in an hour. Be ready, 'cause we'll be late as it is." He glared at Lance. "You come with me now. No more drinking. You need a sharp mind for tomorrow."

Barry nodded. "Yeah, okay. No problem. I'll be ready, but I don't know why you won't tell me the way to your camp. I've proven my loyalty."

"Not yet you ain't, but soon you'll get the chance."

"What about Dane?" Barry asked. He glanced at Lance, looked back at Ira. "If I can find him and he can come, is it all right to bring him, too?"

Ira didn't respond right away. He looked around the tavern. Finally he said, "Yeah, why not. Tomorrow, we'll need all the help we can get."

Jeff Hart stepped back from the podium, bathing in the thunderous applause that washed over him from the partisan crowd in Charleston. He thrust his hand high in the air, waved, then returned to the podium and leaned close to the microphone. "Thank you all. Don't forget to vote."

Laughter erupted in the room. His supporters had paid thousands of dollars to be placed on the list of attendees, so Hart and everyone else in the grand ballroom of the Charleston Inn knew they would all vote—and vote for Hart. Some even had been promised positions in Hart's administration, while others had come to ensure his support for their own future campaigns, or to gain access to his ear for special causes they would lobby for once he became president. All appeared upbeat and happy, for good reason. Just that morning, the new polls had come out showing that Hart's lead over President Flint had jumped another point.

Upstairs in Hart's suite, Adam Cromwell paced. He walked over to a large arrangement of cut flowers and paused to sniff a white rose. Then he plucked a red grape from a bowl of fruit, before stepping toward the bank of windows overlooking Charleston's famed historic district. He tossed the grape into his mouth as he looked out over the city.

He liked this suite, this hotel. He thought he might even like to stay, maybe even with Creighton Lansford, Grayson Locke's not-so-secret lover, whom he had met earlier in the evening.

Cromwell had never married. He had never really dated anyone who cared more for him than for his money, but he didn't mind. Women were arm dressing and eye candy, entertainment for rich and powerful men like himself. Nothing more. They meant no more to him than a fine sailboat or a plush limousine. Still, they lined up to be seen with him, to have him lavish gifts on them. He had never wanted for their attention. And the best part—they did whatever he wanted. Some even competed to see who could shower the most pleasure on him, who could fulfill his every erotic fantasy in exchange for their own materialistic indulgences.

He smiled as he thought about a night in D.C., a spring night when he used a powerful senator's wife, a woman twenty years younger than her husband, to teach the husband a deadly lesson in survival of the fittest. The more powerful the men, the more satisfying it was for Cromwell to seduce their women, and this woman had been more satisfying than all the rest.

*The senator believed he had all the power, was untouchable,* Cromwell thought as he watched a horse-drawn carriage roll down the street beneath his window. He smiled. He had met the beautiful redhead, who had a movie star's body, weeks before at a State Department reception. She had been a woman in need of attention, married to a man drunk with power.

Cromwell and the senator's wife went out to dinner on several occasions following that first meeting, and he bought her jewelry and special things to wear—just for him. In return, she brought him pleasure in ways he had never before enjoyed. He often wondered why her husband wasn't more attentive to such a beautiful wife, a woman with such special talents. At one point in their relationship, Cromwell even wondered if he could learn to love her, but deep down, he knew she was like all the others. She represented nothing more than a means to an end.

After weeks of secretive, sensual rendezvous between the two, the senator learned of the affair just the way Cromwell had planned. Enraged and proud, not wanting the Beltway rumor mills portraying him as weak, the powerful senator sent an aide, who threatened Cromwell physically and promised to send government regulators to tie up his holdings and corporations, even drown him in IRS audits. Cromwell found the attempts to intimidate him amusing and told the aide as much. He pointed out that the senator would never be in the same league as Cromwell when it came to intimidation and ruthlessness. He told the aide to wait and see, then judge for himself.

A few nights later, Cromwell met the senator's wife in her Georgetown home. At the same time, in a private Baltimore home, her husband visited his real lover, the male aide who had delivered the threat.

Over the evening, Cromwell filled the redhead full of pills and alcohol. He made her grant his most bizarre sexual requests, then he beat her and ended her life by cutting her throat so deep that he nearly decapitated her.

In the weeks that followed, Cromwell enjoyed watching the senator being attacked by the press. The police zeroed in on the brutal way the woman died, and news reports speculated the senator may have killed her in a jealous rage. Just as Cromwell planned, the politician had no way to establish his alibi without divulging his secret life. Then when the senator's aide disappeared with the million dollars Cromwell had paid him for his silence, the senator found his world closing in on him as the police narrowed their investigation and focused only on him as his wife's killer.

Colleagues on the Hill soon spoke out, denouncing the man they had once kowtowed to for legislative favors. The vultures of the media beset him. In the end, the news reports showed little remorse when they told of how the senator committed suicide while police investigators stood outside his Georgetown home with murder warrants in their hands.

The time had been Cromwell's finest hour. For years, he believed no one, not even the members of the Board, knew the truth about what led to the senator's suicide, or the role Cromwell played when the senator's former aide tragically died in a fall from the balcony of a hotel in Rio. He believed his secret safe, until Locke shocked him with his knowledge of the crime, including the death of the aide.

Cromwell slammed his hand against the wall next to the window. He had always despised Locke for his insistence at leading their little group. Now he hated him more than ever for the hold he presently had over him.

Cromwell looked down on the busy Charleston streets below the hotel window. All the loose ends had been carefully tied and knotted, he had thought, but somehow one had come undone. As the door opened behind him, Cromwell vowed to retie that loose end. Maybe he'd shame Locke, just like he had the senator. Or maybe he'd arrange to send Locke to Rio, as he had the senator's aide.

He turned and smiled at Lansford, a beautiful woman with flowing blonde hair, who had entered the suite. He noted how her looks rivaled those of the senator's redheaded wife, and he felt his loins stir as he wondered if her sexual prowess was as intense.

"Welcome, Mr. Cromwell."

He nodded. He savored the thought of controlling this powerful woman, who meant so much to powerful men. Locke had exquisite taste, much like his own. He conceded that men had to be careful of women like Creighton Lansford, lest the siren's call seduced and neutered them. Cromwell grinned. He loved a challenge.

"I trust you had a good trip from Washington," she said in a pleasant, if somewhat terse, tone. "Senator Hart will be up in just a minute. He's looking forward to meeting you."

"And I him," Cromwell said, wondering if this lovely liked diamonds as much as his other conquests.

# Chapter · 23

COLUMBIA, SOUTH CAROLINA

Jefferson pulled his bulky camera toward the back of his Bronco and slipped the battery pack off of the end. He snapped on a new, fully charged battery and dropped the old one into the nylon storage bag. He glanced at his watch, picked up the camera, and walked across the hotel parking lot to the front entrance. As he set the equipment down on a nearby bench, a horn honked. He turned to see a black, canvas-top Jeep pull into the drive and stop beside him.

Tree leaned across the front seat and peered out the window. "Yo, Cuz. Heard from your girl yet?"

"What happened to—"

"Where we're going, we need a rugged ride, not a classy one. Besides, this one's got options the T-Bird didn't." He held up an olive-colored, single-lens scope. "Night vision, my man. And in the back, we have a couple of truly mean semiautomatics and a couple cases of ammo."

"I take it you found your informant."

"I did, and he was holding . . . three crack rocks." Tree's mouth spread into a wide, toothy grin. "Looking at felony possession has a way of loosening up a body's tongue."

"He told you where the camp is?"

"Best he could. He hadn't ever been there, but he knows folks who have. He told me what he'd heard."

Jefferson grabbed his cargo and placed it between two backpacks in the back of the Jeep. "Planning on camping?"

"From what my man said, I'm not sure what to expect. Just as we suspected, this place is somewhere out in the middle of the Congaree."

"Think you can trust him? The Swamp's a big place," Jefferson said as he stepped inside the Jeep and settled into his seat. "How you planning on finding the exact location?"

"I've been in there a few times looking for dopers; and at least once, we chased an escapee who used to hunt in there. The land is largely muck, and the water that covers it looks like somebody's sewer, but I recall a couple of places dry enough to build an encampment."

"I feel a little bit like the British going in to find the Swamp Fox, back in the Revolutionary War."

"Whoa, Cuz, I'm impressed. You really *did* study in school."

Jefferson half grinned. "Yeah, us football jocks get a bad rap on our study habits. Fact is, I don't recall which swamp he hid in, but I do remember reading how hard of a time those Redcoats had finding the homeboy. He ran 'em around in circles and got 'em lost in a big-time way." He slapped the dashboard. "But if we're gonna have any luck, we gotta get this swamp buggy rollin'. I'm worried 'bout that li'l Yankee girl."

"Truth."

Cassie awoke with a jerk. She tried to sit up but found her arms bound to a small wooden bed. She pulled hard, tried to free her right wrist, then the left. Both were tied tight with what felt like nylon cord.

Her head pounded, and she could see very little out of her left eye. It felt swollen and achy. *Where is this place? What happened?*

She opened her mouth to call out for help, but she could muster little more than a groan before a cutting pain in her chest overcame her. Her breath formed a tiny cloud in front of her face, then disappeared in the dark. She sucked air in tiny bursts, filling her lungs, then moved her lower jaw from side to side. She opened wider, felt a dull soreness, but decided she didn't have any broken bones, except maybe her nose, which throbbed with every beat of her heart.

Drawing slow breaths through her mouth because no air would come in through her nostrils, Cassie surveyed her surroundings through one eye. She couldn't make out much in the tiny room. Icy cold, pitch darkness enveloped her. Extending the fingers of her left hand, she could feel a rough wooden wall next to her bed. Her right hand touched nothing.

Leaning up just enough to make out the shape of a door in the darkness, she tried to see if any light came from underneath. None did. Her head fell back onto the pillowless, hard mattress. *It must still be night.*

Trepidation of being confined in a small, dark space gripped her senses. As she fought to maintain control by drawing slow, steady breaths, holding them, then releasing them in the same slow way she had inhaled, she recalled the first time the terrifying realization of being claustrophobic hit her. She was 12, lost in a network of caves deep inside a mountain in Virginia.

Her family had decided to take a tour of the cavern while on vacation. Once inside the vast system of underground catacombs, she grew bored with the pace set by the tour guide. Always independent, eager to do her own thing, she had run ahead of the rest of them, wanting to explore on her own. The last voice she heard was that of her father's, calling her back. She didn't listen, and somehow she took a wrong turn, got lost in the maze of crevices and narrow paths. By the time she realized her error, she had no idea how she had gotten to where she was or how to return. She called out to her father. No one answered.

Hours passed with her lost in a darkness so thick, she couldn't see her hand when she held it up in front of her face. Every time she tried to reach out to feel for an opening to walk through, her hand hit damp cold rock. Nothing but stone walls surrounded her, and they seemed to be closing in.

Panic had set in almost immediately. She screamed and cried for hours, until her voice became no more than a raw whisper. By the time rescue workers found her, she was in shock, almost delirious, and suffering from hypothermia. Nearly a year went by before she could stay in a dark room alone, even her bedroom in her own home.

She thought about the ever-present night-light still plugged into a socket in her bedroom back in Atlanta. She sucked air past her tender lips. *My kingdom for some light.*

Determined to direct her thoughts away from the cold darkness and close quarters around her bed, she listened to strange noises permeating the walls of her cell. She hoped she could detect the sound of a human, someone she could somehow get to come help her.

Night creatures chirped and croaked a faint but steady chorus. She even thought she heard an owl hooting, off in the distance.

*Where am I?*

A door slammed somewhere. She was almost certain it had been a door she had heard. She strained to listen, thought she heard voices rising over the din of creatures. If so, they weren't all that far away.

"Please come here. Please help me." She could barely hear her own voice.

Wincing as she tried to raise up, she turned her head toward the door, which stood no more than five feet from the foot of her bed. She looked for signs of someone approaching, the beam from a flashlight slipping under the door. She listened for the sounds of footsteps or more voices. She waited, remaining still, holding her breath, but no one came. Worst of all, she no longer heard the voices. Her face drew taught, and her gaze picked at objects in the darkness.

She remembered leaving the hotel, remembered the cab ride, the man who spoke little English. *Did he come back for me? When he didn't find me, did he go back to the hotel? Did he call Jefferson?*

She rocked her head from side to side, trying to recall what happened next. Pain shot up the side of her face. She closed her right eye, tried to remember.

*Lights!* She remembered bright lights coming at her. Her eye popped open.

*The wreck! The car was hit.*

*What happened to the driver?* she wondered. *The sleazy, scary man who took me out on that lonely road—where is he? Did he die?*

A desperate thought overcame her. *Am I going to die?*

When Finley Sawyer answered his phone, Bryson James's voice sounded more concerned than the director had ever heard it in all the years they had known each other.

James talked in quick bursts without explanation, an uncharacteristic manner for the always calm, never easily ruffled deputy director. "Something's happening tomorrow. We've got serious problems."

"What's happening?"

"Don't know. That's the worst of the problems. I just got a call from Johnny Reb. Direct. He didn't use the security of filtering the information through his controller so it couldn't be traced to the agency. He called direct. If he took that kind of risk, you know it has to be bad—and urgent."

"What did he say?"

"He said he was sure something major was going down tomorrow, somewhere in South Carolina. He thinks there will be an attempt on one of the candidates."

Sawyer sat down in his favorite leather chair and muted the sound on his television with the remote control. He had been watching a discussion on CNN about the upcoming election. "The President's in Charlotte tomorrow. It must be Hart he's talking about."

"That's right. Hart's in Charleston tonight." James sighed. "According to the itinerary I saw earlier, he should be finished with his dinner talk and safely in his hotel suite by now. He has the entire floor. I'll check with the agent in charge, but if there had been any problems, we'd know it by now."

"What about tomorrow?"

"His next event is in the afternoon, on the College of Charleston campus—two-thirty."

Sawyer stared at the silent program on his television. "If Johnny Reb's right, Hart is the target and the campus is where it will go down. The speech is scheduled to be outside, isn't it?"

"Yes. He'll speak in a courtyard in front of the administration building."

"Why Hart? Any threats against him?"

"Just the usual fruitcake stuff we get directed at every candidate. Johnny Reb said that one of the leaders of that fringe group he's been working to get inside of talked about an operation tomorrow."

"He didn't say what kind of operation?"

"Nope, but if it's that group, I'm not sure why they'd target Hart over Flint. They're antigovernment, so you'd think they'd go after the President."

"Yeah, if it's them. I don't have a good feeling about this. Call it a hunch, but something's not ringing true. Have you heard anything from your source over at Langley?"

"He's going to call me from a secure phone, but it may not be tonight. He didn't want to call from his office or home. He'll go to a neutral site that can't be traced back to him."

"Then he's found something sensitive. Hopefully, it'll give us a motive and tell us who the assassin will be."

"Hopefully."

"Call me as soon as you hear. It doesn't matter how late, because I won't be sleeping. . . . You won't either. Pack a bag. We're flying to Charleston first thing in the morning."

"What about the President?"

"Notify his supervising agent. Tell him to have his folks keep a sharp eye out for anything unusual. But also tell him not to alert Flint. The Vice President is in Washington this week. I want both of them to think it's business as usual." Sawyer sighed. "Damn, I hate elections."

# Chapter · 24

CONGAREE SWAMP, NEAR COLUMBIA, SOUTH CAROLINA

"Do you remember hearing the old folks talk about an eccentric aunt who lived out in the boonies?" Tree asked Jefferson as he turned onto a little-used sandy road that ran through the Congaree Swamp.

Jefferson's forehead wrinkled. "Sort of . . . I think."

"Way I remember Mamma telling it, she lives out in the middle of nowhere and is some sort of conjurer, a root doctor. She supposedly casts spells for those poor folks who have been beset by evil spirits."

"Yeah, I've heard about her. Some called her crazy; others swore she had some kind of magical powers. Why do you ask?"

"'Cause, Cuz, she's supposed to reside out here in the swamp, and I figured if there was a bunch of white folk being rowdy around these parts, she'd know about it."

Jefferson beamed. "Yeah, bet she would. Especially if they've been shootin' automatic weapons and testing explosives, like I've heard about."

"Truth. If I'm right, her shack's somewhere up ahead. Keep your eyes peeled for a side road that looks like it leads to nowhere. That'd be her driveway."

"How'd you find out where she stays?"

"Grandma Yost. She knows everything about our family."

"Ain't that the gospel," Jefferson said, thinking about the last time he saw his grandmother, a woman with big eyes and blue-tinted white hair. "I miss those reunions we used to have down at her place near the waterway. All those stories 'bout hants and spirits roamin' the Lowcountry. Used to scare me silly when she told 'em."

"I remember all the eats," Tree said. "Oysters and shrimp and fish—"

"Shut your mouth. I'm hungry enough as it is, and there ain't no tellin' when we'll get something to eat." Jefferson noticed a piece of dry land jutting out from the murky water. "Is that a road?"

Tree slowed the Jeep. He stopped in the middle of the roadway, grabbed a flashlight, and hopped out. Jefferson watched as his cousin shined the light into the surrounding woods.

Seconds later, Tree climbed back behind the steering wheel. "That's the road. There's a post about twenty yards farther on that has an old skull mounted on top. A warning, I guess, to trespassers."

"Skull? A human skull?"

"Nah," Tree said, laughing. "It looks like an old possum or coon. Some animal like that." He steered the Jeep through tall reeds onto the old road.

"Make sure you keep sharp," Jefferson said, watching the narrow strip of land stretching up ahead of them. "I sure as hell don't want to end up drinking swamp water."

They had traveled less than two hundred yards when the land area widened. "There," Tree said. "A cabin. There's a light on inside." He stopped the Jeep beside the ramshackle building and opened his door.

Jefferson's nostrils bridled at a foul stench hanging in the damp night air. "Shoo, what's that? Rotten eggs?"

Tree shook his head. "More likely, sulfur. Root doctors use it in their concoctions to ward off evil spirits."

"I'd say it would ward off bad, good, and behavioral-conflicted spirits." Jefferson said. "That's about the worst smell I've come across—anywhere."

Before the two men could climb out of their vehicle, the front door to the shanty opened. A flickering glow poured out into the darkness as an old owl hooted a warning from deep in the swamp.

"Who be comin' here?" an elderly woman asked as she poked her head out the door. "State your business."

The bone-thin woman, with leathery skin stretched tight over her skeleton, stepped barefooted through the doorway. Wearing only a sack dress made from gingham material, she looked ancient, just like the cypress shanty she lived in. Only the windows and door of the gray-weathered structure were painted—indigo blue, a color believed to protect a home's entries from evil spirits.

"Aunt Cora, it's Tree Calhoun and Jefferson Lee. Granny Yost's grandsons."

The old woman stepped farther out onto the porch. She squinted, straining to see her visitors in the darkness. "Step closer, boys. Come into the light where I can see you."

Tree led the way, with Jefferson close behind. Leaning to within inches of the big man, Cora studied Tree, then did the same with Jefferson. "You boys be fed good," she said with a chuckle. "I can see the Yost resemblance in your faces." She stepped to the side and motioned them into the house. "Come on in and tell me what troubles brought you out disturbing da spirits so late at night."

Inside stood a lone table with melting candles all across the top. Hoodoo trinkets and charms hung on the walls, and amid all of the magical artifacts, a picture of Jesus Christ rested on the top of a wormwood chest of drawers. The room was warm and smelled of sulfur.

Jefferson's nostrils flared, and he wrinkled his nose. He hoped they could hurry and find out what they came for.

"You boys sit a spell and tell Doctor Owl what ails you."

"Doctor Owl?" Jefferson asked.

Tree winked. "All Gullah conjurers take the name of an animal." He looked back at his aunt. "I didn't know you were Doctor Owl."

Pride filled the woman's face. "You heard of me?"

"Indeed I have," Tree said.

Jefferson wondered if his cousin had really heard her referred to as Doctor Owl or if was he merely schmoozing her. Whatever, Aunt Cora was eating up the attention.

"We need your help." Tree pulled his chair close to the one where Cora sat.

"Of course you do. I saw it before you arrived."

Tree glanced at Jefferson, winked, then turned to Cora. "We're lookin' for a friend. A woman who may have been captured by men pretending to be soldiers. They have a camp somewhere out here in the swamp."

Cora, sitting in an old rocker, rocked back and forth, her stare never leaving Tree as he spoke. When he finished, she nodded but didn't speak.

Tree waited for a response from the old woman, but when one didn't come, he continued. "Have you seen any signs of these men out here?"

"Yes, I seen 'em. I seen 'em through da eyes of da hawk that glides o'er da swamp in dayclean and through da owl at night."

Jefferson rubbed the back of his neck. *The woman's nuts. At the very least, she's grown senile living out here all alone.*

Tree didn't flinch. "Where did you see them?"

"Not far away. Near the crooked oak landing."

"Can you show us how to get there?"

"Tonight?" She shook her head and continued to rock. A low chortle rolled from her throat. "Swamp can be deceiving in the dark. Mean-spirited hants and plat-eyes are out, and they will toy with you, get you lost so's nobody'll ever find you."

"We have to take our chances," Tree said. "It's important we find our friend tonight."

Cora shook her head. Without a word, she stood from her rocker and walked to the back of the one-room shanty. She pulled back a blue curtain, stepped past it, then pulled the curtain closed behind her.

Tree looked at Jefferson, who shrugged his broad shoulders and walked over to his cousin, where he could talk without being overheard. "What do you think?" Jefferson asked.

Tree gestured with his wide hands. "Beats me."

After several minutes of clanking jars and pounding something on wood, Cora emerged from behind the curtain. She hobbled over to the men, handing both an oily pouch made of red flannel. Each one had a string around it and smelled like the sulfur they detected when they first arrived. "Wear these around your necks to keep the spirits on your side. They will protect you."

Jefferson took his pouch. He looked it over, then asked, "Is this what they call a mojo?"

She nodded with a faint smile. "Some call it a gris-gris, a good-luck charm." Her smile faded, and her voice grew stern. "Wear it to stay safe in the swamp."

Jefferson slipped the string around his head and tucked the mojo inside his shirt. Tree followed suit.

When they had done as she asked, Cora turned to Tree and handed him a folded piece of paper. "This will take you where you want to go. Be careful. Evil spirits surround these men."

"Yes, we know," Tree said. He patted the pouch hanging from his neck. "Thank you for the protection and the map. We'll be back to visit someday."

Cora escorted her nephews to the front door. "I'll watch the animals and listen to the spirits to know if you come back." She pointed to the lump under Tree's shirt. "Keep your gris-gris for three days, then throw it into running water. The evil around you will be drowned." She looked up at Jefferson. "You do same."

"Thank you," Jefferson said as he followed Tree out of the cabin.

The woman watched as they climbed into the Jeep and started back down the sandy drive.

"Here," Tree said. "Let's see if we can make heads or tails of her map."

"Strange little woman, huh? And she's related?"

Tree laughed. "Yeah, but you know, somehow I feel safer for having stopped by to see her. Where does that map say we need to go?"

# Chapter · 25

THE FREE CONFEDERACY ENCAMPMENT IN THE CONGAREE SWAMP

When Barry climbed into the backseat of Ira's Humvee, he expected to be asked to wear another black hood on his ride to the compound. Ira never mentioned it, so Barry didn't either.

For the first few minutes, the ride had been suspiciously quiet, especially on the part of Lance, who almost always had something to say. Barry didn't press him. He figured his friend had received a verbal lashing for allowing himself to get drunk enough to compromise whatever mission was set for the next day.

Besides, Barry was thankful for the minimal conversation. The lack of distraction would make it easier for him to keep track of every turn and curve on the way to the Free Confederacy's secret camp.

"You keep looking back here. Is something wrong?" Barry asked, after noticing Ira's continual glances at him through the rearview mirror.

"Thought you were going to call Everett and have him meet up with us." Ira replied. "Where is he?"

Barry had never tried to contact Dane like he said he would. The fact was, he hadn't heard from the man since shortly after Jimmy Joe got hurt, and didn't know how to get in touch with him. He suspected Jimmy Joe's mom had told Dane the same thing she had told Barry. Stay away from her son. He couldn't blame the woman, given all that had happened.

As he bounced on the truck's hard seat, he thought how someday he could tell her about his part in all of this. Maybe then, she would forgive him. "I tried but couldn't get up with him," he said to Ira. "I don't know where he is."

Barry figured Dane may have been spooked by the bombing and had given up on the idea of joining the militia after Jimmy Joe got hurt. *After being kicked out of his aunt's home, Dane probably went back to Georgia or the Midwest, wherever he was from.* That little inconsistency still nagged Barry, causing him to wonder what had prompted the man to lie.

"Didn't you tell me he was living with his aunt? If you want, we'll swing by and see if he's there."

Ira seemed insistent. Barry wasn't sure why.

"That's part of the problem. His aunt kicked him out. He's not there, and I'm not sure how to get up with him now."

"Kicked him out? Why?"

"Beats me," Barry replied. "You know how families get sometimes. I guess he wore out his welcome."

Without saying a word, Lance hit Barry with a wary glance.

Staring out into the darkness, Barry wondered what Lance knew about the bombing that hurt Jimmy Joe. Ira had confided some of the plans to Lance, and Barry hoped after the upcoming meeting he would be trusted enough for someone to tell him what they had planned. If he did learn their plans, he had the added problem of getting to a phone to alert his people. Cell phones were too easy to trace. That was why UCs like himself didn't trust them or carry them.

As Ira's black Humvee stopped at the closed gate, Barry retraced the entire route in his head one more time. The trip had taken less time than before, when his head had been covered. He figured Ira had driven around to confuse the riders before, but now he was in too big of a hurry.

Barry went back over the landmarks he had seen. He was confident he could lead others to the encampment, but he wasn't at all sure he could verbalize the directions, and that was the important part. He looked at the green luminous dial of his watch as one of the camp's guards opened the tall gate. As the Humvee passed through the gates, Barry blinked in disbelief at the sight of dozens of cars and trucks parked all around the area. He glanced back at his watch. *Almost one in the morning. Something's definitely up.*

"C'mon," Ira said. He jumped out of the Humvee, motioning toward the front door of the church. "We're late." He jogged the short distance to the church steps, then ascended the six wooden planks two at a time.

As Lance rushed by, Barry slowed to do a quick count of the vehicles he could see. He also took a second to glance up at the top of the church steeple, wondering if the militia members had taken up positions where he and Dane had spotted what looked like gunports.

Spotlights, charged by gas generators that he could hear running somewhere off in the darkness, lit up the area well, but their beams didn't extend to the top of the steeple. He squinted as he stared straight up into the night sky. *Too dark to tell.*

Ira hollered from the top step leading into the church. "C'mon, Lynch. Let's go. We have a special guest at tonight's meeting."

The vestibule was empty of guards with metal detectors as they entered the church, and the doors to the sanctuary were closed, but Barry could hear a muffled voice coming from inside. Ira pushed open the doors. The speaker in front grew silent. Barry walked up behind Lance, who had stopped beside Ira.

The man stepped away from the pulpit. "Glad you could make it, boys," he said in a scalding tone. "Come in and have a seat."

Barry recognized the firm, sculpted jaw and steely, close-set eyes. *Colonel Ambrose Thornton, United States Army, Retired.* Dressed in green fatigues with five stars in a circle on each collar—the symbol for the rank of a wartime general—and pants bloused into the top of laced boots, he stood beside a map that looked like the city of Charleston.

Years before, Barry, a Marine lieutenant at the time, had met him in Washington at a military reception honoring the retirement of career soldiers from all branches of the service. Hundreds of young officers had been in attendance. He hoped the military man's recall wouldn't be so acute that he would remember him. He couldn't imagine how he could. Nevertheless, he made sure he maintained as stealthy an image as possible by walking in step behind Lance as the trio started down the aisle. With luck, they would sit near the back.

Barry's luck didn't hold. Ira led the two men to the front of the sanctuary, where they slid into the middle of the second row—directly in front of the colonel.

Once they were seated, Thornton cast a long look at the three men. His right eyebrow raised, and he returned to his speech, without taking his eyes off them. "As I was saying, tomorrow at 0600 hours, our primary diversionary force will leave here, arriving in Charleston no later than 0830 hours. The advance group, including me, will leave soon after our meeting this morning to meet with operatives already in place."

Thornton reached over with a wooden pointer and tapped on the center of the map. "We shouldn't have trouble with cover. There is still a lot of construction activity going on. Workers are all over the streets and yards, like an army of ants. For those of you who have received orders to create a diversion, I want you to dress as handymen. Wear jeans and overalls. Carry hammers and tool belts, and make sure your plastic explosives are well concealed."

Barry, careful not to draw attention to himself, cut his eyes right and left, trying to gauge the reaction of those seated around him. Everyone—many of them young men in their teens, twenties, and thirties—sat in rapt attentiveness. *These folks are ready to die for their cause.*

A man who appeared to be in his early fifties stood from his pew on the front row, across the aisle from where Barry sat. He also wore green fatigues and, on his collar, bars denoting the rank of captain. "What about schedule changes. With all the construction going on in the city, how can we be sure the target will appear as scheduled?"

Thornton nodded. "We have that contingency covered. We have a source on the inside. If there are any schedule changes, we will know about them, so you will know about them."

A gasp slipped from Barry's mouth before he could prevent it. He glanced at Ira, who looked at him.

Barry feigned a cough. "Throat's dry," he whispered.

Thornton didn't seem to pay attention to Barry's gaffe. His eyes roamed the gathering of would-be soldiers. "We've had a couple of unexpected developments recently that have caused us some concern." He looked around the room, timing his surprise for optimal impact. "We have our first POWs."

A buzz of whispered reactions rose, and many in the crowd exchanged glances. Thornton waited as the hubbub subsided.

Barry looked at Ira, who leaned close to whisper, "Your old friend Yates and some woman reporter. Last I heard, Yates was near death. Injuries he sustained in a wreck last night. The reporter's banged up but okay."

"Two were brought in last night," Thornton said. "One was an impersonator, a man who could have undermined our cause, had we not stopped him. He died this morning, so he won't be a problem in the future." Thornton's demeanor revealed his military bearing. No remorse and no regret could be detected. "The person brought in with him is far more dangerous. She's alive, and we have to decide what to do with her."

"Her?" a man said. "I have a couple of ideas of what we can do." He laughed until a woman sitting beside him rammed her elbow into his ribs. Air rushed from the man's lungs as he doubled over in obvious pain.

The room erupted with uneasy laughter. Even Thornton appeared amused for a few moments, then he held his hand high and gestured for the crowd to grow silent. "We will treat her as a POW. She will have her time to be heard." He shrugged and pointed back at the map. "She might even be useful as a way to get our message out. Back during the Gulf War, the enemy used some of our own reporters to get their propaganda out. Maybe we can use her for that purpose too."

Thornton stood wordless for several seconds. He glared out into the crowd of onlookers. Anger flared from his eyes. "We also have had a spy infiltrate our group."

A stunned silence fell over the followers of the Free Confederacy. Barry held his breath. He felt every head turn and look at him, but when he glanced around, all attention focused on Thornton.

"Who?" shouted a voice near the back of the church.

"Treat 'em the same as they would be treated in war," said another voice across the aisle. "Shoot 'em."

When Barry looked, he saw that the remark came from the same woman who had elbowed her husband in the ribs. The cries for execution came from every corner of the sanctuary. Barry's throat constricted. His breaths came in short bursts.

"Don't worry," Thornton said. "He is with us tonight, but he won't escape, and we will deal with him in our own way, in our own time. Just like the reporter, he will be treated as a captured enemy soldier. His crime is far more serious than hers, however. In due time, there will be a trial; and if the tribunal deems it necessary, there will be an execution."

Eustace Hanley rose from his chair beside Thornton. His face appeared flushed, his eyes red. "Let this be a lesson to us all. We have to be careful who we associate with and especially who we bring into our trust." He looked down at his son. "This man won our trust, then took that trust and betrayed us."

Ira shot from his seat. He seemed as surprised as the others. "Bring him in. Let's see this traitor."

Hanley pointed at his son. "You know him. You brought him here."

Ira paled. He flashed an angry look at Lance, who glared at Barry.

"I demand to know who it is," Ira said angrily. "If he used me to embarrass my father in front of these loyal soldiers of the Free Confederacy, I deserve the opportunity to face him and then kill him. I should be the one to carry out retribution."

Barry's heart leaped into his throat. He watched the drama playing out in front of him and wondered if he was about to be snatched out of his seat and tortured.

Hanley and Thornton conferred with each other, then Thornton nodded to two men in black BDUs standing in the back. The men disappeared through a side door and seconds later emerged with a bound and gagged man who looked like he had been beaten into unconsciousness. As they marched down the aisle holding the man under his arms, letting his feet drag along behind them, Barry turned.

A lump formed in his throat. *Dane!*

The men dragged Dane to the front and dropped him onto the floor at Thornton's feet. He landed limp, without a sound.

Barry leaned forward, rubbing his mouth, wanting to act. Both of Dane's eyelids were swollen shut. Purplish bruises dotted his cheeks and chin. He could see a red welt on the brutalized man's neck. *Did they try to hang him?*

Barry fell back in his pew. A side glance revealed Ira glaring at both him and Lance. *Who is Dane Everett?*

The answer came as Thornton walked over and propped his arm on the back of a chair near where Dane had been dropped. "This is what a special agent for the FBI looks like after he has undergone our interrogation. This is war, ladies and gentlemen. We have to know what the spies have learned, and most importantly, we have to know what they've conveyed about our operation to the enemy."

*FBI!* Barry realized Dane's slipup about where he was from made sense now. Jimmy Joe's mamma knew that her cousin's son was from Georgia, so that was the story Dane gave around Jimmy Joe and the others. But Hanley wanted to hear he was a downtrodden Midwesterner who had witnessed, even felt, the government's oppression. A costly mistake.

Now Barry had to think of a way to get him out without getting them both killed. He had to somehow get alone and make a call. Then he had to find this reporter who had managed to stumble into hell.

## CHAPTER · 26

OUTSIDE THE FREE CONFEDERACY ENCAMPMENT

"What are you seein'?" Jefferson asked. He was crouched on the ground beside Tree, several hundred yards from a tall wooden fence. He couldn't see anything in the dark.

Tree held the night-vision scope up and peered into it. "Two men in a tower. They're both armed. Looks like they're carryin' assault rifles. Maybe AR-15s." He handed the scope to his cousin. "Here, have a look."

Jefferson pulled the lens close. For a second, everything became a bright fluorescent green, but when his vision adjusted, he began to make out images. He saw trees and the fence. He looked up toward the top of the tower Tree had described. Two men held rifles and leaned back against supports for the tower's roof. He could even tell they were smoking cigarettes. *Amazing.*

As he watched the men, he saw one look down into the fenced area. The gate swung open, and a car drove through.

"Whoa." Jefferson jerked the scope away. "Those headlights are bright through this thing."

"Yeah, they don't do much good around bright light. Let me have a look." Jefferson handed Tree the scope.

"Four or five folks just left in that car. Wait. Here comes another one. I see several coming out behind it. They must've had some sort of meeting in there."

"Can you see inside the cars? Can you see a woman?"

"Nah, can't tell that. But I can tell we don't need to be going in by ourselves. We need help. We also need a warrant."

"Let's go get one and get her out."

Tree chuckled as he flashed an amused look at his cousin. "We don't have nothin' to get a warrant—no probable cause. We don't even know if she's in there or if she's bein' held against her will. What if she went willingly?"

"She'd have called me. She's a TV reporter. She needs tape to document what she's covering. Meeting with an informant is one thing, doing the story is another. No, if she went there without me, then she didn't go on her own."

"That won't convince a judge."

"Then we go in without a warrant."

"And get ourselves killed?" Tree said. "I don't think so."

"Then what? I know, deep down, she needs help. I know her, and I know she's done gone and got herself in a jam."

"Let's get back to our Jeep. Maybe I'll come up with something."

Creighton Lansford tossed down the last of the Scotch on the rocks. She had poured it after returning to her room following Jeff Hart's reception at the Charleston Inn. She shut off her laptop, having read all her new e-mails, including one she had received from a trusted friend at the Internal Revenue Service. Pleased with the news, she was just about to call Hart to tell him, when her cell phone rang.

"Hello," she said after recognizing the number on her caller ID as belonging to the candidate.

"How did you gauge the reaction of the crowd?" Hart asked. "I thought they believed me, believed we could turn around the slumping economy and return integrity to the Office of President. You agree?"

She unbuttoned her blouse and slid her arms out of the sleeves. "Jeff, relax. Save the media pitch for the folks who matter. Not me. You had them eating out of the palm of your hand." Cradling the phone between her chin and shoulder, Lansford removed her half slip and walked barefoot across her hotel room carpet. She pulled off the back of one diamond earring and took it out, switched the phone to the other ear, then took out the second earring. She dropped the pair into a velvet-lined box on the dresser.

"Yeah, I thought so too," he said. "Do you think the next speech should hit harder on—"

"It went great. Everything's coming together. I just read an e-mail from our pollster, and you've picked up another half a percentage point. Just keep doing what you're doing. Stay with the plan, and you'll win. Everything's on target."

"Have you heard from the governor? He's about as unpredictable as anyone I know. Is he still planning on showing up tomorrow?"

"Everything is a go. The governor's people said he'd arrive thirty minutes before your speech. He's a crafty son of a bitch. He wants to be the next education secretary, so he's not about to piss you off."

"Ha. That bastard couldn't educate a classroom of overachievers. No way he sits on my cabinet."

"I know that; he doesn't. His endorsement, and the South Carolina citizens believing he's our man, will tally a lot of votes. Without that hope and endorsement, you lose the state."

"What you're saying is, suck up to the pompous bastard."

"Yes, that's exactly what I'm saying—until after the election."

An irritated silence drifted through the phone. "What about this Cromwell fellow, who all of a sudden shows up wanting to make a large contribution. He's loud, obnoxious, and generally disgusting. On top of everything else, I think he's seedy."

"You always were a good judge of character."

"Do you know him?"

Lansford stood in her bathroom and sneered at her reflection in the mirror. "I know *of* him. A friend told me he was interested in your campaign. He's one of the top-fifty wealthiest men in America."

"I'll be damned. Sure can't tell it by the way he carries himself. Fat bastard."

What Lansford didn't tell Hart were the sordid details that Grayson Locke had revealed to her about Adam Cromwell, when he warned her to be careful around the man. "Look, take his money. I'll handle his braggart ego."

"He said he wanted to be onstage with me tomorrow. A chance to be seen as a supporter."

"Yes, he told me. He's a parasite and generally disgusting. But if he's willing to pay for his spot, then what's the harm? It's just one appearance."

"I hate having to pamper these rich assholes. Especially when I'd rather tell them to pound sand."

"You wanted to be president, and sucking up to assholes goes with the job."

"I suppose." He sighed. "I feel like I've sold my soul."

"Oh, you have, sweetheart, you have. That's what being president is all about."

A long yawn could be heard. "I'm going to bed," Hart said. "It's been a bitch of a day."

"Get some sleep. You have to start all over again tomorrow morning with a breakfast for the big contributors—including Cromwell."

"Wonderful, I can hardly wait," he said, sarcasm dripping from his tone as he hung up the phone.

Lansford unhooked the back of her bra, slipped it off. *Don't worry about Cromwell. That bastard will wish he'd never heard of Creighton Lansford.*

***

Sawyer hung up his phone, then tapped his fingers on the desk in his home study. Calls in the middle of the night for the director of the U.S. Secret Service weren't all that unusual; calls in the middle of the night from a worried FBI director were.

He picked the receiver back up and dialed the deputy director's number. "Your bags packed?"

"Yes. Are we leaving now?" James asked.

"Have you heard from the CIA contact?"

"Nothing yet."

"He'll have to contact you in Charleston. Can you get word to him?"

"Yes, I think so."

"Good. Call the hangar and have our plane readied. I just got off the phone with the FBI Director. They've lost one of their UCs."

"Undercover? Where? Do you know what happened?"

"All he could tell me was they were working on the infiltration of the Free Confederacy—"

James's voice rose an octave. "Free Confederacy? The same one—"

"The same. He didn't know for sure about Johnny Reb until I told him."

"Then why'd he call?"

"Our guy must have slipped up somehow. Their guy had relayed a suspicion about ours a few weeks ago. He called to see if I would confirm, and I did. We need to try and make contact again. See if he can locate the Bureau's agent."

"Do they think he's burned?"

"They don't know. He's missed three scheduled check-ins with his controller. They're understandably worried, and they've dispatched a special tactical unit out of Quantico. They're planning on hitting the camp around dawn."

"I'll make sure the plane's ready, then I'll try to reach our man." James grew silent for a moment. "I don't like the sound of this, not with our UC having gone there tonight. What if he's mistaken for one of the bad guys?"

"We discussed that possibility. I passed along a description. At least they know he's there. Hopefully, he'll be able to identify himself amid the chaos."

"Hopefully," James said, his voice filled with trepidation.

"Meet me at the airport in half an hour."

Tree had parked the Jeep off the road and out of sight on a patch of dry ground surrounded by thick bushes and vines. When he and Jefferson left their vantage point near the entrance to the Free Confederacy camp, they hiked back up the road and found a hiding spot in a grove of trees. For almost three hours, the two men watched trucks and cars leaving the compound. Tree used the night-vision scope to peer inside each passing car, then to read the tag. Hoping to track down the members of the militia, he called the tag numbers out as the car went by, and Jefferson wrote the information down on a pad. They were also hopeful one of the members would know—and tell—where Cassie had been taken.

Jefferson looked up and down the road, making sure no more cars were coming. Not seeing any, he stood and stretched his arms over his head. He glanced through the trees toward the brightening sky. "Almost daylight. What are we going to do?"

Tree stood up and bowed his back, pushing in at the base of the spine with his fingers. "My muscles feel tighter than Grandma's ukulele strings."

"You're getting old."

"Beats the alternative." Tree stepped out from the trees and stared in the direction of the encampment. "Judging by the number of cars that passed by us, I'd say most of the folks have left. Guess about all we can do now is go back and run the tags, then go out and see how many good ole boys we can convince to give us some straight answers."

Concern draped Jefferson's expression. "How long will that take?"

"A while, but it has to be done."

"I don't like leaving her in there. There's no telling what those yokels will do."

"Listen, Cuz. I want her out as much as you—if she's even in there—but chances are, all we'll do is get ourselves killed, and that sure ain't gonna help her none."

Jefferson paced, rubbing his hands together. "Probably ain't nobody much left inside. Let's chance a look."

"Maybe we can—" Tree's broad body stiffened. He inspected the darkness beyond the trees. After several seconds, he spoke in a low voice. "You hear that?"

"What?" Jefferson said in a normal voice.

Tree's forehead wrinkled. He glanced around again. "I could've sworn—"

Before he could finish the sentence, two men in dark clothing, their faces blackened, popped out in front of Jefferson and Tree. They leveled their rifles on the startled men's chests. "FBI! Don't move."

Both Tree and Jefferson stood with their mouths gaped open. Tree reached for the chain around his neck, but before he could explain, one of the agents grabbed his hand and swept a leg against the back of Tree's leg. The big SLED agent's knees buckled, sending him hard onto the ground.

The second agent shoved his automatic rifle closer to Jefferson's heart. "On your knees. Now!"

Jefferson dropped, holding his hands over his head.

"Wait a damn minute," Tree said in an angry voice. "I'm a cop. State law enforcement—SLED!"

The agents looked at each other. "You got identification?" the first said.

Tree brushed dirt off his shirt and vest. "If you'd been a damn sight more patient, I was about to show it to you before you dropped me." Without making any quick or sudden moves, he lifted his hand toward his neck. "It's here, attached to this." His fingertip touched the chain. "Can I pull it out?"

The agent nodded. "Go ahead." He trained his rifle barrel on Tree's head.

Tree pulled up the chain, but instead of his badge appearing, the gris-gris Cora had prepared peeped out above his shirt.

"What is that?" the agent asked, wrinkling his nose as the sulfur wafted into his nostrils.

Tree glanced down, shoved the concoction back down his shirt. "Not that, this," he said, producing his badge.

The agent lowered his weapon. Tree stood up as the agent turned to Jefferson. "You SLED, too?"

"No," Jefferson said. "He's my cousin. We're—"

The agent turned back and directed his question to Tree. "What are you doin' out here?"

Tree motioned toward Jefferson. "It's a long story, but to make it short, we think a reporter's been kidnapped and taken into the camp." He pointed in the direction of the militia base, then nodded at the agent. "That's why you're here. Y'all are getting ready to go in, aren't you?"

"You know how many are inside?" the agent asked.

"Not nearly as many as a few hours ago. Most have left. Guess they went home."

"What about sentries? Any besides the ones in the tower?"

"Don't think so."

Jefferson stepped beside Tree. "Listen, we want to go in with you." He looked around. "There are others . . . aren't there?"

The FBI agents exchanged glances. The first said, "There's more. We were just starting to move in when we spotted you two."

"We need to help this friend of mine. She's a reporter—"

"You can come in after we've cleared the camp," advised the second agent.

"Until then, stay here. I'll send someone back for you once it's safe."

"But—"

Tree put his hand on Jefferson's shoulder. "He's right. They've got a lot more firepower, and they don't need to be lookin' out for us at the same time they're fighting those knuckleheads inside." He nodded at the agents. "We'll go back and get our Jeep, then wait here for your all clear."

"This shouldn't take long," the second agent said. "I'll radio the others about the civilian inside." He motioned to his partner, and both disappeared back into the forest.

After the federal agents had gone, Jefferson looked at Tree. "Where the hell did they come from?"

# Chapter · 27

OUTSIDE THE FREE CONFEDERACY ENCAMPMENT

A bright sunny morning filtered light through the forest canopy as Tree drove the Jeep back to where he and Jefferson had encountered the FBI agents. He parked on the side of the road.

"Shouldn't we get out of sight?" Jefferson asked.

"Nah. Besides, we want the feds to be able to find us when they're done." He pulled his .40-caliber Glock pistol out of its holster, popped out the magazine, and checked to make sure it was full of bullets.

Jefferson watched from the passenger seat. "What about the rifles in the back? Want me to get them?"

"Nah. I figure we won't need to tote them after the feds finish. This li'l thing won't get in the way, and it still packs a punch if I need it." Tree slammed the magazine back in the opening of the pistol's grip and pulled back the slide. It snapped forward when he released it. "Ready," he said with a huge grin. "Bring on the rednecks."

No sooner had the words left his mouth than the two men heard a series of fast popping sounds off in the distance. A brief moment of silence followed, then another rapid burst of shots rang out. An explosion thundered.

Tree glanced at Jefferson. "Grenade."

"What if there're more soldiers than they figured?"

"If I know the FBI, they've got plenty of manpower. We only saw two, and that was because they wanted us to." He began to chuckle.

"What's so funny?"

"I was just thinking. Those feds probably studied every contingency that they might face. They knew they were going to be taking on a bunch of right-wing militia nuts capable of doing almost anything. They knew they were white supremacists." He snickered. "What they didn't count on was running into a couple of big black dudes just outside the camp. Bet we caused them to question their intelligence."

Tree's laughter became contagious. Jefferson began too. Soon the Jeep was rocking from side to side.

"Wonder how long they hid out there, watching us, before deciding we didn't belong," Tree said "Sometimes the feds can be a little slow on the uptake."

"Listen."

Tree raised his pistol. "What?"

"It's stopped. No more shooting." Jefferson looked at his cousin. "Think it's over?"

Tree opened the door and climbed out onto the sandy roadway. He looked toward the camp. "Probably." He climbed back into the Jeep. "I'm going to ease on up there."

"You sure that's a good idea?"

"I'm just going to roll down around the curve, where we can see. No farther."

"Wait." Jefferson jumped out and ran to the back of the Jeep. He popped open the tailgate and pulled out his camera. "Just in case," he said as he settled back into his seat, resting the bulky camera on the floorboard.

Tree drove to where they could see the compound gate wide open. No one stood in the tower, but one fatigue-clad figure lay sprawled on the ground at its base. Inside, Jefferson saw two men dressed in black, like the agents they had encountered earlier. They carried rifles and looked back as the Jeep stopped.

Tree stepped out of the vehicle and held up his shield for the men to see. Jefferson remained seated as the two agents approached. One, a dark-featured man with wavy black hair, asked with a Hispanic accent, "Are you two the cops?"

"That's right," Tree said.

"You can come on in. We're still searching a couple of buildings, but we've quelled the resistance."

Jefferson grabbed his camera and climbed out. The agent flashed a suspicious look.

"I'm not a cop. I'm working for CNN. Okay to get some shots?"

"Wait here." The agent looked ill at ease. He glanced at his partner, who seemed to be in charge. The partner grimaced. The pair whispered back and forth, but neither took their eyes off Jefferson.

The man in charge finally spoke. "No faces of our agents or our prisoners. Understood?"

"Understood." Jefferson pulled the camera to his shoulder. He captured footage of six handcuffed members of the militia lying facedown on the ground. Then he focused on two more, who had been wounded and were being treated by a paramedic dressed in the same black uniform as the other agents.

He taped a church off to his left, its door wide open. There seemed to be an extraordinary amount of activity inside. Several agents exited, then returned with two more. "What's in there?" he asked.

The supervising agent's response was terse. "That's off limits."

Jefferson lowered the camera, looked at Tree, and shrugged.

Tree asked, "Have you found a woman?"

"No—"

Another agent rushed up before the man could complete the answer. He whispered in his supervisor's ear.

The agent in charge looked at a nearby cabin, then back at Jefferson. "Yes, follow me." He pulled his walkie-talkie to his mouth as he walked.

Jefferson followed, overhearing him tell someone to get over to the cabin right away. Instinct caused him to look toward the agent treating the wounded across the compound. He saw the paramedic with a walkie-talkie in his hand, saw him grab a black nylon bag and start their way.

"Is she hurt?" Jefferson asked.

"I think she'll be okay. We just want her checked out." The agent motioned at the camera. "She a reporter too?"

Jefferson nodded.

When they got to the door of the cabin, the agent stopped Jefferson. His voice softened. "Wait here until the medic checks her, then you can come in."

Again, Jefferson nodded. Leaning back against the porch railing, he looked over at Tree, who stared out across the camp. Tree pointed toward the church. Several FBI agents carried a stretcher down the steps, toward a green Army ambulance with a red cross painted on the side. Jefferson propped his camera on the railing and angled the viewfinder so he could look down into it without drawing a lot of attention. He began to record the scene.

Just as the door to the ambulance was slammed shut, the agent stepped out of the cabin. "Medic says she'll be okay. She's pretty bruised and battered, though. He wants her to get checked out at a hospital."

Jefferson turned to see the ambulance leaving the compound. "Don't we need to stop the ambulance?"

The agent shook his head. "There's a couple more on the way. They're only a few minutes out."

Inside the dimly lit room, Jefferson sat beside Cassie's bed. Her face looked bruised, her left eye puffy. He took her hand, held it, and tried in vain to keep her from talking.

"What took you so long?" she asked in a joking tone as she tried to sit up.

He could tell she tried to smile, but she winced instead.

"Just lie still. Ain't no hurry for you to get up." Concern shrouded his expression. "And what do you mean, 'what took so long?' We had to find you first. Looking in a swamp wasn't exactly the first place that came to my mind."

"Swamp? Don't know how. . . . The last thing I remember was being out on the highway. Bright lights, then *boom*, and nothing." She reached up and rubbed her forehead. "My head aches. It's like having a hangover without all the fun that comes with getting it."

Jefferson grinned. "Ambulance is on the way. You'll be okay."

"Ambulance? What for?"

"Your head, for one thing. The medic wants you checked by a doctor."

"I'll be okay. Did I hear shots?"

"Yeah, 'spect you did. A while ago. Everything's cool now."

She shut her eyes, spoke in a hoarse voice. "What happened?"

"FBI versus the Free Confederacy. Good guys won."

Her right eye opened wide; her left opened as far as the swelling would allow. "You did get footage?"

Jefferson laughed. "Girl, don't you think of nothin' else?"

"Did you?"

He nodded. "Yeah, I got some good footage, but we can talk about that later."

Tree stepped through the doorway. "Ambulance is here."

Cassie sighed. "Do I have to?"

Jefferson said, "Yes."

"I'll go, but as soon as the doctor finishes, we're back on this story."

Jefferson looked at Tree. "Can't imagine how such a hard head could be hurt."

# Chapter · 28

DOWNTOWN CHARLESTON, SOUTH CAROLINA

Arriving at the Charleston airport just after sunrise, Sawyer instructed the Secret Service agent driving their car to ride by the location where the federal office building had stood. He wanted to witness, firsthand, the damage he had seen on television newscasts. As the car slowed to be admitted into the secured areas, Sawyer looked at the crumbled buildings, where workers busily removed debris.

The hurricane's devastation to the city was much more than the director had expected, even given the extensive national coverage of both the destruction and now the attempt to rebuild. As they got close to the historical district, the road became impassable.

He directed the driver to park. "We'll walk from here," he said as he opened the door and stepped out. When James had exited the car, Sawyer turned to him with a look of dismay. "How did we allow Hart to speak here? This is insane."

"Yes, sir. We tried to dissuade him. He wanted to appear here, and his chief, Lansford, insisted. She went as far as saying he would appear here, with or without our protection."

"The man's too crazy to be president." Sawyer paused, looked at James with a thin smile. "On second thought, he'll fit right in."

Standing in front of a pile of debris that had once been the federal office building, he worried about the presidential campaign speech scheduled for the afternoon. "Last night's dinner was one thing, but today's speech is just plain insanity. There's way too much that could go wrong."

"They won't listen. Especially Lansford. And Hart takes his cues from her. We either protect them the best we can or leave. They're hell-bent on going on as planned."

Sawyer felt a stab of anxiety in his gut. "Then we don't have a choice. Have I ever told you how much I hate politicians?"

"Yes, sir," James replied, "I believe you have."

"Anything from Johnny Reb?"

"Not a word."

Sawyer caught motion out of the corner of his eye, turned, and saw his driver running toward them. He thought the scrubbed-face youth looked too young to be an agent. "I meant to ask earlier," he whispered to James before the boyish agent got close enough to hear, "are we hiring straight out of high school now?"

The young agent stopped in front of Sawyer. "Sir, the FBI director wants you to call. Says it's urgent."

Sawyer pulled his cell phone from his suit pocket and dialed the number he knew from memory. He walked to a corner where no one else could overhear his conversation.

"We hit the camp," the FBI director said in a grave tone. "No casualties, but our UC is critical. They all but killed him—maybe even thought they had."

"Did your folks run across our man?"

"No. I double-checked with our guys. No sign of anyone identifying themselves as Secret Service. Fact is, the place was nearly deserted."

"Anybody talking?"

"Not a one. Three militia were shot, one fatal. We're questioning a half dozen more, but no one's opened up. In fact—you're not going to believe this—they claim they're protected under some sort of prisoner-of-war treaty, like the Geneva convention. Bunch of idiots."

"Dangerous idiots. Hopefully, our guy still has his cover and he'll be able to get word out to us."

"Yeah, I hope so, for all our sakes. These folks are dangerous with a capital D. We found a reporter in the camp too. She's been banged up pretty good, but I'm told she'll be okay."

"Reporter? Local reporter? A sympathizer?"

"No, according to my information, she's from CNN. I think she's the one a year or so ago who uncovered the . . . shall we say, somewhat unscrupulous attempt by the DEA to bring down that drug cartel. If you recall, her report stirred up a hornet's nest all over Capitol Hill. Name's Cassie O'Connor."

"O'Connor," Sawyer repeated. "She's the reporter who found the senator's body down here. Right after the hurricane calmed. Any idea what she was doing at the camp?"

"From what I understand, she had gone out to meet an informant, apparently someone linked to these nuts. When she didn't come back, a SLED agent and one of her friends set out to find her."

"Interesting." Sawyer looked back at James and the young agent talking beside the car. "Thanks for the update. I'll send someone up to talk to O'Connor. Maybe her informant told her what these lunatics have planned."

"No need to send anybody up here unless you just want to. You've got your hands full, with Hart speaking this afternoon. My guys will question her, and if she knows anything, we'll relay it to you."

"Okay. Keep me posted, and I'll reciprocate." Sawyer turned off the phone, thumped it on his leg as he stared around at the busy workers.

The black Humvee carrying Ira and Eustace Hanley, Barry Lynch, and Lance Mackenzie pulled into a self-service fuel center in Manning, South Carolina, to fill up with diesel fuel. The older man got out with his son, while Barry and Lance remained inside the vehicle.

"Did you know Dane had been caught and beaten?" Barry asked, talking low so the Hanleys wouldn't overhear him.

"Hell, no. Then again, I didn't know he was a lousy fed, neither. He could have ruined everything."

"What exactly is 'everything'? What's happening, Lance? Where are we going, and what is going to happen?"

Lance glanced toward the back of the car. "Ira doesn't want me talkin' 'bout nothin'. He'll tell you when we get to Charleston."

Barry also glanced back. He saw Ira filling the vehicle's tank, but he didn't see the man's father. "Where's Ira's dad?"

"Saw him heading inside. Guess he had to relieve himself."

"So we're going to Charleston, huh?"

Lance's face wrinkled. "Don't let on that you know. Ira will kill me."

"I won't say anything if you'll tell me everything you know. I ain't crazy about ridin' into something where I might get killed, without knowing what's going on."

Suspicion clouded Lance's features. "Why you want to know so bad? You ain't no stinking fed, too, are you?"

Barry laughed. "Do I look like a fed? Besides, if I was, Dane would have known. From the looks of him, they likely beat the truth out of him. He would have given me up just to get them to quit."

"Reckon you're right. They did whup him purty good."

"So what's gettin'—"

"We're almost ready to roll," Ira said as he yanked open the door. "Pa's gone in to use the phone. He's afraid if we use our cell phones or the satellite phone the general gave us, them New World assholes will track us down and send in the black helicopters. They'll do anything to keep us from completin' our mission."

"You never did tell me exactly what our mission is," Barry said.

Lance fidgeted in his seat. He looked out the side window, pretending not to listen.

Ira turned around and stared straight at Barry. "Nope, never did, did I?" He pointed out the back window. "Yonder comes Pa. Now we can get on down the road, where you'll find out for yourself what our mission is."

Hanley crawled into the front seat. He glared around at all three men. Fire shot out of his eyes. "Sons o' bitches attacked the camp this mornin'. Right after we left. We took casualties, and they took prisoners. "I 'spect they're out lookin' for us right now."

"Traitors," Ira hissed. "Now what? Do we go on into Charleston or lay low?"

"Drive on," Hanley ordered. "We'll stop at the black water creek site and hide out there until a little closer to time. The feds won't know any of our folks who're already in the city. The diversions will be in place by the time we roll in."

Barry sat silent, watching the two men discuss their options. Panic masked the face of the older man; confusion, the younger.

In Charleston, Lansford called Cromwell's room. "Trust you slept well?"

"Alone but well, darling. Will you be joining us for breakfast?"

She grimaced at the disgusting thought of spending any more time with the vile creature than she had to. Locke had told her what had happened between Cromwell and a senator, years before. She knew he'd also played a major role in another death—just like Locke had—and in time, she would settle that score with both men.

"I really wish I could, but I have to meet with the media, then the Secret Service. Those security types are a real pain in the ass when it comes to the senator being able to get close to his people."

"Yes, that is important." Cromwell's voice sounded distant, as if he was preoccupied with some other thought. "Maybe dinner, then. After the speech."

"Yes, maybe so. I called to make sure you got your credentials. You'll need them to get up on the stage."

"I got them. When should I go over to the campus?"

"I'll send someone for you. They'll get you through the security. Enjoy your morning." She hung up the phone. *Death would be a more welcome dinner companion than you, you parasite.*

Leaning against a gleaming wall, Jefferson watched as the emergency room doctors rushed in and out of the rooms where Dane and Cassie had been taken. At the same time, he looked over at Tree, who was talking to a couple of FBI agents farther down the crowded corridor.

A young nurse with a coffee-and-cream complexion stepped out of a nearby room. She flashed a malicious smile. "Might you be Jefferson Lee?"

Pushing away from the wall, he cleared his throat and grinned. "Not only might I be, I definitely am. And what can I do for you?"

The woman's brown eyes scoured his face. "Not for me, tall, dark, and henpecked. For her." She pointed toward the room she had just left. "Scarlett O'Hara in there wants you, Rhett, and she won't have it any other way. So go in there and calm your girl, so we can get on with making her better."

"We're not—"

"Don't explain, just go in and calm her down. Please." She folded her arms across her chest. Her pupils glowed like angry beacons.

Jefferson frowned as he walked passed the pretty nurse. Inside the room, Cassie lay on her back, one eye open, staring straight up at the ceiling, the other covered by a gauze patch.

She turned to look at him as he stepped beside her bed. "I want you to get my stuff from my room at the hotel and pick me up here. We need to get to Charleston."

"Has the doctor—"

"Forget the doctor. I'm feeling better. All I need is more pain medicine."

"But—"

"No buts. Florence Nightingale and Doctor Livingston gave me some pain medicine, but they won't let me go. They say they want to observe me a little while longer, but while I'm here, the biggest story of my career is developing in Charleston."

"How can you be sure?"

"After the wreck, some goons threw me into the back of a truck and drove to hell-knows-where, before dumping me in that vile cabin. They thought I was unconscious. I was, for a while, but not the whole time. They were talking about attacking Charleston and shooting someone there."

"Hart? He's speaking this afternoon."

"They didn't mention names, but after I got some of my senses back . . . yes, that's who I think they were talking about."

"What else did you hear?"

"Not much," Cassie replied. "Who's the other person everyone is scurrying around trying to save? I heard one of the nurses saying he had been beaten worse than anyone she had ever seen."

"FBI agent, I think. From what I heard, he was an undercover agent who had infiltrated the group and got caught."

"FBI?"

Jefferson nodded. "That's who got you out."

"That's why they were in here asking all those questions. Did they get the leaders of the group?"

"Don't think so. There weren't but a handful of folks left in the camp when they went in."

"Then something big is still planned for Charleston. I just know it. We've got to go there. I'll use my ears and one good eye. Your camera can be my other one." She reached up and touched the gauze bandage.

Jefferson sighed. "You're impossible."

"Have you seen Brock?"

"Tree called him after we got here. He's been across the state on a murder investigation, but I think he's on his way back."

"I wondered—"

"He cares an awful lot about you, if that's what you're wondering. When he does get here, you'd better—"

"I know, I know. Believe me, I know. But right now, we need to get to—"

"You won't be gettin' anywhere until you get the doc's okay." The voice came from behind Jefferson.

Cassie scowled as he stepped aside and turned to see who was talking. A momentary glow appeared on her face. "Brock!"

He winked at Jefferson. "Don't let her bully you into going against the doctor's orders."

"Okay, okay," Cassie replied. She tried to sound irritated, but the sparkle of joy in her expression revealed her true feelings.

"Tell you what," Jefferson said. "I'll get your things while you take your medicine, then we'll see if the doc will let you go. This cop can keep you company while I'm gone."

Brock glanced at his watch, shrugged his shoulders. "I guess I can stay a while."

Cassie hit him with a scorching stare. "I guess you'd better."

He smiled and winked.

Jefferson headed out of the room. "I'll get your stuff. At least get some rest until I get back."

She waved him away from the bed. "Hurry."

"Yeah, yeah," he said, waving his hand as he left.

# CHAPTER · 29

CHARLESTON POLICE HEADQUARTERS

James opened the door to the room where the final Secret Service briefing was being held for the afternoon's speech by Senator Hart. He motioned to Sawyer, who excused himself and stepped out into the hallway.

"Better late than never." James held up his cell phone. "I just talked to my man at Langley. He's come through with some interesting information."

"Don't keep me in suspense." Sawyer pulled the door shut behind him.

"Back when the Gulf War was winding down, there was a faction of the military command who wanted to go on into Baghdad and take out Hussein. They argued at the time that there would never be a better opportunity to take control of Iraq. As you know, that didn't happen."

"Yeah, I knew there had been a lot of discussion about going in. International politics forced the President and Joint Chiefs to scrap the idea."

"Did you know that a Ranger unit went in anyway?"

"No."

"Neither did anybody else, except a few top generals and some folks at the CIA. The unit took out some strategic targets, killed—assassinated would be a better way to say it—top officials, and their next target was to be Hussein, but their little mission got compromised by one of their former officers."

"Who?"

"Jeff Hart."

"Hart? Hart participated in an unauthorized military attack on a foreign country?" Sawyer whistled. "That's one hell of a campaign issue. I'm surprised Flint hasn't clubbed him over the head with that one."

"The Administration, then and now, won't acknowledge it ever happened. The international fallout would be too severe."

"So, if I hear you right, someone out there is after Hart because he blew the whistle on an unauthorized and illegal operation."

"The leader of that renegade unit was Colonel Ambrose Thornton. And, besides Hart, one of his other officers was Eustace Hanley, our Free Confederacy leader. Fallout from the illicit raid included Thornton being forced out of the Army—just before he was to be promoted. Hanley received a dishonorable discharge, and after he left, he began training his own militia, one dedicated to overthrowing the government and getting even for what they had done to him."

"I know of Thornton," Sawyer said. "I heard he was running some mercenary, soldier-for-hire operation, mainly in South America."

"Well, apparently he's operating here for now, and his primary target is Jeff Hart. According to my source in the CIA, Thorn, as he is called, will do anything to stop Hart from becoming president."

"Including assassination?"

"Especially assassination," James said.

"Did your man know where and how this plan is to be carried out?"

"Nope, but he did say that he'd bet good money on Hanley's group being heavily involved. If that's so, then right here in good ole Charleston is where it will likely happen."

"Damn. There are construction workers all over the place, on top of buildings, everywhere. We've cleared the area immediately around the speaking site, but we'll need as many spotters as we can get to watch other buildings and the surrounding grounds." Sawyer sighed. "Maybe, with this new information, we can talk Hart out of his appearance?"

"Like I said earlier. He's been very insistent. And you can't blame him. He's waded into this disaster, been photographed meeting with the workers, encouraging them and promising continued economic support for the area to ensure that the rebuilding continues. The speech could very well be his coup d'etat for this election."

"What about his attractive lioness, Lansford. Maybe she'll care enough about her boss to want to do something."

James shrugged. "You met her. Do you think she'll scrap the most important appearance Hart will make?"

Sawyer opened the door to return to the briefing. "You've got to try to convince her. Meanwhile, I'll update everyone in here, then we need to get our folks deployed and on the lookout for trouble."

Parked alongside a river in a heavily wooded forest north of Charleston, Barry leaned back in his seat inside the Humvee, watching Ira and Eustace

Hanley's lively exchange in front of the vehicle. Lance opened the side door to climb back in after going behind the vehicle to answer nature's call.

"What's all that about?" Barry asked. "They look pissed at each other."

"Not sure." Lance shook his head. He rubbed his chin. "Maybe they're trying to decide what happens now that the feds are onto us."

"What's supposed to happen? What's going down in Charleston?"

A look of concern fell across Lance's face. He didn't answer, just blinked excessively.

"What did you and Ira do in Charleston?"

"We helped rebuild houses."

"You know what I'm talkin' about. You helped him deal with a situation that came up. What happened?"

Before Lance could answer, Ira and his father returned to the car. Both shot hard glances toward the two men in the backseat as they climbed into the front.

"We're going on into Charleston," the older man said. "When we get there, we'll split up. Nothing can stop our mission."

Jefferson pushed Cassie's wheelchair out the sliding glass doors of Richland Memorial Hospital's emergency room and rolled the grumbling reporter up beside the waiting blue T-Bird. Tree opened the back door.

"Okay, we did it their way." She hopped out of the wheelchair. "Now let's get to Charleston. Hart's scheduled to speak in a little over an hour, and I'd at least like to have a shot at a post-speech interview."

"You be careful." Brock took her arm. "And don't overdo. You still owe me a date. Besides, the doctor said you needed to rest."

She pecked a kiss on his cheek. "When this is over, I promise to take a long-overdue, restful vacation. So be planning to take some time off yourself." She smiled. "I hear Cancún is nice this time of year."

Inside the car, Cassie stretched out across the seat. She propped her head on a pillow the hospital had given her.

"You sure this is a good idea?" Jefferson asked as he slid into the front seat. "I don't want you fallin' out on us halfway there."

Tree, who had already cranked the car, laughed. He glanced in the rearview mirror, patted the dashboard. "Yeah, this baby ain't exactly equipped like an ambulance."

Cassie winced as she shifted her position. She closed her eyes. "Just drive. I'll be all right."

\* \* \*

Sawyer looked overhead as he and James walked through an arbor tunnel leading onto the campus of the College of Charleston. "Hart couldn't have picked a harder place to secure if he'd tried." He pointed to the heavy foliage lining the pedestrian path known as the Promenade.

"No, you're right. Our folks pointed all of that out to his advance team, but nobody seemed to care. Least of all, Lansford."

"Of all the damn locations in Charleston, why here? Students are everywhere." Sawyer kicked a small limb that had fallen out of one of the trees still standing in the aftermath of the hurricane. "All that damage, and these trees look as if they weren't even fazed."

"The whole campus—buildings and trees—escaped having any major damage. The entire place looks like the hand of God wrapped around it and protected it until the storm passed."

"Well, for our purposes, that's bad. Hart could have spoken in front of city hall or inside an auditorium. They're a whole lot easier to secure than here." He stopped and looked up toward the roof of a nearby clapboard building, where a police officer with binoculars stood. "Restricted access to the speech area?"

"Yes, sir. We have agents at entrance points. The rest of the area is roped off. Local police are stationed along the perimeter, to keep out folks who don't have an invitation. We're using handheld metal detectors to wand everyone who comes through the perimeter."

"Rooftops?" Sawyer asked as the two men walked past the student center, heading toward the stage where Hart would be speaking.

"We have spotters and snipers on the Science Center, the School of the Arts building, and a nearby parking garage. As you'll see in a second, the stage has been constructed on the Cistern that sits in front of Randolph Hall. The guests will gather across the lawn in front."

Sawyer stopped as soon as the stage came into sight. He studied the columned brick building directly behind the temporary wooden structure, the raised grassy area that James had referred to as the Cistern, where the stage was standing, and the tree-filled lawn in front. "Shit! There's enough cover to hide the 101st Army division." He gazed through the treetops, rubbed his forehead. "This is nuts."

"Yes, sir."

The Humvee pulled into an alleyway off Rutledge Avenue in Charleston and parked inside a fence behind a construction office. "A member owns this place," Hanley said. "We'll change vehicles here."

Ira climbed out onto the asphalt lot and motioned to Lance. "You come with me." He pointed toward a gray pickup, then walked to the back of the Humvee.

"What about us?" Barry asked Hanley.

"Just sit tight. As soon as they're gone, we'll move."

Lance stepped out just as Ira slammed the tailgate of the Humvee. As he glanced back at Barry, trepidation shrouded his face.

"Here." Ira handed Lance a backpack and a suitcase. "Toss 'em in the back of the pickup and climb in."

A couple of minutes later, Barry watched the truck drive through the gate and turn, heading back toward the street. He looked at Hanley sitting quietly in the front seat. "Now what?"

Hanley opened his door. "Let's get out and stretch our legs. I'll fill you in." He eased out of the vehicle.

When Barry hopped out, Hanley leveled a .45 in his face. "Keep your hands where I can see 'em, boy. Now step back."

"What the—"

"Come on, boy. We ain't all as stupid as you federal smart-asses think we are. You're just like the other one—cocky and thinking you're smarter than everybody else."

The hairs on the back of Barry's neck stirred. "I don't know—"

"Shit, boy. You know. I spent too much time in the Rangers to not recognize when somebody's lying. Your eyes give you away."

Barry weighed the bulk of his nemesis. He watched the pistol in Hanley's right hand, wondering when the older man figured him out. He glanced around. There were homes and other businesses close by.

*Is Hanley going to shoot me, out in the open like this, or make me walk inside the construction office, where the noise of the shot won't be easily heard?*

He decided to wait and see if he would be taken toward the building behind him before making his move. "Why do you think I'm a fed? Where'd you hear this bullshit?" His voice held a hint of concern, but it remained strong and firm. Somehow, he had to convince Hanley he wasn't a threat, at least cast enough doubt for him to gain an advantage.

"Hey, you were good," Hanley said with a grin. "Actually, both of you were. But your friend slipped up a couple of times, and when we checked him out, his story didn't jibe with what my intelligence on him revealed."

Barry thought about the slip he had detected when Dane claimed to be from the Midwest. "Look, I didn't really know the guy. We only met a few weeks before I met you and Ira."

"Yeah, I know. We beat the boy good, but I don't think he knew who you were, either. I suspect he's dead now, and if he knew about you, he took it to the grave with him. He'd've made a damn good soldier."

"I don't—"

"We heard we had some spies among us. We just didn't know who they were. And you did a real good job foolin' us. I didn't know for sure it was you until we stopped and I made the call back to check on everything. That's when I heard about the raid on our camp and the questions being asked of our folks about you."

"Where's Ira taking Lance?"

Hanley grinned. He stroked his beard with the tips of his fingers. "It's killing you not to know, ain't it?"

Barry shifted his feet for a better stance, in case he had the opportunity to jump Hanley. His back calf rested against the running board of the Humvee.

"Easy, boy. Don't go gettin' no ideas." Hanley glanced down at his watch, then back up, before Barry had a chance to move. "I still have a little while before I have to leave, so I'll answer your question. Lance is gonna shoot that yellow-spined son of a bitch Hart. The bastard damn near got our whole unit pinned up in Iraq without any support."

Barry's forehead furrowed. "Hart? You know the senator?"

"Know him?" Hanley laughed. "Shit, boy, I trained the pantywaist. He got scared and compromised our mission. We barely got away from the swarthy bastards."

Barry didn't totally understand the connection between Hart and Hanley, but he understood the hatred the man held, and he understood he had precious little time to stop Ira and Lance. "Why Lance?"

Hanley shook his head. "Damn good question, boy. I have my doubts about him, to tell the truth, but Ira says he can do it. We'll see. Besides, Ira's got another target, and he likely won't have time to get both."

*Another target?* "Who is the other target?"

"Doesn't matter to you, now does it? We take our marching orders from the Almighty himself. Orders straight from as high up as you can get." Hanley pointed his free hand toward the heavens. "We're puttin' an end to the Zionist bastards wanting to take over the world. Shit, boy, by the time the smoke clears, we're gonna have us a friend in the White House. We'll put an end to all of this crap that treasonous bunch up in the United Nations is selling. The conspiracy to take our guns and land will be put to rest, and the true patriots will control America, maybe even the entire world."

"White House? You're crazy. You know that? There's no damn conspiracy to take your land and guns—or anything else, for that matter."

"You're brainwashed, boy, just like all them bastards who stormed Ruby Ridge and Waco. Patriots died at their hands, and you're gonna die at mine. Once today's targets are down, Ira's going to kill your friend, too. Just to tie up loose ends. Weren't for him, you and that other treasonous fed wouldn't have gotten in among us." The old man began laughing. "Yep, when you boys arrive together, you're gonna crack hell wide-ass open."

Noticing the gun barrel dip just a little, Barry pushed the back of his legs away from the Humvee and lunged toward Hanley's gun hand. Before the surprised man could squeeze the trigger, Barry wrapped his fingers around the semiautomatic's frame. Squeezing to prevent the slide from working, he popped the back of Hanley's wrist with his free hand, twisted the gun back toward the man's fingers, and pried the weapon loose.

He turned the gun on Hanley. "U.S. Secret Service. You're under arrest."

"Never take prisoners, boy." Rage flamed in Hanley's eyes as he dove at Barry.

The gun barked just as the old man's thick fingers wrapped around Barry's neck. Barry heard the rush of air escaping the man's lungs as the bullet penetrated the chest. He glared into Hanley's seething face. The man's fingers squeezed tighter.

Gasping and coughing, Barry fired, with the barrel pulled back away from Hanley's body just enough to allow the slide to work. The weapon thundered, then thundered again.

Hanley's fingers loosened. His body dropped to the pavement. Barry sucked oxygen through his bruised windpipe.

Looking around to see if the sounds of shots drew spectators, Barry was surprised to see no one. He slid the pistol into his waistband and bent down to check Hanley. He held his fingers against the man's carotid artery. *Dead.*

He stood and checked his watch, even though he wasn't sure what time the senator was scheduled to speak. He remembered overhearing the talk about the College of Charleston campus and about Free Confederacy members deployed to set off explosives as a distraction. He jumped into the Humvee and backed it out of the fenced-in construction yard.

He had to hurry. Trying to get up with any of the agents at the scene would be next to impossible right now. They had gone into their heightened security mode, and the only communications they would be receiving would come over their radio system. All he could do was drive like hell. Try to get to the speech before the shooting started.

# CHAPTER · 30

DOWNTOWN CHARLESTON, NEAR THE COLLEGE OF CHARLESTON CAMPUS

Ira parked the gray pickup in a secluded corner of a parking deck behind a hotel on Meeting Street. He and Lance climbed out and began preparing for their mission.

"We're walking from here," Ira said as he dropped the tailgate. He pulled the suitcase toward him and unlocked it.

Lance watched. Inside was a canvas belt like carpenters wear, but this one was different from anything he had seen. There were specially sewn loops, sleeves, and pouches. "Ain't never seen a belt like that before."

"Reckon you ain't. Thorn had this made special."

"He's the general, right?"

"That's right. And when it comes to warfare, he knows how it's done." Ira grabbed a rifle barrel from a foam insert inside the suitcase and slid it into one of the custom-sewn sleeves. He put a rifle magazine into one of the pouches, then he slipped a metal bracket that looked like it might be the gun's shoulder stock into a couple of the loops. When he finished, he looked around to make sure no one had been watching them, then dropped his baggy pants and put on the belt. He pulled his pants back up, concealing the belt and all it carried.

"Your turn," he said, pulling up the foam and revealing another layer of rifle parts and another belt.

Once Lance was properly outfitted, he walked around to test his movement. "This stuff's light. You sure it's safe for a gun barrel?"

"Yeah. It's made of some special space-age shit Thorn got ahold of from NASA." He rapped his knuckles against his pants leg. "But don't worry about it blowing up in your face. It's stronger than steel, according to Thorn."

"So, now what?" Lance asked. A hint of nervousness hung on each word.

Ira looked around the shadows inside the parking lot. Apparently satisfied no one was around to overhear, he pulled a folded piece of paper out of his back pocket. "We go over to the campus, blend in with the crowd, and find the place marked on this map." He slapped the map against his open palm. "Everything's been studied and planned, just like for any covert mission. Just think of the campus as enemy territory."

"What about when it's over? What if we get separated?"

"We'll meet back here." Ira reached into the pickup bed and pulled out the backpack. He stuck his arms through the straps and positioned the pack between his shoulder blades. "You ready to go?"

Lance stared at the pickup truck, then he looked at Ira. He didn't say a word, just drew a deep breath and nodded.

Cassie sat up in the backseat of the T-Bird and rubbed her bruised face. She tried to clear the cobwebs from her brain.

The sound of a rapper and music with a deep bass filled her ears as she looked out the tinted windows, hoping to spot a familiar landmark. "How much farther?"

"Ah, Sleeping Beauty is awake," Jefferson said, his voice loud enough to be heard over the music. "Feel any better?"

"Some." The word dissolved into a wide yawn. She sniffed. "Does anybody besides me smell rotten eggs?"

Tree patted the lump beneath his shirt. Jefferson glanced at his cousin, a smirk spreading across his face. Both men began laughing.

Cassie grimaced. "What's so damn funny? And where are we?"

"Funny? Nothing's funny," Jefferson replied through a broad grin.

"We're 'bout twenty minutes out of Charleston," Tree said.

Cassie saw him use the rearview mirror to look back at her, so she smiled and nodded. "That's good." She checked the clock on the dash. "Hart's about to make his speech. We should get there before he's finished."

Jefferson looked over his seat back. "Yeah. Cuz, here, has pretty much punished the speed limit."

Cassie fell back against the plush leather upholstery. "Far as I'm concerned, he can punish it all he wants. We need to get there before something happens." She sat silent for a few seconds, then leaned forward and tapped Jefferson's shoulder. "Hey, no offense, but would you cut the music and find a news station, one that might be covering Hart's speech."

Jefferson nodded at Tree, who shrugged his indifference. "I'll try some of the local stations. Maybe one of 'em is civic-minded."

* * *

Creighton Lansford hurried up the steps of Randolph Hall, located behind the stage where Senator Jeff Hart would soon speak. Just inside, she saw Hart primping in front of a mirror. "You look great. Sound's been checked, and the crowd is gathering. We'll go out in ten minutes."

"Where the hell is the governor?" Hart asked. "He's still doing the introduction, right?"

Lansford straightened his tie. "I saw his motorcade pull up just as I came across the lawn. He should be here any second now."

"Am I supposed to introduce that new contributor? What's his name?"

"Cromwell. Adam Cromwell, and no, you don't have to introduce him. Just refer to him and all the others on the stage with you as generous contributors who support the same values you do."

"Anything else?"

"That's pretty much it," Lansford said.

The door opened, and in walked the South Carolina governor, who wore a shiny silk suit. Two burly troopers, wearing dark suits and sunglasses, filled the doorway behind him.

Hart watched the arrival with a cold eye. "Your entourage looks more like one for a Mafia don than a governor."

The governor's eyebrow lifted as he extended his hand to Hart. "Can't be too careful these days. There are nutcases everywhere. I understand the latest state poll has you three points ahead."

"So I hear, but we have to keep the pressure on. If I know Flint, he'll come up with some last-minute surprise." Hart looked at Lansford. "Are we ready to go out?"

She walked to the door. "Let me make sure everyone out here is ready. If they are, then the governor can go on out. We'll position you out of sight until he introduces you."

Dressed in baggy painter's pants, like many of the other carpenters and construction people hovering around the campus, Ira and Lance had entered the school grounds from the west and made their way back toward where Hart would be giving his speech. They weren't close enough to be challenged by any of Hart's security detail just yet, and the local police, who were so used to seeing contractors all over the city, hadn't given them a second glance.

Thornton had told Ira not to worry about the Charleston officers, who had been working twelve-hour shifts, with no days off, since the hurricane hit. He had assured them that fatigue dulled the usually vigilant police instincts.

Ira pulled out the map he had been given by Thornton. "Okay, we're going to ease our way around behind the student center." He pointed to a nearby building. "That's it over there. I'm going to put the backpack behind that house." He pointed again. "According to this map, it's a faculty office building. When that bomb goes off, most of the attention will be focused there for a few seconds. That should give us our opportunity." He looked at Lance. "You ready?"

Lance swallowed hard. He nodded, with a faraway stare. But just like back at the parking deck, he remained silent.

Barry pulled onto King Street and sped through the usually busy shopping district, toward the College of Charleston. At Calhoun Street, a roadblock had been set up to divert all traffic away from the campus. Cars were backed up, and Barry saw no way to get around them.

He turned the Humvee to the right and drove up onto the sidewalk. He was able to go another block before he encountered a crowd watching the snarled streets and the police officers rerouting traffic.

He stopped the military vehicle, left it in the middle of the sidewalk, and jumped out. A man exited the store where the abandoned Humvee blocked the entrance. As the irate man yelled at him, Barry ran toward the northeast corner of the campus.

After he passed the roadblock, he heard another voice shout out. "Hey. You there. Stop."

Barry glanced over his shoulder to see a lanky, uniformed police officer chasing after him. Barry slowed for a moment but sped up when he saw the angry glare in the officer's eyes. *No time for explanations*, he decided. He hoped his pursuer would radio ahead to alert the Secret Service that someone was running in their direction. Maybe he could buy time while everyone, especially Hart, waited for him to be caught.

Overhead, he saw the police helicopter appear and hover. He heard the loudspeaker crackle, then he heard a harsh command for him to stop.

He ran past a row of shops, toward the entrance to the campus. Just ahead, he saw trees draped with Spanish moss. *Almost there.* He spotted a brick walkway leading between clapboard buildings. If he could just make it to an agent who knew him, before he was stopped, he'd be all right.

His lungs burned and his legs grew heavy. He heard footsteps coming up fast behind him.

As he turned to look, a shoulder bore into his left side. His knees buckled, and he hit the pavement hard, felt the air rush from his lungs. Pain shot through his wrists. Someone yanked his arm and wrenched it behind his back.

A woman's voice barked orders. "Hold it right there, mister. You're under arrest."

Ira disappeared behind the faculty office he had pointed out to Lance. When he emerged, the backpack was gone.

"Think anyone will find it?" Lance asked. Try as he might, he couldn't stop the quavering in his voice.

"They'll hear it, but they won't see it," Ira said with a grin. He reached down the front of his pants and pulled out a scope. "Come on, I want to get to our spots and see what kind of a view we have."

The two men walked at a fast pace, away from the stage. As they came to a hedge of oleander bushes, Ira pointed to the thickest part. "You're in there."

Lance looked all around. He saw no one close by, and most of the people up ahead were facing in the direction of the stage. "This is an awful long way off. You sure I'll be able to see Hart?"

"That stage is built on a raised area, and it's a good five feet off the ground. You'll be able to see. Come on." Ira snuck a quick glance around him, then shoved Lance's back.

Lance hesitated, then spread apart the thick bushes. Inside, he was surprised to find a tiny clearing, as if the hedge had been planted in a circle. "Can you see me in here?"

"No. You're good. Can you see the stage?"

Lance pulled his scope from the tool belt and raised it to his eye. He pushed the powerful viewer into a tiny opening and peered toward the stage. "You were right. I see four people up there, and I see the podium."

Ira whispered into the hedge. "Put your rifle together. I'm moving to my location."

Lance's pulse began pounding in his throat. As his shaky hands retrieved the rifle parts inside his pants, he couldn't dismiss the sensation that a trapdoor had just opened inside his gut. He ran Ira's instructions through his head, then repeated them in a low, whispered voice: "As soon as you hear a second explosion, take out Hart. I'll take out my target at the same time. Leave your rifle and slip out during the chaos. We'll meet back at the parking deck."

A cold sweat beaded Lance's forehead. If he could just pull his nerves together, the mission would soon be over and he could stand proud with the others, knowing he had dealt a blow for freedom.

\* \* \*

Barry squirmed on the pavement in the middle of King Street, his hands cuffed behind his back. He couldn't get back to his feet.

Men and women in suits and dresses gave wide berth to him and the officers surrounding him as they hurried toward the brick walkway that led to where Jeff Hart would soon speak. From his prone position, he could see the crowd forming, through an opening between two buildings. Hundreds of people were on their way to see a United States senator assassinated, and he couldn't stop them. "I'm secret—"

The woman slapped the back of his head. "I said, shut your mouth."

"What's his story?" a deep voice asked.

"Don't know, sir. He was running—"

"I've got to get over there!" Barry yelled at the top of his lungs. "There's going to be a shooting."

He saw the spit-shined shoes appear in front of his face. As he looked up, a tall black man, in a blue Charleston Police uniform with gold captain's bars on his collar, knelt down in front of him.

"What did you say?" the police captain asked.

"I'm Secret Service—working undercover. Someone's trying to kill the senator."

The captain stared for a second. "Stand him up." The command held a sense of urgency.

As Barry was pulled to his feet, the captain looked him in the eye. "You got any ID?"

"My sock. My ID is in my sock."

A loud explosion sounded, off in the distance. Seconds later, another ripped the air in the opposite direction.

"What the hell?" the captain yelled.

"Diversions. You've got to let me loose, so I can warn the others."

Hart had just begun his address when the first explosion echoed from the harbor. He stopped his speech, looked surprised, then jokingly asked, "Are they firing on Fort Sumter again?"

An uneasy laugh rose from the crowd as they exchanged concerned glances. Secret Service agents, standing in front of the stage, snapped their attention in the direction of the sound, then back at the surrounding crowd. One agent on the platform eased closer to Hart.

The second explosion came from somewhere on campus and shook the ground under the stage. It sounded much too close to suit three agents, who sprinted in the direction of the thunderous noise and black smoke rising beyond a hedge of tall shrubs.

The crowd moved in different directions all at once, then pushed together, like a herd of stampeding cattle, toward the closest street leading away from the campus. The agent who had sidled close to the candidate grabbed Hart's arm.

Amid the confusion and turmoil, a shot rang out. The fleeing crowd screamed. Some dove to the ground, while others ran for nearby buildings and trees. Secret Service agents in front of the stage drew their weapons and looked around, trying to spot the location of the shooter. The agent holding Hart's arm jerked the senator to the stage floor. Another agent, his weapon drawn, aimed, and ready for any suspicious movement, dropped to one knee in front of the senator's prone body.

On the side of the stage, a woman screamed. Beside her, a man who would later be identified as Adam Cromwell, a wealthy contributor to Hart's campaign, lay lifeless, blood pooling under his head.

Jefferson hadn't had much luck finding a station carrying the senator's speech. "I don't think anybody cares," he said as he stopped on a country music station. The twang of a steel guitar filled the elaborate speaker system.

"You've got to be kiddin'," Tree said. "Don't leave it—"

An abrupt interruption in the music severed the conversation as quickly as a sharp cleaver slicing meat. "There's been a reported shooting on the campus of the College of Charleston, the location of presidential candidate Jeff Hart's speech today. We have a reporter on the scene. Jennifer, what's happening there?"

As the woman began her assessment of the chaos on the college campus, Cassie slapped the back of Jefferson's seat. "Dammit! I knew something was going to happen. How much farther?"

"We'll be there in five minutes," Tree said. "That is, if we can get near the campus."

She groaned. "Can't you flash a badge or something? We need to get inside the perimeter."

"Inside the perimeter?" Jefferson said with a chuckle. "You sound like a cop yourself."

"I'll get us as close as I can," Tree said. "Are you sure you're up to this?"

Cassie pulled out her makeup mirror. "Oh, yeah. I may not be much to look at, but inside, I'm ready to go."

# Chapter · 31

A PARKING GARAGE IN DOWNTOWN CHARLESTON, SOUTH CAROLINA

As police and Secret Service agents scoured the area around the College of Charleston campus, Lance cowered in a dark corner of the parking deck. His ears trained on every sound that echoed in the concrete-and-steel structure. When he first arrived, he heard a siren approaching, thought he had been seen, and believed his days of freedom were about to come to an end. The police car streaked past, however, and as he listened to the shrill noise fade into the distance, he felt the force of his own heart pounding inside his chest.

Footsteps—fast-running footsteps—caught his attention. Recoiling into a corner formed by two support columns, he cast a long, searching look toward the daylight pouring into the parking deck opening.

The steps drew closer, grew louder. He watched, crouched as low as he could get, reluctant to even crane his neck high enough to see over the hood of a nearby Mercedes-Benz.

The steps began to slow. They shuffled against the concrete floor.

Lance eased up out of his corner and looked through the windshield of the Mercedes. The dark figure had stopped near the truck taken from behind the construction office. Lance recognized the lean physique, the narrow, hatchet-faced profile. "Ira. Over here."

Ira's head snapped in Lance's direction. "Where are you?"

Lance eased out of the shadows and ran toward Ira. He wiped his sweaty palms against his pants. "I thought they had you."

"Where'd you get to?" Ira asked with a probing glare. "You get Hart?"

Lance didn't respond right away. He glanced out into the sunlight. "We need to get out of here before the cops arrive."

"We're blocks away. They're mostly over on campus, trying to figure out what happened." He scrutinized Lance's features. "You did get Hart . . . didn't you?"

Lance cleared his throat. He shuffled his feet.

Ira's voice took on an air of desperation. "You killed him—right?"

The sullen man drew a deep breath. "I couldn't hold the rifle, couldn't keep it steady."

Ira looked around the deck with the glare of a lion about to pounce. "You didn't shoot at all?"

Lance's gaze swept the concrete floor. He shook his head. "I left the rifle in the bushes and came back here."

"You *what*? You didn't even try to kill the bastard? You left me there to be caught."

"I couldn't pull the trigger." His voice quaked. "I couldn't breathe. I had to get out."

Ira slapped the side of the pickup. He stormed to the driver-side door, snatched it open, and reached inside. When he turned around, he held a pistol, with a silencer on the end.

Lance's face transfixed with terror. He stumbled back.

Ira scowled as he walked straight toward the shrinking man. "Daddy told me you were a coward. He said you wouldn't be able to carry out our mission." He shook his head. "I thought, after you helped with that street woman, you'd be ready. I told Daddy not to worry. Now he's going to blame me." He looked stricken. "Thorn will blame me, too, and the general doesn't tolerate failure. We have to go back and clean up your mess. Hart has to die."

"We . . . we can't go back. There are too many cops."

Ira stared in silence. "You're right. We won't be able to go back." He raised the handgun and deposited one shot into Lance's forehead. "I'll have to do it." He shoved the gun into the waistband of his painter's pants, hopped behind the steering wheel of the pickup, and drove out of the deck.

Trapped behind a police barricade, Cassie fought back a yawn as she listened to the Charleston Police press-relations officer describe the events that took place on the campus. Standing off to one side, Jefferson had his camera focused on the melee two blocks away.

"The senator was not harmed," the police spokesman said. "One man is dead, but we're not releasing an identity until we can contact next of kin."

"Can you tell us if the victim was a member of Hart's entourage?" a young female reporter asked.

As Cassie watched the girl, she wondered if the youthful questioner represented the college newspaper or maybe a local high school publication. Whichever, the question was a good one. Cassie turned her attention to the police officer, awaiting his answer.

"No, I can't tell you anything about the victim's identity."

"What about the governor?" asked another reporter, a man with perfect hair and flawless teeth.

Cassie had seen him anchoring the local news. She wondered if the man, clad in blue blazer and gray slacks, had grown up in Charleston. His accent was Southern, and he looked more like a blue blood than a reporter. *Way too preppy for a reporter,* she thought.

"He's fine. Only the one victim was injured, and unfortunately, his injury was fatal," the spokesman said.

Someone quipped, "We heard the governor sprained his ankle diving off the back of the stage. Can you comment on that?"

Laughter rose from the crowd of reporters. "Yeah," another male voice said. "When the going gets rough, you can count on our governor to get going—the other way."

"We're not doing any good here," Cassie whispered in Jefferson's ear. "All we're getting is the PD's spin on everything. As soon as Tree gets back, we need to start doing our own digging." She started back toward the parking lot where they had left the Thunderbird. "If you've got enough footage, then let's go. I want to find someone in Hart's campaign to talk to. Maybe we can find out why these fanatics want him dead."

"Mr. Director, this is agent Barry Lynch," James said. "You know him better as Johnny Reb."

Sawyer cast a slow, appraising look at his agent. He noticed the blood-stained shirt, the rosy abrasion on his right cheek, and what looked like bruising on his neck. "What happened to you?"

"Seems everyone, good guys and bad guys, wanted to stop me, but I got through, sir." He glanced around the area known as the Cistern, on the College of Charleston campus, looked up at the now vacant stage. A wounded look appeared in his eyes. "Albeit a bit too late."

Sawyer patted the agent's back. "I'm just glad you're okay. When we heard about the Bureau's man, we were concerned about your status."

Barry flashed a half smile. "I appreciate that, sir. How is Dane?"

"Dane?"

"Yes, sir. The FBI UC. Is he . . . alive?"

"Oh, I understand he's in bad shape, but they think he'll live."

Barry shook his head. "When they dragged him into that church at the Free Confederacy camp, I thought he might already be dead. I hope he'll be okay."

Sawyer nodded. "I'm going to get with the FBI Director after this is all over. We have to do a better job of keeping each other informed when we have operations that might overlap into the other's jurisdiction."

Barry acknowledged the need for better cooperation. "Good idea. I hear Hart's okay."

James spoke up. "Yes, he's fine. Banged his knee good when our man took him to the floor of the stage, but under the circumstances, he's not complaining. Fortunately they missed him, but they accidentally hit some poor guy who happened to be a contributor. I hear this was his first appearance with Hart."

"I don't think his shooting was an accident," Barry said.

Sawyer blinked with surprise. "Why's that?"

Barry narrowed his eyes as he looked at his director. "Sir, do you know General Ambrose Thornton?"

"Yes, I know him, and I understand he may have some involvement in all this."

"Yes, sir. But it's more than just an involvement. He's one of the men directing this lunacy."

"One of the men?" James asked.

"Based on Thornton's comments when he appeared to spur on the troops last night, there's at least one other person at the top—maybe two."

Sawyer and James exchanged glances.

"Eustace Hanley was the leader of the Free Confederacy. His son, Ira, came here today with Lance Mackenzie. Lance was to kill Hart, but the father told me Ira had another target. From the looks of things, Ira carried out his mission, Lance didn't."

"Where is this Eustace Hanley?" Sawyer asked.

"He's dead." Barry pointed to his bruised neck. "He tried to take me with him after I wrestled his gun away from him. I'll show our folks where they can find his body."

"Why do you think they targeted this other guy?" James asked.

"Don't know for sure. But as for Hart, Hanley told me before he died that when the smoke cleared, they'd have their own man in the White House. Guess they wanted Hart out of the way. Who do you suppose their man in the White House could be?"

"Who has the most to lose if Hart wins?" Sawyer asked in a suspicious tone as he looked at his deputy director.

James held a look of incredulity. "You're not thinking—"

"That's exactly what I'm thinking," Sawyer said to James, then turned to Barry. "Our new Vice President just may be ruthless and desperate enough to spearhead this insanity."

"The Vice President of the United States?" Barry asked.

Sawyer nodded. "Scary, isn't it?"

"And the reason Thornton is involved is because Hart was part of his Ranger group, until they decided to go into Iraq after the Gulf War. Eustace Hanley was an officer in that unit. Hart's the one who blew the whistle on the covert mission, nearly causing the unit to be trapped behind enemy lines. If that had happened, the United States would have had to deny knowledge of the operation, and no one would have tried to rescue them."

"That explains Hanley's loathing of Hart," Barry said. "He was a target for revenge."

"And a threat to their controlling the White House," Sawyer said, completing the theory.

James looked up at the white fluffy clouds floating across the blue sky. "But with Hanley dead, how do we make charges stick to Randall's hide? If anybody has Teflon skin, he does."

"We have to find Thornton," Sawyer said. "He won't come willingly, either, so tell our folks to be extremely cautious as they look for him."

"You think he'll give up Randall?"

"I don't know. But right now, he's our best shot at linking the Vice President to this . . . and maybe another conspiracy."

# CHAPTER · 32

CHARLESTON, SOUTH CAROLINA

Cassie hung up the newsroom phone and looked to Jefferson with a self-aggrandizing grin. "Barbara Walters, look out. I just got the interview of the campaign."

"Hart? He's been on every talk show that has a political twist, even some that don't. I'm surprised he hasn't shown up on 'Saturday Night Live.'"

"You're right. Hart wouldn't be a coup. But his image-maker, Creighton Lansford, would be, and she's agreed to sit down this afternoon before they leave. This will be a behind-the-scenes what-makes-the-candidate-tick."

"I get it. She wants to maximize on the publicity surrounding the assassination attempt. She'll talk about the commitment one has to have to serve the people, to make sure our great nation remains great." Jefferson's voice mocked the political ads running on all the networks.

Cassie pulled her lipstick from her purse and walked over to a nearby mirror. "Something like that, yeah." She applied the makeup, mashed her lips together, and dropped the black cylinder back into her purse. "Come on. We're supposed to meet her at Marion Square."

"Marion Square? The Secret Service isn't going to let her go to an open place like that. Not after the attempt today."

"They're not protecting her. They're guarding the candidate, and he won't be there. Besides, hardly anybody, outside of those who follow the campaign closely, even knows who she is." A broad smile slid across her face. "Of course, I plan on changing that."

Lansford had just finished packing her overnight bag and setting it on the floor beside her suitcases when she heard a knock. She opened the door, and Hart stepped into her room.

His expression wrinkled into a pronounced scowl. "I just heard you're meeting a reporter in Marion Square. Are you crazy?"

"Crazy like a fox," Lansford replied, grinning to reveal pearl-white teeth. "This interview will allow us to capitalize on the assassination attempt. When I'm finished, you'll be seen as the All-American boy next door who wants to be president, no matter how risky it is to your personal health."

Hart walked to the window and looked out over Meeting Street. "I don't like it. Not right now." He turned, with his arms folded across his chest. "They haven't caught the assassin yet. Hell, they don't know for sure how many are out there."

"They want you, not me. I'll be fine."

He shook his head. "I don't like it. Why can't the reporter come to the hotel, do the interview here?"

"I wanted to do it away from the hustle and bustle of the campaign. Doing it outside with birds and sunshine will make it look all the more natural."

"You're impossible. I could order you not to do it, you know."

"Yes, I know. You could, but you won't." She winked at him.

Hart crossed the room and opened the door to leave. He looked back at the woman who had seemingly appeared out of nowhere to run his campaign and whom he now credited with his success to this point. Her insistence at being involved in his campaign had been so passionate that he agreed without really knowing that much about her. It wasn't until a week after she began working for him that he learned the real reason for her wanting Wagner Flint defeated. Then he understood the passion and made her his lead strategist. "All right, but I'm going to ask a couple of agents to be in the area."

"No, just the driver," she said. "No others. They'll spoil the mood."

He shook his head. "I give up." The door slammed behind him.

Lansford picked up her overnight bag, unsnapped it, and pulled out a framed picture of her brother. As she studied the tender smile, the caring look that had so often reassured her when she was a little girl, she wondered what Grayson Locke would say if he knew the real reason for her intimacy with him. The irony was that if she had done the same to someone else, she knew Locke would have admired her for her ruthlessness.

Staring at her brother's cheerful expression, she recalled the day her mother called to tell her to turn on the news. Lansford's heart had sunk at the sound of grief filling her mother's voice. Right away she knew something was wrong. She flipped on CNN, and there was Samuel's picture covering the entire screen. They were accusing him of corruption, of taking illegal monies from rich Middle Easterners. They were accusing him of selling out the office he loved so dearly. She knew it was a lie the instant she heard it.

One week later, she received a large envelope in the mail. Inside, a smaller envelope instructed, "Open only in the event of my death." Attached was a note from her brother. Attempts to contact him in the days that followed were unsuccessful.

Then the news came that her brother, the Vice President of the United States, was found dead. The talking heads at the White House claimed he had taken his own life, but she knew that had also been a well-orchestrated lie. She knew he didn't kill himself, that he would never do such a thing, but at the time, she thought she had no way to prove it. Then she opened the envelope he had sent her. Inside she found a lockbox key and a note telling her how much Samuel loved her.

Grief stricken, she didn't realize the magnitude of what had happened to her brother until she removed what had been hidden in the lockbox. There, she learned the truth. Her brother believed he would be killed, and the story about his betrayal and death had all been fabricated for a bigger, much more sinister purpose than she could have ever imagined.

News soon came that her mother had collapsed upon hearing of Samuel's death and, two months later, died. Standing over her mother's grave, Creighton Lansford vowed to do more than clear her brother's name. She wouldn't rest until she had brought down all the men who were responsible.

Drawing on her considerable family wealth and the friendships it had bought her, she soon learned the dirty secrets of power politics in the nation's capital. A Harvard-educated lawyer with an undergraduate degree in political science, she made the right connections and became a D.C. power broker too. She developed a strategy, used her beauty and her brains, and now she was ready to see her deadly plan of retribution come to fruition.

"They'll all pay, Samuel. Every damn one of them."

Tears stained her cheeks as she closed the overnight case. She went into the bathroom and stood before the mirror to repair the damage to her makeup. If, after her interview, she felt right about the reporter she had called, then Lansford would choose her to expose everything. She feared that if accusations came out of the Hart camp from her, they would be downplayed by the President's people as nothing more than political rhetoric. They might be seen as a desperate attempt to discredit the President and Vice President, nothing more, then ignored. But if a nationally known reporter broke the story—a reporter who had already rattled the walls of the Capitol by exposing another conspiracy—heads would turn and, just maybe, the right people would take it seriously.

Lansford finished with her makeup and looked at her reflection in the mirror. *Ms. Cassie O'Connor, play your cards right, and you'll get the story of a lifetime.*

She flipped off the bathroom light, looked around her room to make sure everything had been packed. Her gaze fell on the overnight case containing her brother's picture. *Today the castles will begin to crumble, and all the king's men will tumble on their swords.*

Ira eyed the row of limousines parked in front of the Charleston Inn. *Hart has to go down, even if it means I go down with him. Daddy won't settle for less.*

He worried about his father's whereabouts. Since the shooting, Ira had combed the city but hadn't seen him. He even went back to the construction office, hoping to find him waiting there, but police were all over the place, and he couldn't get close enough to see what had happened.

If everything had gone according to plan, he already knew what they were there for. His dad planned to kill that other spy once he and Lance had left. That must've been what the police were doing. *They found the asshole's body.*

Still, concern shrouded his thoughts as he watched a lithe, long-legged blonde stride down the steps of the hotel and slide into one of the waiting limos. As the woman settled into the backseat of the shiny black Lincoln, Ira glanced around, still hoping he would spot his father somewhere down the street. Instead, all he saw were workers carrying lumber and plywood toward a lot where more men and women were busy framing a clapboard house, rebuilding it to look as close as possible to the original. *Where in hell could he be?*

Ira straightened as two people who looked like Secret Service agents rushed out the hotel door and started down the steps. Then he recognized the man jogging down behind them. *Well, now, Mr. Commander-in-Chief-wannabe, just where are you headed?* He stroked the butt of the pistol stuck in his pants.

As Ira watched, Jeff Hart hurried after the agents, one a man, the other a woman. The agents stopped at the car and stepped aside to give Hart access to the woman inside. While he leaned into the window, the pair stood straight and alert at his side. Their eyes scanned the street.

Ira pressed back against a stack of lumber to avoid being seen. *She must be important to the senator.*

If he had only known Hart was coming out, he could have been waiting nearby, taken out the candidate, then gotten away before anybody knew what had happened. One of the mercenaries who had trained him and the others back at the encampment once said the easiest way to get away after killing someone is to just walk up, shoot, and walk away at a brisk pace. He said the shock would prevent a reaction long enough to escape.

Ira shook his head. He wasn't so sure that would work with trained Secret Service agents. He figured all he'd be doing was committing suicide. There had to be another way to please his father and the general.

He watched as the limo drove off. *Maybe she's the key.* Ira eased away from the lumber and jumped into the truck parked just a few feet away. *Maybe Hart will come to rescue his lady friend if she's in danger.*

Barry walked out of the Charleston Inn with Sawyer just as Lansford's limo pulled away from the curb. Earlier, he had learned that Lance's body had been found in a parking deck a few blocks away, but Ira had not been seen. "What now?" he asked the director.

"Thorn's the key. We have to find him. I think we may have enough to charge him with treason, not to mention multiple counts of murder. Maybe that'll loosen up his tongue a bit. I think the attorney general will bargain to make a case against the Vice President."

"If we—" Barry stopped when he spotted the gray pickup as it turned the corner, heading in the direction the limo went. He saw the name of the construction company stenciled on the side. "There." He pointed. "That's the truck Ira Hanley and Lance McKenzie drove out of the construction lot. That's got to be Ira."

Sawyer grabbed a walkie-talkie from a nearby agent, radioed the truck's description. "If that's him, we'll get him."

Ira kept one eye on the rearview mirror as he turned onto King Street. He pulled the pistol from his waistband, laid it on the seat beside him. If anybody followed him, he planned on ditching the truck and running, and he wanted the gun where he could grab it if needed.

He mashed his foot down on the accelerator, cussed the old truck's engine when it didn't respond. Forty miles per hour was about all he could get the hunk of junk to do, and he didn't know if that would be enough to catch up to the Lincoln carrying the woman.

As he drove down the busy commercial street, he glanced down alleys and side streets he passed, making sure he didn't drive by the one where the limo had turned. The woman had a substantial head start, and that could put her almost anywhere. His only hope was that the signal lights and traffic would slow her car enough for him to catch up.

After making sure no cops were around, he drove through an intersection after the light turned red. He hoped the limo driver would do a better job of obeying the law.

At the intersection of King and Society streets, his face brightened. The limo had been stopped by the traffic signal up ahead at George Street. Two cars sat between his truck and the black Lincoln. *Perfect.* He'd hang back now and watch to see where the car headed.

To Ira's surprise, the limo traveled less than a block more before it turned into Marion Square and stopped. As he pulled the truck to the curb, he watched the driver hop out and rush around to the back passenger-side door. The woman stepped out and looked around the park. She appeared to be looking for someone.

Ira mused about making the blonde his captive, taking her back to the compound, where he'd torture her in his own special way, releasing her only if Hart himself came to the rescue. Thoughts of the encampment and the raid by federal agents saddened him. He had to think of another place to run. *Daddy will know where a new camp can be built. And this time, we'll booby-trap its perimeter to thwart any surprises.*

He watched the leggy blonde stride across the grassy park toward a couple, a white woman with a muscular-looking black man, standing near a tall column with the statue of some man on top. Ira shook his head in disgust, then recognized the woman. *That damn reporter. She's as good as dead.*

A sinister grin spread across his face as he picked up the semiautomatic and unscrewed the silencer. *Accuracy is more important than being quiet,* he thought. Besides, the noise would help to disorient witnesses—at least that's what he had been taught in his training.

He glanced back at the limo, saw the driver standing outside, keeping a close watch on his passenger. Ira figured he worked for the government, wondered if he was armed.

The blonde continued toward the couple. Ira didn't want to have to take on both men, especially if they were carrying guns. He studied the guy with the reporter. *He might be armed, too.*

He decided to take out the driver once the woman returned, just to be on the safe side. *If I move fast enough, I might not even have to worry about the black guy.*

He planned to ditch the truck and force the woman into the Lincoln, then he'd head out of Charleston and get lost in the countryside. His only real concern was his dad. *What could have happened to the old man?*

# Chapter · 33

MARION SQUARE IN CHARLESTON, SOUTH CAROLINA

Cassie had just extended her hand to greet Lansford when the siren blast drew her attention toward the street. She saw a policeman jump from his patrol car, heard two shots, and saw the officer dive for cover. With her attention focused on the police cruiser, she didn't see the man running toward her and Lansford until Jefferson hollered behind her.

"Duck. Get down," Jefferson's voice rang out with a sense of urgency.

Lansford's expression looked stricken. She whirled around. Cassie froze, her attention drawn to the man bearing down on them.

Ira had been watching the women, not the rearview mirror, when movement behind him caught his attention. He glanced up and saw the black-and-white patrol car stop behind him, blue lights flashing on top. He grabbed the gun off the seat, threw open the door, and jumped onto the pavement. He fired at the officer exiting the cruiser, then dove across the hood of the truck and slid to the ground in a full run.

Ahead of him, he saw the limo driver's hand thrust inside his jacket. Ira fired as he raced by. The driver's face contorted in agony. His knees buckled, dropping his tall torso on the pavement.

Not stopping, Ira glanced over his shoulder. He didn't see any police officers pursuing him, so he focused on the women up ahead. If he could get to the blonde, maybe take both of them, then he'd have hostages to shield his escape. He looked past the women, decided to kill the black man before the bastard had a chance to react.

The shorter woman held a startled look; the other, the statuesque blonde, glared at him with a fierceness he didn't quite understand. She dropped the purse she carried. By the time Ira saw the small pistol the blonde brandished, he had little time to react. She lifted the gun, leveled it at him.

Surprised, he skidded to a stop on the grass. He raised his pistol. Lansford's revolver fired. Ira squeezed off two shots from his gun, heard the reports just as his shoulder exploded with pain. He spun around, saw more police, but never heard the shots from their guns.

As if caught up in some surreal out-of-body experience, Cassie felt someone hit her from behind as she saw the shooter fall. Buried under Jefferson's weight, she raised her head in time to see the police race over to disarm the assailant.

One officer dropped to his knee, checked for a pulse by placing his fingers against the man's neck. The officer looked at the other one, shook his head. Cassie heard him say, "He won't be shootin' at anybody else."

She looked to Lansford. "Are you—"

The woman was on the ground; blood soaked the beige pantsuit she wore. She didn't move.

Cassie squirmed from under Jefferson and ran over to Lansford. "She's been shot. Help her," she said to anybody who would listen. She felt helpless, inept to stop the bleeding.

As she watched the policemen approaching, the ground and sky began to spin. Cassie stumbled forward, then everything went black.

When Cassie opened her eyes, starbursts from bright lights overhead blinded her. She couldn't see anything, but dozens of voices buzzed in her head, as if she had been captured by rogue insects. "Where am I?"

"Welcome back. You had us a little worried there."

She strained to see the face that went with the familiar voice. "Brock? Is that you?"

His laugh echoed a sound of relief. "You were expecting somebody else?"

She tried to grin, but her face ached. "What happened? One minute I'm seeing all this shooting, bodies falling all around. . . . What about Creighton Lansford? Is she—"

"Ms. Lansford's alive. She's upstairs in surgery."

Cassie recognized Jefferson's voice, too.

"Could somebody kill this light?" she asked. "I can't see a damn thing."

As if on command, the light went out. Cassie blinked several times to make the beach-ball-size spots disappear from in front of her. The first face she saw belonged to Brock. "When did you get here?" she asked.

"I must have just missed all the action. They sent me down right after the attempt on Hart. When I got to Marion Square, you had already been transported."

She rubbed her forehead. Fiery pain streaked from her temple. "Did I get hit?"

"Yep," Jefferson said. "Just a graze, though. You can be thankful God gave you a hard head."

Brock grinned. "I've always said—"

"Don't even go there." Cassie looked up at the man who had made trip after trip to Atlanta to see her, but whom she had been too busy to visit even once. "Lean down here, handsome. I need a kiss."

He winked at Jefferson. "See? All it took was a bullet to the head. I should have shot her myself a long time ago."

"Very fun—"

Brock's lips smothered the words before they could escape. He pulled back, smiled at her. "The doc said you were clear to leave, once you regained consciousness. I'll take you back to Columbia, if you want."

Cassie sat up and swung her legs over the edge of the bed. She still felt swimmy-headed, and inside, she felt like someone was pounding on an anvil with a ball-peen hammer. "I'd like to see Lansford, see how she's doing. I feel responsible for her being out in the park when that idiot tried to kill us."

Brock took her hand, squeezed it. "I doubt anybody can get close to her right now. Once she's out of surgery, Senator Hart has asked for a Secret Service detail to be assigned to her room."

"I want to get word to her. Not to a press secretary for the senator, but to Lansford. Can you help me do that?"

He sighed. "I doubt a howitzer shell could penetrate that noggin of yours. I'll talk to the agents, see what I can do. Meanwhile, you need rest."

Jefferson said, "She . . . you both can stay at my place, if you want, Brock. I have room."

Brock looked at Cassie, shrugged his shoulders. "Up to you."

She grinned, squeezed his hand. "Sounds good . . . real good."

# Chapter · 34

HILTON HEAD ISLAND, SOUTH CAROLINA

One hour from Charleston, Locke watched the news coverage of the events unfolding to his north. When the breaking news announcement interrupted the stock market report he was watching, he felt a flutter of excitement charge through his body. *This is it.*

But now, sitting in the living room of his Sea Pines estate on Hilton Head Island, he watched and listened in disbelief as two reporters described how one man had died but Senator Jeff Hart escaped an assassination attempt unharmed.

*How can that be? The son of a bitch has more lives than a cat.*

He hadn't quite come to grips with the failure of Hart's assassination, when one of the reporters announced that another shooting had just occurred and this victim was rumored to also be a member of the Hart campaign. Locke walked to the wall of windows looking out over the Calibogue Sound, trying to think of someone to call and find out what had gone wrong.

*Hopefully,* he thought, *Cromwell was one of the victims. But who was the other? And how could they have possibly missed Hart?*

Locke picked up the cordless phone on the table next to where he stood. As he watched a flock of seagulls and crows swoop down on edible remnants brought ashore by the recent high tide, he dialed a number for a contact he had in the Secret Service. Maybe he could find out something from him.

In Washington, Vice President Clark Randall sat red-faced as he watched CNN's account that one of their reporters had been taken to a local hospital after being wounded at one of the shootings. The female anchor described how the reporter, Cassie O'Connor, working on a story related to the assassination, had even been held captive for a short period of time by a right-wing militia group suspected in the attempt on the presidential candidate's life.

"Word from the hospital," the anchor said, "is that Cassie is okay and is being released. We hope she will be able to continue her coverage of this breaking story."

"Son of a bitch!" Randall grabbed a snow globe of the nation's Capitol building off his desk and hurled it against the wood paneling in his office. It shattered as it crashed against the wall, spraying water and shards of glass onto the thick-pile carpet covering the floor. He grabbed the phone, held it momentarily, then returned it to its cradle. He needed a secure line.

Dressed in army fatigues, Ambrose Thornton waited in a Lowcountry barn behind a farmhouse owned by a member of the Free Confederacy. The barn, located just a few minutes from Charleston's historic district, had no hay in the loft or cattle in its stalls. There were no tractors parked under its roof. Inside the rustic, weathered building, covered boxes of rifles and ammunition towered toward the pitched roof.

His walkie-talkie crackled as a call came in. "Thornton," he said.

He listened in indignant silence.

"Do we have reports on Hanley or his son?" Thornton asked.

"Ira's dead." The static-filled words of the caller hit like a bolt of lightning. "Killed in a shootout with police. No one's heard from his father. He may have been apprehended or killed."

Thornton looked up at the beams of timber crisscrossing the underside of the roof. Given all that was at stake, he hoped they both were dead. He didn't want anyone being questioned. "Anything else?"

"Word is, the reporter we captured got away in an early morning raid. And there might have been another infiltrator in the camp."

"I heard about the raid. So, if there was another spy, the authorities know who we are."

"Yes."

Thornton leaned back against a stack of crates. "So be it. That's why it's important to tie up loose ends. Is Hart leaving for Atlanta, as scheduled?"

"Yes, but I doubt we'll be able to get close to him. Security is tighter than ever."

"Yes, I imagine it is. That's why sometimes a soldier must be prepared to die for a cause." Thornton clicked off the two-way radio.

# Chapter · 35

MEDICAL UNIVERSITY HOSPITAL, CHARLESTON, SOUTH CAROLINA

Cassie waited while the Secret Service agent in the hospital lobby searched her purse. He pulled out a tape recorder, held it up, and popped the tape out.

In the past, the extra scrutiny would have driven her into a state of angry delirium, but not now, not after everything that had happened. In fact, she welcomed the extra security. "Tools of the trade," she explained.

The agent nodded. "I've seen guns made to look like recorders. Can't be too careful."

Cassie glanced back at Brock with an appreciative wink. He had driven her to the hospital that morning, after she had received the surprise call from Hart's staff, telling her that Lansford was doing well. Even better, she wanted to see Cassie. The only rule was, she had to come alone—without a camera.

Brock had agreed to drive her and wait for her in the hospital lobby. In fact, he insisted. He hadn't left her side since the shooting in the park.

Jefferson wasn't available, anyway. He had been dispatched by his station to cover a story about a raid of a nearby barn full of military weapons and ammunition. Before he left, he told Cassie and Brock that word on the street was that the barn belonged to a Free Confederacy member, who had been discovered during the raid with a bullet hole in his head.

When the agent finished with her purse and had passed a metal-detection wand along her sides, Cassie stepped into the elevator, where another agent waited. She leaned back against the wall and watched as the doors closed and the floor numbers began to appear and disappear. The elevator stopped on the fifth floor.

As Cassie exited, the agent stepped out and waited by the elevator. She saw two Charleston police officers sitting outside one of the rooms. "Must be the place," she joked, trying to calm her nerves.

The Secret Service agent ignored her.

Cassie knocked before entering the room and waited until she heard a weak voice beckon her to come in. Inside, the room was bright. The curtains had been opened all the way, and sun poured through the window. A huge bouquet of flowers sat on a table, bathing in the sunlight.

"Good morning," Lansford said, smiling. "I'm glad you could come."

Cassie walked over and stood next to the bed. She noted the dark circles under the woman's eyes and the tube running into her arm. "I appreciate your asking me. Are you sure you feel up to this?"

"Wonders of modern medicine. Besides, I owe you an interview."

Cassie nodded appreciatively. "It could wait."

Lansford's features dropped, her smile faded. "No, no it can't. I have a story you're going to find hard to believe, but I have proof." She pointed to a thick file folder on the foot of her bed. "You can take it with you when you leave. I also want you to know that what I'm about to tell you is not about helping Jeff Hart win the election. It's about seeking justice and righting a wrong."

Cassie's eyebrow raised. She pulled out the tape recorder, showed it to the bedridden woman. "Do you mind?"

Lansford stared at the recorder for a brief moment, then shook her head. "No, go ahead."

Cassie clicked on the recorder, raised it to her mouth. "Cassie O'Connor, October 28th, interview with Creighton Lansford in Charleston." She placed the recorder on the woman's pillow.

That afternoon, on the steps of the Georgia state capitol building, Jeff Hart looked out into the faces of an enthusiastic crowd of supporters. As a bright sun gleamed off the golden dome behind him, he spoke of a new direction for the country, one where jobs would be plentiful and corporations would be held accountable for their business practices. The speech lasted forty minutes.

As the applause died down and he started down the steps to shake hands with a group of nearby supporters, a voice rose above the babble of congratulatory responses. The loud cry caused him to freeze and look in the caller's direction.

"Coward. You're not fit for leadership."

In an instant, Hart recognized Thornton's face and saw the semiautomatic thrust up in front of him. Shots rang out as Hart was knocked to the ground. He heard a woman scream, and someone shouted, "Gun!"

Then it was over. A Secret Service agent pulled Hart up, as two more surrounded him and shoved him through the crowd to his car. The agents pushed him inside, and the car accelerated before he could draw a breath.

"What happened?" he asked as Thornton's face flashed in his mind. "I knew him."

At Jefferson's canal-side home, word of the second assassination attempt on Jeff Hart, in as many days, garnered Cassie's attention as she read the file given to her by Lansford. Brock grabbed the remote, increased the volume. Jefferson settled into a custom-built recliner, one that fit his six-foot-eight-inch body.

"Incredible," Cassie said as she watched the national feed from a local station in Atlanta. "I just read about that Thornton guy in this journal. He's a real psycho."

"A real dead psycho now," Brock said.

Jefferson sat mesmerized by the news. At a commercial break, he looked over at Cassie. "Do you believe the President and Vice President are involved?"

"I believe at least one of them knew what was happening. I'm not sure about Flint, but if you can believe this journal, handwritten by Samuel Griffith, Clark Randall was the mastermind of the entire conspiracy, including Griffith's own demise."

"You're going to have to turn that over to the FBI," Brock said. "You know that, don't you?"

Cassie nodded as she thumbed through the pages. "I know, but they don't get it until I've broken the story. I don't want a federal judge sealing this and slapping a gag order on me."

Jefferson shook his head. "They ain't gonna be happy."

"They'll have to get over it," she said. "You two leave me alone for a couple of hours. I've got what I want from this stuff." She looked at Jefferson. "We'll tape it on the campus. If CNN wants to do a live spot, and I'm betting they will, can your station provide a satellite hookup?"

Jefferson laughed. "For this story—are you kidding? They might even buy a brand-new truck."

"Good. Brock, once we're live, you take the documents and give them to the FBI."

"I'll call a friend in the Bureau, tell him I have a career-maker for him. He'll latch onto it like a fat tick on a hound dog."

She looked up from her papers with a mirthful expression. "You have such a way with words."

"Thanks, babe. Just let me know when."

Cassie dropped the papers on the table. She gave Jefferson a thumbs-up, then leaned over and kissed Brock on the cheek. Excitement twinkled in her eyes. "Okay, now out, you two. I have work to do."

# CHAPTER · 36

THE WHITE HOUSE OVAL OFFICE

Creighton Lansford stood in the Oval Office, her arms folded across her chest, as she watched CNN reporter Cassie O'Connor sum up the day's events in Clark Randall's trial. Charged with one count of conspiracy to commit murder and one count of treason, Randall had remained defiant; but he was in custody, and his attorneys had little to say on his behalf. The trial was in its first month, and some legal analysts predicted it could run through the rest of the year.

Six months earlier, just days after Cassie's investigative report blew the lid off the Capitol, Jeff Hart won the presidency in a landslide vote. Lansford, now the White House chief of staff, glanced at President Hart, who sat behind his desk, fixated on what was being revealed on television. She recalled watching Cassie's first report from her hospital bed in Charleston, followed by another CNN reporter's attempt to solicit a statement from then-Vice President Randall. The fury in his eyes as he refused to comment lifted her spirits. Now she knew he had experienced the same anger she had after learning her brother had allegedly committed suicide.

The indictments hadn't come until after President Hart's inauguration. Prior to then, the only recourse was to impeach Randall—something many on the Hill advocated—but calmer minds prevailed, and indictments waited until a thorough investigation had taken place and the Vice President had left office.

Of course, Lansford had been questioned over and over again, and Samuel's journal had undergone tremendous scrutiny to ensure it was, in fact, written in his hand. Early on, some in President Flint's camp cried foul, alleging the story was little more than a political ruse to gain an advantage in what was purported to be a close election. But as more and more evidence mounted, the truth became obvious. Statements taken from several influential corporate power brokers—a group known as the Board—implicated the Vice President. Flint's supporters quieted, and, just before leaving office, President Flint himself denounced Randall's actions, as well as the actions of others involved in the conspiracy.

The rats began jumping from the sinking ship almost from the start. Locke had called Lansford within days of the election, attempting to assure her he knew nothing of what had been planned.

She knew better. Her brother's journal described Locke and Cromwell in a way that undressed their viciousness for all to see. Dates and times of despicable acts, including murders, even one of a senator's wife, were revealed in detail.

She had worried at first as to how Samuel knew all the sordid details without having gone to the authorities, but over time she let that worry fade. In the world of international politics, she had learned, one had to hold back hole cards to use as trumps in the next power play. Even when those trump cards might reveal murder.

She visited Locke once in federal prison, where he awaited his day in court, without bond, just to let him know she knew his true self. The meeting had been short, and she assured him that their relationship had been nothing more than a means to an end, a necessary evil she had to endure to bring her brother's killers to justice. As she got up to leave, she actually thought she detected a hint of admiration in his cold eyes. She never would know for sure.

She knew she should be experiencing great self-satisfaction in every moment of what was unfolding, and afterward, if the death penalty was invoked, she knew she should exalt in achieving the ultimate vindication for what Randall and his thugs had done to her brother. She knew she should feel all those things, but she didn't.

The ultimate vindication could only be if Samuel were sitting behind the president's desk, and she knew that was impossible. Samuel was gone, so now she had to use her influence on the new Commander in Chief to accomplish those objectives she felt Samuel would have embraced.

As Lansford watched Cassie wrap up her coverage from the front of the federal courthouse, she likened the young reporter's drive to her own. A wry smile creased her lips. *Wonder if she's ever thought about being the White House press secretary?*

*ALSO BY DANIEL BAILEY*

**Justice Betrayed**

A violent murder, a capture, an all-too-convenient escape. What fledgling television reporter Cassie O'Connor thought would be a routine assignment in a tiny South Carolina town turned out to be the biggest conspiracy to rock the Eastern seaboard in years. Ambitious Cassie wants a job at a major network; when she senses a sinister cover-up following the cop killer's jailbreak, she knows the story could be her big chance. Her dogged determination leads her into the mouth of the lion—a dangerous place filled with government operatives, a crazed drug lord, and homicide. Having become a part of the game she sought to expose, Cassie must guard her own life against a host of characters, all eager to see justice betrayed.

"*Justice Betrayed* is a fascinating tale of how far the federal government will go to win the war on illegal drugs."

—*Midwest Book Review*

"Wrapped in Southern charm, this action-packed realistic view inside law enforcement and crime is reminiscent of Michael Connelly with a Southern drawl."

—*Foreword Magazine*

"Bailey . . . knows the Lowcountry and he tells a good story while probing the underbelly of drug investigations where sometimes it's hard to tell the good guys from the bad guys."

—*Jekyll's Golden Islander*

Trade Paper 1-57072-210-2 $13.95 · Hardcover 1-57072-209-9 $23.95

## www.mysterysouth.com

# TAKE A STAB AT THESE MYSTERIES COMING SOON

The Ohio River Valley Chapter of Sisters in Crime has compiled these mystery stories surrounding one of the world's greatest sporting events—the Kentucky Derby. Amidst the glamour of fast horses, beautiful women, and great bourbon is the underlying current, as deep as the Ohio River, of danger and deceit.

**Derby Rotten Scoundrels**

a SinC anthology

**A Stroke of Misfortune**

by

Nancy Gotter Gates

When her favorite neighbor in her Sarasota condominium dies suddenly, Emma Daniels expects the grief that follows. What she doesn't expect is having to help fight to clear the name of the widower, who suffers a major stroke shortly after his wife's death and soon finds himself the prime suspect.

If Williamsburg shop owner Emma Spencer wants to live, she has to find out why someone wants her dead. Her investigation ranges from the swamps of South Carolina to a deserted farm in Virginia, and Emma uncovers more than anyone expected: family secrets, an old murder, and deadly connections.

**Death by Any Other Name**

by

Ellis Vidler

## SILVER DAGGER MYSTERIES

WOULD YOU LIKE TO WRITE A REVIEW OF A SILVER DAGGER MYSTERY?
VISIT OUR WEB SITE FOR DETAILS

### www.silverdaggermysteries.com

ALL SILVER DAGGER MYSTERIES ARE AVAILABLE IN BOTH
TRADE PAPER AND HARDCOVER AT YOUR LOCAL BOOKSTORE
OR DIRECTLY FROM THE PUBLISHER
P.O. Box 1261 • Johnson City, TN 37605
1-800-992-2691